TWISTED

Parsons was in what he figured was some kind of weird dream, carrying a harpoon. The whore in the low-cut, floor-length dress stood in front of him, shaking her head no.

"I told you before, I've got bucks aplenty to keep me amused. I don't need your money to pay my bills. I will not do it with a married man."

"Here's the money, swine of Satan," Parsons heard himself say. "You're a whore. You have to do it."

"Yes, I am a whore, but I always pride myself on living up to what my enemies say of me. And you are married, sir, so let's have an end of it. Good day."

The whore turned her back on Parsons. He grabbed her and pulled her dress up. She fought like a wildcat, but he gouged her eyes out with his thumbs. That shut her up. Then he tied her down, but there was still a problem.

As the whore lay whimpering something about never being able to see a star again, Parson got an idea. He reached for the harpoon....

TWISTED

Sue Hollister Barr

LEISURE BOOKS   NEW YORK CITY

A LEISURE BOOK®

February 1992

Published by

Dorchester Publishing Co., Inc.
276 Fifth Avenue
New York, NY 10001

TWISTED

Chapter 1

"Simba's a killer."

"Girl, you got to be crazy."

"Like, nobody ever believes me, man. It's the curse of my life."

Ronna peered out from under her faded Bambi bedspread at the two women who had awakened her with their talking. The one who'd spoken first was taller and thinner than Ronna with stringy dark hair. Her pallid skin was even paler than Ronna's complexion which was typical of blondes. The second woman was athletically built with yellow-brown skin and was even taller than the first. Ronna wasn't into drugs, but she did have to give these two strangers credit for originality.

Everybody else occupying the mattresses scattered all over the floors of this off-campus house which Ronna shared was into grass and acid. These two women had apparently been snorting coke all night and had now settled down to do the last few lines in the corner of what used to be Ronna's bedroom.

It was now merely another space for the hippie hordes that wandered in off Telegraph Avenue in search of a place to crash.

"Ursula, honey," the yellow-brown woman said to the pale woman, "Simba's no big thing. What he got over any other boy worth you breaking your heart this way?"

"Another two, maybe three, inches."

A gangly boy on a mattress on the floor next to Ursula whipped a sheet around his crotch and disappeared into the kitchen.

Ronna blinked at the bedroom that once enshrined an innocent childhood she now ached for. A carved sesame wood table covered with the stems of what must have been a grade D lid of grass sat digging its clawed feet into her prized Mickey Mouse rug. Someone's bell bottoms and Mexican poncho, the 1966 school uniform at the University of California at Berkeley, had knocked over the pink alarm clock Ronna's mother had given her four years before for her sixteenth birthday.

Ronna twisted her head sideways. 7:30 A.M. She'd stayed up till 3:00 listening to one of the girls upstairs who actually contributed to the rent as she did. No one else had the patience to listen to this girl because she'd had such a run of bad luck. Ronna managed to listen long enough to suggest solutions. She was then able to bolster the girl's ego by prodding her into discovering these solutions herself.

Meanwhile Ronna had a ton of school work she should have been doing instead. If it was to be completed anytime before 1967 rolled around, she would have to get more sleep. She yanked her Bambi bedspread about her shoulders.

"Girl, there are too many fish in the sea," pointed out the athletically built woman. "Did you check out that sho' 'nuff tough-stuff Simba brought in with him last night? Muscular as all get-out."

"The Negro?" Ursula shoved a greasy strand of dark hair away from her deathly white cheek. "Revoltingly healthy. You take him, Josephine."

"I did," Josephine answered. Did Ronna detect a flatness in her eyes, or was it just an odd reflection of the brownish yellow of her skin?

Ursula leered. "Like, tell me about it—in detail. Is it true what they say about the size of a Negro cock?"

Josephine started to answer but was silenced by a crash in the kitchen, followed by a curse by the gangly boy. Ronna sighed. She didn't even know his name. Anyway she had to get back to sleep right away or she might not be able to.

Another curse from the kitchen was followed by what sounded like a sob. Ronna got up. On her way to the kitchen she noticed that Ursula held a compulsively detailed pastel drawing of a man with black hair and beard and hypnotic blue eyes.

Ronna found the gangly boy huddled by the back door. He was breathing deeply with rigid muscles, moist eyes, and a bitter set to his jaw. Ronna figured he couldn't be much more than 16. When he saw her, Ronna spotted the hurt he hid behind the slimiest leer she'd ever seen.

"Hey, baby," he drawled somewhat awkwardly, "I don't remember seeing you around here before."

Ronna's first instinct was to slap him; her second was to wonder if some girl who had slapped him previously had, perhaps, followed it up with an insult about his size.

"We haven't met," she said carefully and then added a lie. "But I've heard about you."

His expression turned belligerent; his muscles went rigid again. "What have you heard?"

"Well, uh, please don't get me wrong. I'm not looking to put this to the test right now myself, but some girl on the Avenue was talking about how good you are in bed."

The boy beamed, his ego as transparent as a child's. Thank God he didn't turn out to be a virgin or Ronna's lie would have blown up right in her face. She was happy, but decided she better exit quickly after a line like that. "Anyway, I've got to get some sleep. Bye."

On her way back to bed, Ronna noticed that Ursula had propped the pastel with the hypnotic eyes up against the lace curtains Ronna's Grandma Evans had crocheted for her when she was seven. Ronna cuddled up with her Bambi bedspread, caught by the contrast between the man's mesmerizing eyes, black hair and the now pastel-smudged white of the curtains.

Life had been simple when Grandma Evans was alive and Ronna's Mickey Mouse rug was new. Everyone had liked Ike, Donna Reed and Lassie. Ronna was glad she'd been able to make the gangly boy feel better but wished she could do the same for herself. Meanwhile she felt emotionally seasick as the old familiar anguish washed over her.

Yet again Ronna relived going home for Christmas. She remembered her mother's face as her mother looked at photographs revealing that her marriage of 25 years had been a farce, a lie, a never-never land that never was. After years of her father's assurances of fidelity despite his disinterest in his wife, the pictures showed he had been screwing any man, woman or child he could get his hands on. Ronna was sure the white picket fence around their house wilted and yellowed as she watched her mother looking at those photographs. It seemed the photographs sucked the life out of her mother, taking on a third dimension while her mother was left a lifeless shell.

The family Christmas tree had become an obscenity by the time the suddenly rootless Ronna stumbled onto a plane back to Berkeley. The first night back she'd slept for exactly one hour and 37 minutes. The second night she'd started letting the hippies in. Maybe what they represented was real; God knew, the world she'd been brought up in certainly wasn't real.

A drowsiness, deeper than physical exhaustion, swept over Ronna. She could feel her mind letting go of consciousness, synapse by synapse. The pudgy preadolescent who lived on in her despite her 20 years stopped worrying about the fat she didn't actually have anymore. The perpetual compulsion over the English paper due next month ceased. Ronna swooned slowly toward sleep. Jerked awake again briefly by a sense of vertigo just before the final drop into sleep, she at last fell headlong into the world of dreams where past, present, future, all things real and all things imagined are one.

In Ronna's dream it is no longer 1966. For one thing nobody is wearing bell bottoms. There are no palms, no eucalyptus. All the trees are pointed like Christmas trees rather than rounded like Californian trees, but worse, they are all twisting strangely as Ronna squints through a mist.

The people are in a clearing barely visible through the painfully distorted trees. Old, old clothes. 19th Century. And Ronna must decide whether to go to these people.

A sole tree in the clearing is the biggest, most gnarled of all. Next to it, a woodpile and the people. Ronna knows she must think clearly, that her decision is important, but the trees are twisting insanely and she doesn't know what is real and what is not.

She goes to the people, struggling through the

ever-moving trees, but there is a great sense of elation—of a freedom soon to come.

A man turns toward her with muscles like the strings of a harp playing under his naked torso, the sharp tang of his sweat sweet in her nostrils, raven black hair and beard, and blue eyes with tendrils of electric green that laser through her. He looks her up and down, his glance warming her wherever it falls.

Hands touch her, but she knows they are not those of the man with the mesmerizing blue eyes. They are pushing her down. Her cheek rests upon a cool wooden surface, fragrant with wood chips. It's smooth against her cheek, but she can't see what's above her and, just as this seems terribly important, a clump of her honey-colored hair blows across her eyes.

A muffled *thunk* pounds through the wood against her ear, and Ronna feels a great coldness next to her collarbone.

"Ya' missed, boy. Almost got my pinkie."

Something frigid is being yanked from her upper chest, working back and forth.

"I can't get it out."

Ronna tries to gasp, but she can't inhale. Sharp shivers of pain convulse her arms as her hands fly about, reaching wildly for the source of the agony. The icy presence is hooked under her collarbone, pulling out now with a relentless suction she can hear through the wood and feel as it tugs at her innards, pulling bits of her out in its wake.

"Can't you do anything right?"

Ronna hears her collarbone splintering, then a

soft, squishy slurp as the coldness leaves her body, tearing things out that yank, before breaking, at their connections in her legs, crotch and gut.

"Watch me now."

At last the wind flips the hair from her eyes, and Ronna looks up to see the ax with its bits of bone and flesh stuck to it. Something red and white and oozy falls on her cheek, splattering blood in her eyes that again obscures her vision.

Ronna feels something alive and shaky dipping into the mess where her collarbone was. With a staccato crawl it reaches her neck before she realizes it's her own hand.

Thunk. As her vision clears she sees something fly by and land above her on the wooden block, then roll leisurely past her nose. It's the upper joint of her index finger. Now her head is falling back, off the wooden block, and she can see her body, one finger-less hand twitching at the gurgling red fountain that used to be her neck.

Simba paused at the corner of Telegraph and Dwight to savor the scream. The real thing. A woman. A part of him wanted to go to the rescue, but he quickly suppressed it.

The scream peaked—a pulsing, living thing seeping into his bones like the fog that dropped at sunset on the hills above Sausalito. Someone's TV? No. In the face of *this* scream, Hollywood's very best suddenly became nothing but a hollow whisper.

It was muffled, definitely inside. Simba looked

west, toward the place where night still lingered in the hills above Berkeley, toward Regent Street running parallel to Telegraph where all the hippies crashed after a rough night on The Avenue. Somebody had a real bad trip? Maybe some day-tripper from Walnut Creek did acid for the first time and found, after the pretty colors faded, the fact that her parents would never love her staring at her in full psychedelic splendor.

The light changed, not that there was any traffic at this hour anyway, and he moved on toward The Forum. The essence of middle-class values in its previous incarnation as a Lucky supermarket, it wisely became a coffee house when the overzealous efforts of the grape boycotters closed the store. The Forum was now *the* coffee house. Bob Dylan, who had recently attained Top 40 stardom through the Byrds rendition of "Hey, Mr. Tambourine Man," had been seen hiding behind sunglasses in a corner. Just now The Forum was closed. Simba would have to settle for American coffee elsewhere.

Simba froze. What the fuck was he doing in Berkeley, two bridges and an easy hour away from his houseboat in Sausalito, anyway? He couldn't even remember getting high. Was he getting so used to these blackouts that he could walk half the length of Telegraph Avenue before it even occurred to him to question how he got there? He tried to think. The really bad ones had started with that cokehead bitch he balled last weekend. Ursula. Gave new meaning to the slang for getting laid—scoring—or rather made him wonder which sex was doing the scoring. There he was, deep inside her, and should have been in ecstasy, but instead he found himself wondering if, when it was over, he was going to get his dick back.

The thing was, he couldn't remember meeting her.

Simba was almost at the end of Telegraph, looking across Bancroft at the campus, the Student Union and the Campanile beyond. Two years ago he'd been a junior there, part of the birth of Berkeley's hippiedom when the Free Speech Movement rocked the University of California. He'd hefted picket signs, scaled the walls of the administration buildings to deliver Pepe's famous pizza to the protesters entrenched within, composed and sang protest songs, and found he could save a considerable amount of money by shunning the local barber. Now he was an out-of-work singer/composer living in Sausalito on a houseboat he'd picked because the airspace within was so compact that five people could get high off a single pipe of hash.

Two opposing feelings pulled at once, wrenching his very soul. He wanted to settle down and find meaning in his life. He also wanted to run wild, wander and avoid it all. Then he heard a woman's scream again, probably in an apartment over a nearby store, but this one brought a quick smile to Simba's lips. Someone was getting his rocks off.

Piper's pendulous breasts swung wildly with her final bounce. The man beneath her let out a low, guttural growl that reverberated perfectly with the orgasmic tingle she could feel all the way to the tips of her toes. Wrinkles interrupted the angled planes of his cheeks as he arched his head back against the bed, making a curly halo of what little hair he had left. His impeccable technique stemmed from an easy quarter century of more experience than she had.

No matter.

Just now nothing could have been more beautiful to Piper than the delicate rosy tint of this man's skin or the tarnished tangle of his platinum gold hair. The glow from coming worked its way over the tops of her cheekbones as he tossed her onto her belly, pressing her flushed body into the bed as he slammed into her from behind.

His turn now.

He sank his fingers into Piper's rear, and she could feel that delicious shuddering intensity that meant he was about to climax. Unable to decide whether he'd managed to provoke her to the next orgasm or indefinitely extended the last, she grinned as she felt him come. Was that pain she heard mixed into his long, expressive cry? It seemed a little bit of everything—very much man yet partly little boy, oddly universal while embarrassingly personal. He buried his face in the back of her neck, and somehow she felt it was all right if she never knew the name of his fifth grade teacher or about the time the kid down the block beat him up. On some perhaps more valid nonverbal level she'd heard and felt it all.

He rolled off her onto his back and lit a cigarette.

Piper giggled. "This is supposed to be your line, but what did you say your name was?"

He laughed, an easy laugh that said he'd been around too long to take anything, even his own generation's values, too seriously. "Eugene. I remember yours, Piper."

"Was it my brilliant defense of Emerson's distinction between freedom and license?"

"It was when you lost the notes." There was a twinkle in his eye.

"Oh, yes! And I had to ad lib and—"

"More to the point, to retrieve the notes from the floor, you had to turn your back on the audience and lean over."

"Thus ripping another patch off my jeans and revealing my fat ass?"

"A rose by any other name . . ." He offered her a cigarette but she shook her head no.

"Eugene, my parents are full of it."

"I'm sure your parents' crimes are many, but they did do one thing very right." He was looking her over.

"They follow the rules without thinking, and think I should too. What's wrong with what we just did, for instance?"

"Extramarital sex? Don't be too quick to assume that a taboo which has existed for thousands of years doesn't have some validity."

"Pooh. What validity? It's like the ancient religious taboo against certain foods or combinations of foods which in biblical times did pose a threat to people's health."

"It may be awhile before we discover the price tag for all this free sex. I hope it's decades. By then I won't be able to get it up anyway."

"This is 1966. Birth control is cheap and effective, and there isn't a sexually transmitted disease around that can't be wiped out by a good shot of penicillin."

"Perhaps."

Piper studied the man, realizing that was a word he used when he didn't agree but didn't want to discuss it further either. She grinned and kissed the tip of his American Indian-style nose. It didn't matter; life was grand, and she wasn't going to let anything or anybody bring her down. No strings. No ties. No bullshit. She sprang out of bed, shoved the curtains aside and leaned out the window resting her naked breasts on the outside sill. The Student Union was dead at this hour, but the spire of the Campanile was glorious in the morning sun. She stuck her tongue out at a great-looking guy with black hair and beard, who was looking up at her from the street, just as she heard the siren.

"Patrol car?" Eugene asked. "Statutory rape squad, no doubt."

Piper watched the car squeal around the corner of Bancroft and Telegraph. "Goddamn pigs." She turned back toward the man in her bed, watching his long stretch ripple through the brown and white fur on his chest. His short hair did look a little out of place against the psychedelic poster

of the Jefferson Airplane on the wall behind him.
"I have a silly question for you. What was the
name of your fifth grade teacher?"

Eugene pursed his wickedly sensual lips. "I
honestly don't remember."

No matter.

Officer Parsons had seen his share of naked
women, on and off duty, so what was the big deal
about a two second shot of some frizzy-haired
hippie hanging out a second story window? He
crossed his legs and checked to see if the young
rookie next to him sensed anything. Nada. Too
busy driving. So inexperienced that the siren
made him nervous. Parsons stretched, rubbing
his paunch, and smiled. He loved to feel smug.

"Real nice of you to come along, Parsons, what
with your being off duty and from a different
jurisdiction and all. Seems like half the force was
out with the Russian flu last night, and we really
came up short and—Oh Jesus!" The rookie cut
the wheel, launching them into the opposing
lanes of traffic with an ear-splitting screech just
as the young girl carrying a huge stack of books
across the street finally looked up.

Parsons noted idly that this young person, despite the demands of a heavy course load that
left her capable of starting across a street without
noticing a siren, found the time to arrange her
honey-colored hair in an attractive bouffant
style. Even as he grabbed the wheel, correcting
the skid in time to avoid a sluggishly driven microbus in an oncoming lane, he felt the familiar

rush of rage against his daughter, the hippie.

"Jesus Christ!" The rookie regained a semblance of control over the vehicle. "Thanks. I don't know what's wrong with me. I've never answered a call for one of these before."

The rookie gulped, and Parsons wanted to laugh. Young idiot. Six foot four, 240 pounds, and he looked like a toddler about to cry because someone said "boo."

"I hope I'm not bothering you what with all this chatter and the driving and—"

"Not at all," Parsons lied. "Nuthin' at all irregular about your behavior there, son. We all get nervous when confronted by a thing like this." What a patsy, he thought. Back in Orange County, Parsons would never have handed this young man a badge. Why did he have to put up with this crap? The world was nothing but incompetents.

They made a right on Ashby that included a terrifying four-wheel drift. Parsons suppressed a snort of disdain and sounded fatherly. "How much further, son?"

"Not far," the rookie barked in an unnecessarily loud voice. "Corner of Ashby and Adeline. You know, where that antique store and all—oh yeah, you wouldn't know being from out of town and all."

Parsons noted that a price war had brought the two corner gas stations down to 26.9. A huge co-op supermarket was now on their left. What the hell was this pinko commie co-op crap? Why couldn't it be something normal like a Safeway or a Lucky? Where was that no-good daughter he'd come 500 miles to get the hell out of all this?

That bitch wife of his, amply deserving of everything he ever did or did not do to her, wouldn't give him his own daughter's address. Just because he hadn't taken much interest in her before, like enough to have her address at college, didn't mean he didn't have the right to straighten her out now. After all, he was paying the bills, and that was all that counted. Kid could have gone to college anywhere—Chico, Santa Barbara or UCLA—and saved him a fortune by living at home. So what did she pick, and what did the wife back her on? Pinko commie Berkeley. Degenerate U.

The rookie squealed to a stop and turned to Parsons. "This is it." He touched his gun.

They piled out of the squad car. "Where?" Parsons asked.

The rookie jerked a thumb toward a huge antique store on the corner, then approached a lone figure standing in front. "You called for the police, ma'am? To report a possible homicide?"

Parsons heard the woman's wail over the siren of the meat wagon which was pulling up behind them and peered over the rookie's shoulder.

The woman was a wisp of a girl with filthy bare feet. Her hair was a matted mass, so long that it reached her thigh, and red—to match her political convictions, thought Parsons. She was dressed, if you could call it that, in some rag covered with symbols Parsons vaguely associated with witchcraft. Goddamn freak. This, he figured, was the ultimate false alarm.

The rookie flipped his pad open. "What's your name?"

"Mushroom." Her voice was both a whisper and a scream.

"Mushroom?" The rookie raked his fingers through his crewcut. "What kind of a name is that?"

"Because I like to eat them."

"Well, gosh, I eat them too, but nobody ever thought to call me—"

"Different kind of mushroom." She was weaving slightly, listing acutely to one side, but somehow didn't seem drunk.

It was then Parsons noticed the window of the antique store behind her. It was broken, but what caught his eye was the ancient harpoon. Suddenly he was rock-hard, thinking of the frizzy-haired hippie in the second story window, and he didn't know why.

"And the," the rookie's voice cracked, "deceased. Did you see—?"

But Mushroom was screaming, an eerie, unnatural explosion of sound that set her hair in motion, like wisps of smoke and flame. She hugged herself, desperately sinking her fingernails into her upper arms. The red light atop the squad car caught her full in the eyes, but Parsons had the uncomfortable feeling that some of the red he saw was in the eyes themselves.

Suddenly she smiled. "The blood was beautiful." Parsons and the rookie looked at each other.

Sue Hollister Barr

Parsons could feel the hairs rise on the back of his neck. Steadying herself, Mushroom extended her hand backwards, ushering them graciously through the broken window of the antique store. "Please. Step into my parlor."

The rookie looked as if he were going to cry. Parsons groaned. Incompetents, nothing but incompetents. On the other hand Parsons had seen enough in his life to know what a wrong step could cost. He would have loved to have screamed himself, but his voice came out like silk. "You go ahead first, son. I have faith in you, and you need to know you can do it." The look on the idiot's face was priceless. The fool went ahead first. Parsons waited a moment or two, giving the tattered rag the girl wore a careful enough look to feel pretty sure she wasn't packing anything lethal. His eyes met those of a burly middle-aged attendant from the meat wagon, and he jerked his head toward Mushroom. The attendant nodded. Then Parsons, gun drawn, left the girl behind and followed the rookie through the hole in the window.

A thick smell of mildew and mustiness settled into Parson's nostrils. He hated antiques and was glad there weren't many of them in Southern California. What was the big deal? He looked around as the red beacon from the squad car swept through dust and dankness. A bunch of beat-up old furniture? To him, the past was depressing and made him feel uncomfortable somehow.

To avoid seeing the harpoon again Parsons had

24

his eyes on the threadbare orientals, covering the floor like erratic fungi, when he first saw the blood. It was pooled on a patch of bare floor in front of one of those Victorian front hall pieces with the big mirror surrounded by clothes hooks. He could barely make out the shape of the bowler hat on one of the hooks, and he probably would have missed the blood if it hadn't been spotlighted by the streetlight outside.

Parsons bent over to take a look while the beacon from the squad car made its sweep. He was about to touch it when he saw an additional drop land in the pool's center, rippling it gently. He yanked his hand back and looked up.

Directly over Parson's head was the bowler hat, except that it wasn't a bowler hat. It was the head of a Negro, staring down at him with a look of almost comical surprise. Parsons jerked sideways, banging his shoulder against the bottom of the mirror. He heard a slurpy, squealing sound, like he'd heard in a meat packing plant once when someone had struggled to get a side of beef off a hook, and the head fell into his lap. Rocking back onto his rear, he felt something warm and wet oozing out of the base of the head to soak slowly through his trousers, as the head came to rest in an upright position in the full light of the street lamp.

Parsons leaped to his feet, sending the head rolling across the floor like some punctured basketball. Directly to his right, the rookie's scream cut through Parsons' nervous system like an electric shock. He turned, saw the rookie's silhouette double over, and heard the sounds of puking. Beyond the rookie was a brass log holder filled with logs which turned out to be two-foot sections of a muscular Negro's arms and legs. The oriental rug in front of Parsons was littered with bits of bone and tissue. The rookie stumbled to his feet and ran from the store. Parsons followed, but with more dignity.

The girl was gone. Parsons looked at the burly middle-aged attendant, who was dabbing iodine on some scratches on his face. "So," the attendant said, "was I supposed to know she had the strength of a demon? When one of you screamed in there, she went mad."

Another incompetent.

"Hey, I'm sure you did your best," Parsons said. "Did she say anything useful to you before she, uh, left?"

"Oh, sure. She claimed she was with a crowd of people last night that included the deceased. She described them all very carefully—names, first at least, where to find them, the whole schmeer."

"You got all that out of her? Good work, buddy."

"It was nothing. She was so far gone on peyote, she hardly had any irises left. If she hadn't been moving around so damn much, I would have declared her dead."

"Any idea who the murderer is?"

"Hard to sort out. She was not the most rational when she started to describe that part of the evening. All I really got was that it was somebody who started to rant on about the virtues of hard work and clean living. Must hate hippies.''

"Oh Jesus," the rookie said. "Just what we need in Berkeley, what with all the weirdos and all.''

"Calm down, son. What are you talking about?" It occurred to Parsons that if he heard one more "and all" out of this rookie, the next person to perpetrate an act of violence might be himself.

The rookie wiped some vomit from his lips with a shaky hand. His eyes said life wasn't acting like the Superman comics he read only a few years ago said it would. "What I'm talking about is a murderer who doesn't like hippies.''

Chapter 2

Ronna couldn't stop trembling.

"Chile, there'd be no way I'd let any boy do that to me."

Ronna felt the Negro girl's arms tighten around her and had no problem believing this.

Ursula ran a hand through her dark hair from her place on the opposite side of the room. "Like, come on, Josephine. It was only a dream. She'll be all right. Help me find the rest of the coke."

"Ursula, honey, listen up. There ain't any. You snorted it all." As Josephine continued to hold her, Ronna sensed a real tenderness and an intensity that puzzled her because she'd never felt it from her own sex. "Ronna, honey, listen—men ain't worth a damn."

The last words, husky and low, sent a shiver

through Ronna. She looked up into Josephine's dark eyes, sensed scar tissue, and at last forgot her own dream.

Josephine laughed, and Ronna imagined a sheet hastily thrown over a corpse. "I had me my very first one when I was seven," Josephine said, smirking.

"Seven?" Ronna couldn't believe it.

"That ain't nothin'. By the time I was fourteen, I could take on five or six, or maybe even seven of them on a good night."

Gravel crunched under a car in the driveway. Ursula was at the window with the speed of a striking snake. "Jesus Christ!"

Josephine rolled her eyes at Ronna. "Don't you worry, now. She's always like this by morning."

Ursula was off in the other direction, down the hall and, by the sounds of it, out the back door, before Ronna heard the knocking at the front door. Now Josephine looked worried.

Ronna wrapped her Bambi bedspread around herself and stumbled into the hall to open the door. Four glum-looking police officers faced her. The youngest took off his hat to rake his fingers through his crewcut.

"Your name, please?" one of the older officers asked.

"Ronna Parsons."

"May we step in, Miss Parsons? We understand a colored woman named Josephine spent the night—or at least part of the night—here."

Ronna could feel Josephine behind her, could

almost smell her fear. "Whatcha' want with me? I ain't done nuthin' wrong."

The young cop looked sickly and impatient. "No woman would have had the strength and all," he started to say, but one of his associates shushed him with a wave of the hand. Ronna looked thoughtfully at Josephine, easily five foot ten with manly muscles tensing under her yellow-brown skin.

Simba was backtracking down Telegraph later that morning in search of the antique dagger he always wore on a leather thong round his neck. While cursing his inability to remember where he'd been the night before, he reached the corner where he'd heard the woman's scream earlier that same morning.

Coming down the block from Regent was a squad car, perhaps the only feature of middle-class America Simba would deign to notice. A Negro girl in the back met his eyes as the car stopped for the light at the corner in front of him. It wasn't the hatred that sent the shudder through him. It was the absolute certainty that this girl knew him, and yet he was sure he had never laid eyes on her.

The girl clawed the partition separating her from the three cops in the front. Simba could see her screaming and pointing at him, although he couldn't hear through the glass.

The cops turned as one to stare at Simba. As their hands flew to the door handles, Simba's flew to the drug stash in his jeans' pocket. Too close.

He'd never get away with plucking it out and discarding it.

Simba fought the lump in his throat, the tingly sense of unreality threatening to freeze him to the spot. Quick, without looking, what was behind him? Shakespeare and Company, one of the campus bookstores. Tall bookshelves. Skinny aisles. Probably crowded already—it always was. He about-faced into the place. As the door slammed behind him, it cut off a "Hey, you!" and the rumble of feet on the pavement outside.

Inside, a scrawny, strung-out girl blocked his way. "Like, wow, do you think you could spare a quarter so I could get an order of turkey dressing at Robbie's? I haven't, like, eaten anything in—" Simba knocked her aside, amidst a hail of "Hey" and "Be cool." He leapt over a pile of books on the floor, plowed through an aisle of lethargic browsers, and turned in time to see a cop—blocked by the crowd Simba had just brushed through—reach for his gun and think better of it.

No, please! roared through Simba's mind with shadowy half-promises to cut his hair and go back to school if he could just this once get away. In front of him was the rear door, but wouldn't the cops think of that? He bolted to the left, down the steps to the basement storeroom.

What if there wasn't a way out?

Simba was digging out his drug stash, hampered by the motion of his legs in running the length of the storeroom, when a burly arm caught him. Simba looked into a bearded face that reminded him more than anything, perhaps because of the name of the bookstore, of a Shakespearean actor.

They both looked up as the sounds of turmoil reverberated through the floor inches above their heads.

Plucking the hashish from Simba's fingers, his captor took a quick sniff and cocked a bushy brow. "Me thinks the alcohol-addicted pigs wish to incarcerate you for the unpardonable offense of smoking a substance that isn't addictive." He pocketed the hash in somewhat baggy, very faded, brown corduroy trousers. "I assume the question of whether I'm honorable enough to return this to you is not foremost in your mind at this time."

Simba looked to the basement window at the front of the store, the one place the cops might not expect him.

"No," the other man whispered. Simba saw a well of tenderness in the warm golden-brown of the other man's eyes. Then he heard a clatter on the stairs and received a shove that almost knocked the wind out of him. He fell backwards into a huge box full of coverless paperbacks.

His captor gave the dusty hardcover he'd been holding all along a rueful look. "First edition. Only 500 in print." Like a discus thrower in the last Olympics Simba had watched, he hurled the book at the front window. It hit the corner, knocking it open with a shattering of glass just as the first cop appeared, and Simba dove under the books.

"Oh, officer, I was so scared!"

It took Simba a moment to identify the voice of the flamboyant homosexual as that of his former captor.

"Christ, just what I need. Higgins! The front! He went out the basement window! Look, buddy, I'm going to have to take a look around, ask you a few questions. Your name?"

"Chutney McLaughlin."

"Higgins! The front, goddammit! You got any identification?"

"One moment."

"He did go through that window?"

"Oh, yes, officer."

"Something wrong with your trouser pocket there?"

"Oh, no, officer! Just a little crowded in there, if you know what I mean. Here's my identification."

"Christ! Work here at the bookstore?"

"I own the bookstore, sir."

There was a moment of silence, during which Simba realized a book was hooked precariously over his left ear. Then he heard the crinkling of paper.

"That's pretty good for someone who's only twenty-two. I took you for the stock boy."

"It was passed down to me by my grandfather."

Scared shitless and uncomfortable as hell, Simba still heard the warmth in the last word. This cat really loved his grandfather.

"Yeah, well, like I say I'm going to have to look around a little."

"Oh, yes, officer, by all means!"

Simba was squeezing his eyes shut, hoping like a little kid that if he couldn't see he couldn't be seen. His sweat beaded up on his nose and dripped on a book below. One of his legs was so badly cramped that even in the midst of his terror it occurred to him that even the electric chair might be a kinder fate than spending another millisecond in the same position.

Simba heard a step in his direction. Every muscle tensed, which caused the book hooked over his left ear to shift slightly. His throat felt like it was going to crack from dryness. He was sure he was about to either cough or sneeze because of the dust and the smell of print from all the paperbacks.

"Can you describe the individual you saw go out that window, Mr. McLaughlin?"

Damn, that was close!

"Oh, yes. Long black hair and a full beard to match. Hypnotic blue eyes. Six feet tall, at least. Beautiful build."

Six one and change, to be exact—and never before in a situation he couldn't fight his way out of. Was this excruciating helplessness what it felt like to be a woman?

"Yummy broad shoulders, skinny little rump. Nice proportions in the front, too, if you know what I mean."

"Christ!"

The cop was right next to Simba's box. The

34

book was slipping off Simba's left ear.

"You know, you're not so bad yourself, officer. Tell me, what has this naughty boy done? Do I need protection?"

"Hey, get away from me. We...uh...want to question him in connection with a murder. You're too much. I'll send another officer back to question you later, so don't go swishing off anywhere."

The book slipped off Simba's ear. To his hearing, it sounded like a glacier falling off a mountain. Then there was a horrible moment in which he heard nothing, followed by the familiar clatter of footsteps going up the stairs. Ever so carefully, he moved his leg. Suddenly the books were shoved off the top of his head.

"Come on out of there!"

Stiff and shaken, Simba stepped out to confront a stern and angry Chutney. He was holding a gun.

"Look, man, I've gotten myself into a lot of trouble because I assumed the pigs were after your ass over a little smoke, but that's not the point. The point is that what's right is right, and I think healthy disrespect for the law stops far short of harboring anyone associated with anything that so clearly crosses Emerson's line between freedom and license to murder. I'm turning you in."

"Wait a minute, man."

"No wait-a-minutes, no disclaimers. The more shit I hear out of you, the more it occurs to me that you're probably guilty of the murder yourself. Get your ass up those stairs."

"That gun isn't loaded."

Chutney stare turned to puzzlement. "How can you tell?"

"The cylinder's hanging to the side." Held by this irate, righteous individual who Simba couldn't help from liking, the gun looked as ineffectual as a limp dick.

Chutney looked down at the revolver. "Oh, shit!"

Simba started to laugh. "I'm sorry, man. It's just that after all I've been through.... I really appreciate everything you did for me, and I'm sorry I got you into this. I swear to God, I didn't have any idea this had anything to do with a murder until just now either." Suddenly deflated, Simba sank to the floor, squatting with his head in his hands. "My ass is grass."

"And the pigs have the lawn mower?"

"And I have no idea why."

Piper stopped walking to tilt her head up toward the sun, closing her eyes. The warmth and glittering orange colors washed over her face like a wave at the beach. The musty smell of eucalyptus filled her nose. There was a moment of absolute quiet, a peace so thick and plush she imagined it had a sound all its own but that, like ultraviolet light, it was outside the human range of perception.

Piper stood still, rejoicing in the gentle play of each little breeze through her clothes and over her skin. A soft sound, a rhythm she never would have picked up if she hadn't been listening so carefully, entered her range of hearing. She opened her eyes.

Someone was watching her intently from the shade of the eucalyptus grove across the street. To her sun-blitzed eyes it looked like the person was leaning against a brown whale. Her vision cleared. The whale was an old school bus, sloppily painted an unhealthy-looking brown. The man reminded her of a hobbit out of the Tolkien trilogy. He was squat with skinny arms, a pot belly, pasty skin and hair all over him that somehow mirrored the unhealthy brown of the bus. As she watched, his gnarled hand fumbled for a decrepit plant resting on the front fender—as if she might steal it if he wasn't careful. He then made an ineffectual attempt at looking friendly.

"Hi. My name's Midas."

"I might have known."

"Excuse me? I didn't quite hear you. I have problems with my hearing, you know, but I couldn't help but notice that you're the kind of girl I'd like to get to know and . . ."

But Piper was hardly listening. Like a radio, she'd gradually tuned out Midas and was happy again, grooving to the beat that was coming closer. It was deliciously complex. She was jiggling to it now, tapping out the beginnings of a counter rhythm with the thick leather sandals she'd had custom-made in a beatnik sandal shop in North Beach years before. Snatches of lyrics and melody had just started to bubble through her when the source of the beat appeared at the corner of Bowditch and Durant and turned her way.

He was the blackest man Piper had ever seen. At once regal and ultra-hip, he sported a red headband, an elegant goatee, a huge grin and glittering white teeth. Although not tall, every inch of him was magnificently muscled. Strong, beautifully sculpted hands drummed out the beat Piper had been listening to on his shapely thighs. Its show-stopping intricacy and precision marked him as a professional.

Piper broke into song with the sexy rasp in her well-trained alto that her mother had always hated. "Liquid sun and whisper breeze. A storybook sky that's sure to please. All I ask is to be alive."

She was interrupted by a deep baritone. "And not brought down by a bunch of jive." The drummer squatted next to her and beat out an elaborate break with whatever refuse was within reach of his remarkably fast fingers—a rock, a stick, some glass, and a piece of chrome off a car. His bare, curvy arms shone like dark satin in the sun. Across the front of his sleeveless black T-shirt bright purple letters read, "The Gizmo Delicious." Piper didn't know what that meant but, acutely aware as she was of his tight clothing, she figured she'd be the last to debate its accuracy if he turned out to be the gizmo.

He smiled up at her as her sandaled feet, making their final break with any conscious control on her part, slapped the pavement with an almost syncopated counter beat. Piper opened her mouth, and there was the next verse. "Feel it with me. Don't be shy. It's too short a time until we die. All I ask is to be alive. And not brought down by a bunch of jive." His fingers were a blur; her feet broke into a stampede. Vaguely she realized they had an audience that was clapping, yelling and beating on telephone polls. Finally they wound down to a halt amidst whistles and cheers. The drummer got to his feet and hefted her onto his shoulders in one continuous motion.

Feeling the thick muscles at the back of his neck against her inner thighs, Piper had to ask, "What is 'The Gizmo Delicious'?"

"The name of my group."

"How many other people in the band?"

He laughed. "None." The crowd was starting to dissipate as he let her down.

"How could this be?" she asked.

He fingered the purple letters across his pectorals. "The group came into being this morning. What amazes me is the paint's dry."

Piper heard someone mutter to one of the few remaining stragglers behind her that this was no time to hang around in public drawing attention to themselves. Other than that they were alone except for Midas, the hobbit, on whose face Piper caught an angry look he quickly suppressed when their eyes met. She turned her attention back to the drummer. "Only this morning?"

"Only last night I was the lead drummer for Sabita."

"Wow!"

"Unfortunately, the manager and I had a slight difference of opinion. Dude felt the honor of being in a top band was all the pay this boy had coming to him. I felt all the gratitude he had coming to him was my fist in his fat face."

His tone was matter-of-fact. Piper decided this was not a person who wasted time looking for pity or dwelling on the past.

"What's your name?" she asked.

"Bell." He beamed. "What's yours, baby?"

"Piper." She bit her lip; she felt electric. She threw her head back, shaking her hair until she could feel it on the back of her neck, and she smiled when it occurred to her how very much her father would disapprove of all this. Just as she was starting to envision an infinity of doors opening in front of her, she heard someone trip over the piece of chrome Bell had left on the sidewalk at her side. She turned to discover Midas, uncomfortably close. He started to clap, and it occurred to Piper to wonder, as she watched him, if his level of physical coordination was such that he would be able to keep it up.

"You were really quite good," Midas told Piper, attempting to conceal his excited admiration behind a mild aura of condescension.

"Thank you," Piper said graciously.

"You should be singing professionally."

"She probably already is," Bell put in.

"I'm not," Piper answered. It was another one of those things her parents had always managed to suppress. "But I'd love to."

Midas continued as if neither of them had spoken. "As it so happens, I know some people in the business. Maybe I could help you out."

"Which coast, man?" Bell asked.

It took Midas a little too long to decide. "Why this coast, of course."

Bell didn't seem to notice. He looked thoughtful as he smoothed his goatee. "Tough coast to break into the scene, man. She might do a whole lot better in New York. That's where I'm headed."

"Yeah?" Piper was ecstatic. "I've never been east! Oh, Bell, do you think there might be a place in The Gizmo Delicious for an inexperienced female singer?"

"You don't happen to have a microbus capable of carrying a righteous set of drums, do you?"

Piper shook her head no, but Midas started jumping up and down and pointing. "Look what *I've* got!"

Bell's eyes widened at the sight of the old school bus. "Outta' sight!" He cartwheeled across the street and scrambled onto the roof, where he stood like a conquering king.

Piper, sizzling with excitement, put an arm around Midas without thinking. "You want to join a rock 'n' roll band?"

"You bet!"

Piper looked down to find her breast wedged under Midas' chin. Judging from the look in his eye, she figured he would have said "You bet!" if she'd asked him to vote Republican. She let him go and bounded across the street.

Bell was sitting cross-legged now, beating out

a new rhythm on the roof of the bus. Piper saw that he was not alone. There were two guys, seeming to hide on the other side of the bus. One was the guy with the black hair and beard that had looked up at her early that morning when she was naked. The other, talking urgently in low tones, had a voice trained for the stage.

Bell turned to her happily. "We are on a roll! Meet singer/composer Simba, who you've gotta' remember from the Free Speech Movement, and Chutney McLaughlin, an independent businessman with some much-needed bread to fund all this. All they ask is one teeny little thing."

"What's that?" Piper asked.

"That we leave for New York by tomorrow."

"Disgusting," Parsons muttered to himself. He quickly looked away from the house he'd been staring at to make sure nobody had heard him, then rechecked the address he'd gotten out of the rookie when, in the midst of a painfully detailed description of the murder investigation, the rookie had started reeling off the names of everybody involved.

Meanwhile, the local head honchos had asked Parsons to help out with the investigation—and he probably would. It would look good on his record if he could show up the local yokels by nailing the murderer himself. The idiots back home would be forced to give him his long overdue promotion.

But first he had matters of his own to attend to.

He looked back at the house. For one thing it was old. Far worse, some commie bastard was using an American flag as a makeshift curtain. Love beads hung from the porch roof. A poster showing two ducks fornicating was tacked onto the front door. At the end of the path a scrawny cat, sporting a pierced ear and a single gold earring, was staring vacantly up at Parsons.

Since no one was around Parsons kicked the cat aside on his way to the door. Its sluggish reaction annoyed him further. He pounded on the door, trying not to look at the ducks.

A gangly boy with hair to his shoulders answered the door. Parsons puffed himself up.

"Come on in, man." The boy flashed the peace sign.

Parsons missed the uniform he'd left at home in Anaheim. "I'm here to see my daughter." He was doing his best to sound intimidating.

The fear Parsons yearned for flickered across the boy's face only to be replaced by an annoyingly serene smile. "I don't know any of the chicks in this house very well. What's your daughter's name?"

"Ronna Parsons."

The boy shrugged. "I'll see if I can find her."

Parsons followed him into the house which was filthy. The boy ambled up the stairs. Parsons looked into one of the downstairs rooms. One of those little, circular, carved-wood, hippie tables covered with God-knows-what was sitting next to the Mickey Mouse rug he'd given Ronna when she was a kid.

Wandering back into the front hall, Parsons could hear the boy upstairs checking bedrooms. How many people lived in this one house anyway? There had been enough mattresses in the room he'd seen for at least ten.

Near the back of the house Parsons paused. He could hear her voice.

"Oh, Josephine, did you know him long? I guess you must have since you went to bed with him."

Parsons came around the corner. Ronna was on the phone with her back towards him.

"Met him last night? Well, I guess if the chemistry is right. Poor boy."

Parsons was steaming. Poor boy? Some slut friend of his daughter's puts out the first night and she's saying "poor boy"?

"How long did they keep you there this morning?"

They? What kind of communism did they teach at the University of Berkeley? Group sex?

"So you were free to go, but they might want to talk to you again?"

Parsons doubted "they" would respect this Josephine enough to ever say as much as hello to her again.

"You're leaving with Ursula for New York tomorrow? Hey, it was nice of her to arrange it for you, even if she is being a little secretive about who you're going with. At least she can think of someone other than herself. I didn't even know you played bass. But what if they want to talk to you again or do something more?"

Something more than Parsons's rage against

his daughter's mother vied for his attention. It had to do with names and police work, but it was quickly buried as Parsons, steaming, fixated yet again on his bitch wife's two most unforgivable crimes—forever expressing her actual feelings and, even more unforgivable, enjoying life.

This daughter of a bitch was telling a friend to hang around for the next all-night gang bang? Parsons could feel the flush on his cheeks.

"You want *me* to join you?"

In what?

"This morning was good for me, too, and I could feel the closeness between us."

Parsons was beside himself. He did note that Ronna had inherited at least enough of a shred of decency from him to sound a little uncomfortable and confused.

"I'll go with you if you stay here and they want you again, but I won't go to New York. Guess I'm not very hip, but I do believe in seeing things through, and my education is important to me. I don't want to disappoint my parents, so thanks, but no thanks."

Parsons snatched the phone out of his daughter's hand and slammed it down. He expected to see shame in her face at the sight of him. What he saw first was a child's pure, unquestioning love, then an anguish that he didn't at all understand except that it didn't seem to be related to shame. He was almost touched. For a moment he almost saw the world through different eyes. Then he saw the old familiar features of his bitch wife in his daughter's face.

"Hello, Father. I haven't seen you in a long time. I didn't know you were coming." Her tone was civil, if somewhat flat. Now she was frowning up at him, studying his face. "Is something wrong?" At last he saw something halfway appropriate in her face—fear.

She could ask such a thing? After stating that the group sex she and a friend had participated in this morning had been good for her, and that she could feel the closeness? She certainly must have felt a lot of closeness. Bang. Bang. Bang. And she'd be glad to go with her friend, if her friend didn't go to New York and they wanted these two tramps again. Parsons wanted to speak, but he'd been trained well and, whatever else he did, he never spoke what he felt. His bitch wife had never let him hit his child either. Well, he'd show her.

Parsons drew back his fist.

Chapter 3

Ronna squeezed her eyes shut. She could feel the tears welling up again and knew too well what their salt could do to her battered face. Touching her face to wipe them away, though, was even worse.

Her own father! He hated her, but she mustn't think about it. It would lead to more tears. Her eyes flickered open. Through a bloody haze Ronna caught a glimpse of the Mickey Mouse rug she held in a sweaty heap in her lap. She closed her eyes again but didn't squeeze this time. That hurt, too.

Ronna's heart started to pound, and she knew there was no physical explanation. Inside her was a scream that couldn't get out, that thrashed and twisted inside her until she was sure it—not her physical wounds—would kill her. She had to find comfort.

A large hand started to stroke her, miraculously knowing where not to touch because of her wounds. "Ronna, you're safe now." It was the deepest, most commanding male voice she'd ever heard. "Nothing more is going to hurt you. I promise." She felt him next to her now. A huge arm encircled her, possessed of the same miraculous knowledge of what not to touch.

Someone else's arm, lacking this knowledge, attempted to encircle her from the other side. "Get your goddamn hands off her!" Ronna recognized Josephine's voice. "Leave it to a knucklehead like you to try and cop a feel!"

"Stupid bitch!" bellowed the male voice. The second arm was whipped away. A shadow fell over Ronna's closed eyes, and she inhaled the sharp tang of a man's sweat. "Can't you see you're hurting her?" Ronna opened her eyes. Shaded by this man, she could withstand the light of day. She looked out over the peeling brown paint on the hood of the bus at a flat, colorless land she knew wasn't California anymore. Then she looked up at him—that black hair and blue eyes with tendrils of electric green that were lasering through Josephine just now.

"Girl," Josephine whined, "I should kick your fucking ass for inviting this cocksucker Simba along without telling me."

"Ditto, bitch," Simba snapped back. "I don't care how well you play bass, except I'm not dumb enough to waste my time trying to talk to Ursula before sundown. When did the two of you stop snorting coke last night? Around noontime?"

Ronna tried to move her neck. Since she couldn't, she used her shoulders to turn herself so she could see Ursula sleeping in the back of the bus. Ursula's brunette hair was a tumbling mess, and her mouth was open. Ronna had never seen her looking so childlike. "Is . . ." It was hard to talk ". . . is Ursula okay?"

Simba gave Ronna a look of wonder, then gently put his fingers to her mouth. "Don't talk." He touched her chin lightly, frowning. "The bruise here, and the fact that you can't move your neck . . . The scum who did this started out with a fist." He paused to look over the rest of her. "Before he got into other things."

Ronna didn't understand, then she felt a new pain between her legs. "No!" Simba's fingers silenced her again, but the scream raged within. Tears scalded the raw flesh on her cheeks. Shaking, her fingers kneaded the Mickey Mouse rug.

Daddy!

Simba wrapped his arms around her, again with that uncanny knowledge of exactly where she'd been hurt. "Don't think about it. Close your eyes." She did. He started to rock her. "Listen to me. Your brain is like half a walnut with two separate hemispheres. Concentrate. A cool, velvet green is pouring into the right hemisphere. Deep inside it is the calm of the forest floor and a hint of mint. The right hemisphere is full now. There is nothing in it except this lush greenness. Now concentrate harder. The green is pouring from the right hemisphere of your brain into the left hemisphere. It's pooling in the bottom of the left hemisphere, then spreading. Now it's filling the left hemisphere and emptying the right. The left hemisphere is full. A new color is pouring into the right, yellow and warm like a million childhood memories of the sun at the beach. It's filling the right hemisphere with laughter and running, giggles and fun."

Ronna was on the beach at Santa Monica with her pail and shovel. Her mother was in the yellow cotton bathing suit with the elasticized gathering up the back. Drowsy from the sun, Ronna stretched out on the warm sand. Was it her mother's hands stroking her, or was it Simba? Then came that brief jerk of vertigo before Ronna's final drop into a much needed and very welcome sleep.

In Ronna's dream she is even further in the past. Mommy is outside in a long cotton skirt, boiling a huge tub full of clothes. Daddy's there, too. She knows it's him although he looks a little different, like a cross between the farmer in "American Gothic" and the hunchback of Notre Dame. He's blocking the sun, and yelling at Mommy. Ronna stands next to him, puts her arm around his knee, pats it with a pudgy-fingered hand, and cranes her head back to look up at him. Little as she is, she can only understand three or four out of every five words he yells, but emotion she can measure with the accuracy of a thermometer.

Daddy is furious again.

Twisted

It has something to do with Mommy not working hard enough again, which seems funny to Ronna. Mommy is always working hard and never has any time for Ronna. Or Lucia, her sister. Or Portia, her other sister. Or her brothers who look out for her, Luke and Eb.

Finally Daddy shakes her loose so she falls on her fanny all the way to the ground. Ronna doesn't mind the shake. She loves Daddy anyway. And now that he's gone the sun is shining yellow all over her, warm and happy. And look, Mommy is looking at her! Mommy is always too busy to look at her, but she's looking now with a look that is as warm and happy as the sun.

The scene is fading. Funny, Ronna thinks to herself in the dream. It doesn't feel like a dream. It has the poignant familiarity of a memory, but it's set in the nineteenth century, so that's ridiculous.

The twisted trees are back again. The sun is gone. The ground is cold and faraway. Mommy's huge washing tub has been left, upside down, to rust under the trees. Daddy is standing before her—grayer, more twisted, about her height. Ronna wants to touch him, to smooth the ugly wrinkles from his face, but he's yelling furiously. This time it's at Ronna. He hates her! She can see it burning in his eyes, scalding her, but she continues to peer deeper. Somewhere behind the hate there has to be a teeny bit of the love she must find in him or she'll go crazy.

There is none.

A scream is born in Ronna. She turns away

51

from Daddy. Next to her is her little sister Lucia, looking to Ronna to find out what to do next, just like always. But Lucia isn't a doll anymore. She's big; she has boobies. There's terror in her eyes, pleading. She needs Ronna, but Ronna doesn't know what to do.

Daddy is holding Ronna now. Is the hate gone? Will he make it all better? Her silly hair blows into her face, and she can't see.

"Ya' missed, boy. Almost got my pinkie."

Who almost got Daddy's pinkie? What is the cold thing near her neck?

Simba stared down at the battered girl sleeping in his arms. Most of the others were outside. The bus was stopped by the side of the road somewhere just west of Elko, Nevada.

The girl's face looked like chum; thrown overboard, it could attract sharks worldwide. Still, he felt her warmth, the soft curves of her body against his. Suddenly her face wasn't a mess. All that was left was the beginnings of a bruise on her chin. She was beautiful, the sleeping princess. Long thin brows arched high over deep-set eyes, closed now with spidery brown lashes peacefully shading her cheeks. A spattering of freckles crossed a gently upturned nose. With the sun-splashed phone on the table behind her she reminded Simba of a high school girl out of *Bye Bye Birdie*. There was a vulnerability in her heart-shaped face he found irresistible.

Simba was shaken. He'd never had an acid flash-back before. It was particularly strange since it'd been awhile since he'd done any LSD. He felt a clap on the back and looked up into the warm golden-brown of Chutney's eyes.

"A face only a lover could love? I give you credit, man."

"For what?" Simba was still shaken and confused.

"For the look of ardor in thy eye. She's a mess. I can't even imagine what she looks like."

It was the wrong thing to say, considering the flashback, but Simba could hear the tender intentions underneath Chutney's theatrical voice. He looked back at Ronna and jumped when he saw that her beautiful face had turned back to shark bait.

Again, Chutney had no way of understanding. "Easy, Simba. It may take you awhile to get over the shock of finding her last night. You didn't know her?"

"Never saw her before last night."

Chutney settled into the seat next to him, tucking a knee up under his beard. In the short time they'd known each other, Simba had already learned to recognize this as Chutney's I'll-be-your-unpaid-therapist pose. "Tell me about it."

"I smoked all the hash you gave back to me. Didn't want it on me in case the cops caught up with me again. Had another one of those blackouts I told you about. Then it was night, and I was in the front room of the place on Regent where Ursula asked me to stop by with the bus and get her stuff for the trip. My eyes weren't adjusted to the dark, but I could see a shape on the bed and thought Ursula might have crashed. Unfucking likely. Bitch probably hasn't gone to sleep before dawn since she was in grammar school."

Chutney laughed. "True."

"Couldn't find the light at first. Knocked over one of those carved wooden tables and made a lot of noise. Ronna started to thrash around on the bed and cry out things like 'Daddy, don't.'"

"Her father beat her up?"

"Worse. Her father raped her."

Chutney opened his mouth but said nothing.

The old familiar desire to avoid it all hit Simba as subtly as the boom on a 50-foot sloop. "You didn't bring anything to trip on, did you?"

"LSD? Acid? No. Less than twenty-four hours has elapsed since the first hint that I might be temporarily abandoning my bookstore to travel east with a band that is—to say the least—in the embryonic stage. I thought I was doing extraordinarily well to remember to bring the three pairs of not too filthy underwear I had to scrape off the bathroom floor." Chutney struck a noble pose—hand to heart, head held high. "Truthfully, the question here is not whether I also remembered a change of socks, which I did not, but rather why am I doing this?" He gazed heavenward. "And what is the meaning of life?"

"I give up; I hate riddles. Go ahead and tell me." The girl stirred in Simba's arms, and he held her closer.

"The meaning of life? Damned if I know. What I have been trying to figure out is what I'm doing in an old school bus full of hippies headed east."

"And?"

"At first I thought it was pig paranoia. Hanging around to be part of a murder investigation after successfully tricking the cops into thinking I constitute the ultimate threat to their brand of masculinity—that is, being homosexual—is not my idea of a secure situation in life."

"Yeah. You would have gotten your balls busted for that. But they'd have figured out eventually that you never even met the guy that got butchered."

"So? Did you?"

"I don't know, man. I was too stoned at the time. Ursula says I did. I don't remember. Considering what happened, I don't want to remember." Ronna jerked in her sleep, startling Simba. "So if pig paranoia was first, what was second?"

"I don't know. I never thought of myself as impulsive. Intellectually, I can't even begin to figure it out. A voice inside says it has something to do with you, man, and something to do with the East."

"The East?" Ronna started to thrash about, and Simba stroked her. Outside he heard voices. The drummer, Bell, who was solidly built but not tall, was trying to kiss the Amazonian Josephine. That bitch, taller than any woman Simba had ever seen, wasn't going for it.

Chutney looked as if he was in another world, possibly another lifetime. "The East. When I was little I had a recurrent nightmare. It was about an old house with a funny double porch in front."

"Haunted?"

Chutney laughed and lost that otherworldly look. "Undoubtedly, but the part that bothered me was the trees. My grandfather made me describe them in painstaking detail, right down to the smell and the feel of the bark. He said what I was describing perfectly were eastern trees, plentiful on the north shore of Long Island but nonexistent west of the Mississippi." The otherworldly look was back. "I've never been east of the Mississippi."

Ronna let out a piercing scream.

Josephine gave Bell a final, nasty push away and jumped back into the bus. "What did you do to her, chump?"

Midas, the creepy little guy who owned the bus, materialized out of nowhere, ignoring Ronna but fussing compulsively over everything else. "Who put a candy wrapper in the green Rubbermaid garbage can? I keep tools there. Who put ashes in the ashtray? What's in this huge box? Somebody's pet elephant? This whole thing is ridiculous. There wasn't enough time to prepare my plants emotionally."

Simba tuned them all out to concentrate on Ronna. Her eyes popped open with the same otherworldly look as Chutney's. She was staring up at Simba. "Luke?"

Luke? Whatever otherworld these others could see into, Simba could not. "No. My name is Simba."

"Luke!"

"Simba!" Was her father's name Luke?

"Luke! Oh my God, Luke! No!"

"Ronna, it's Simba. Your father is gone. Hundreds of miles are separating the two of you by now."

The otherworld look faded—and with it the horror he'd seen in her eyes. Oblivion was a relief until confusion replaced it. Ronna put a hand to her face, rediscovering its condition. Simba knew that the hurt he saw flooding her was far more spiritual than it was physical. "Daddy?"

"Look here, Mr. High and Mighty!"

It was that bitch Josephine, her face inches from his.

"I know you think you're God's gift to women, but what she needs is a hospital."

"Back off, bitch." Simba could feel the snarl deep in his throat. "I've seen my share of fights. Looks bad, but there's nothing wrong with Ronna I can't handle with that first-aid kit of Midas's."

Josephine's nostrils flared, but she backed off. Simba noted that the stormy look she gave him was a mere squall compared to the typhoon in her eyes when she turned to glare at Bell. He returned his attention to Ronna, whose battered body so craved sleep that she kept slipping in and out of consciousness despite her anguish.

"Daddy!"

Chutney leaned in toward Ronna, knee still tucked in under his beard. "What is Daddy doing, Ronna?"

Ronna's eyes opened. "He snatched the phone out of my hand when I was talking to Josephine about yesterday morning, about how she comforted me and how long the police kept her with them for questioning." She strained to find Josephine. "I was going to go with her if they wanted her for more questioning."

"I know, honey." Josephine's voice was husky. "I knew something was strange when you cut me short and hung up the phone. I should have come over and checked you out right away, chile."

"Then what happened?" Chutney prompted.

Ronna's smile clashed with the agony in her eyes. Her voice was even softer than usual. "He used to snatch the phone out of my hand when I was in high school. It took me back to a time when all was right with the world, a time I've since lost." Tears started down her cheeks. Simba saw she was oblivious although he knew their salt must sting. "Worse than lost. Found out it never even was. Far better to have never had than to discover that you only thought you had."

Simba knew he loved her.

"Then what happened?" Chutney repeated.

Ronna started to sob. "I don't know! I was trying to be civil, despite all I felt, when I saw the look of fury he often directed at my mother, although I never understood why. Only this time, for the first time, it was directed toward me." She stopped, puzzled.

"And?" Chutney prompted.

"And all of a sudden I was looking backwards, instead of forwards, and my feet were off the ground. The next thing I knew I was falling backwards, like in slow motion."

Simba remembered an incident in grammar

school a long time ago. "You were hit by a fist for the first time in your life. Didn't even see it coming."

"And then?" Chutney's query was gentle.

Josephine's eyes glistened with tender empathy.

Simba wanted to be someone else, somewhere else. He wasn't sure he could take it.

Even Midas, busy with a plant, paused and looked up.

"And then I woke up in Simba's arms."

"Say what?" Josephine said. "Girl, your face has seen a whole lot more than one punch."

Simba shared a puzzled look with Chutney, then studied Ronna. The bruise on her chin had lost some of its initial pink. It was older than all the others. "You were lucky, Ronna."

She frowned up at him.

Simba stroked her chin tenderly. "Glass jaw. Out with the first punch and spared the rest."

She tried to smile.

Simba tried to look reassuring because, even as he spoke the words, he realized that wasn't all there was to it. Why had her father hit her once, knocked her out, waited awhile, and then beat the shit out of her? He found himself reaching over to turn on the dashboard AM radio.

Midas started to stop him, then appeared to think better of it. "Watch the knob. It comes off if it isn't handled properly."

"It comes off because it's broken and you haven't fixed it," Simba pointed out as he turned it on and started sorting through the static. A few minutes before the hour. Perfect if the signal was still strong enough.

"I gather," Chutney was saying to Ronna, "that your father's only lapse in an otherwise perfect record of making the world a hideous place for all was the act of siring you?"

Josephine's voice throbbed with emotion. "A man who beats on his own child after he knocks her out cold should have his balls stuffed down his fucking throat."

"Yeah," put in Simba. "While he's still attached to them."

"Sunny, thank you for the..." Bobby Hebb sang sweetly from the radio. Simba stopped turning the knob. "My sunny one shines so sincere. Sunny one so true, I love you." The song ended. Eddie Floyd started in with "Knock On Wood."

Simba turned his attention back to Ronna. "At least I think you were lucky. I am beginning to wonder if oblivion is always the answer."

Arms snaked around Simba's neck from behind. Small breasts pressed insistently against his shoulders as Ursula's voice hissed in his ear. "Like, oblivion is always—most definitely—the answer, man." Ursula moved seductively to the music.

Simba ignored her. "Ronna, do you remember anything between that first punch and my finding you?"

"Dreams. Only dreams."

Chutney leaned in even closer. "Maybe they weren't all dreams. Maybe some of them were vague snatches of consciousness. Which seemed the most real?''

"They all seemed real. I dreamt a lot about you, Simba.'' Her cheeks turned even pinker, and Simba grinned as he realized she was blushing. "In one dream, you were, um, interested in Josephine but she didn't want to have anything to do with you.''

"Girl, that was real!''

"But Josephine, you were working in a field in a floor-length dress, and Simba was in a sailor's outfit carrying a harpoon. And I hadn't met Simba yet, except in Ursula's painting.''

"What else did you dream?'' Chutney asked.

"A lot of things. In one this gangly young boy who sleeps in my room a lot was trying to get me away from somebody else. I remember it was in the hallway between the back room where the phone is and my bedroom.''

"What about the clothing?'' Simba asked. "Present or past?''

"Present.''

Simba put a finger to his lips, silencing them all.

"And in the San Francisco Bay Area,'' the radio newscaster said, "Berkeley police report the second in what is now being called the Hippie Hack Murders. The dismembered body of a young boy was found in the backyard of a Regent Street crash pad. Forensic experts estimate the killing took place just before sundown yesterday.''

"Latest form of self-expression for so-called normal people?'' Chutney was bitter.

The radio continued. "The police say they are taking every step possible in order to quickly locate the person or persons responsible."

"Shee-it!" Josephine looked nervous.

Ronna looked stricken. "The gangly young boy?"

"Do you remember anything else about him?" Simba asked her.

"No. Nothing."

"Like, who cares?" Ursula was moving to the music again. "I may be hip, but nobody's going to hack me." She moved away from Simba long enough to peer out the window. "Wherever the hell we are, it's a long ways from Berkeley."

Midas let out a scream. Simba turned to see him staring into the huge box he'd suggested might contain a pet elephant earlier.

"Very funny, man." Ursula sneered. "Like, I'm supposed to suppose there's a body in there?"

Midas's dazed expression, staring back at Ursula, was pathetic. Simba disengaged himself from both Ronna and Ursula, took a giant step over a seat and joined Midas in the rear where the seats had been ripped out long ago.

The body inside the box moved. Green eyes with flecks of red in them stared up at Simba. A fist as pale as death reached up towards him, then opened to expose the biggest mushroom of peyote Simba had ever seen. "Wanta' get high?"

The voice sent a chill through him, but his answer was instant. "Yeah." He took the mushroom and started to chew on it. "What are you doing here?"

"Gravel."

"Huh?"

"I was outside, floating through the last of the sunlight. Gravel crunched in the driveway, and there was this brown whale. Inside was this huge brown bus, and inside was this huge box with a bunch of stuff in it that I stashed in the corner over there. I was very tired, and I needed to get out of town." She seemed to levitate out of the box, her red hair a surreal spiral about her head and so unnatural that it reminded Simba of something out of Flash Gordon.

Midas confronted her with all the flamboyance of an angry toddler. "Well, whoever you are—"

"My name is Mushroom."

"—you weren't invited, so buzz off!"

"No!" Simba snapped. It occurred to him that Mushroom might have more mushrooms. "We don't turn away someone who needs us." Using the commanding voice that never failed him, he found nothing but acquiescence in the faces around him. Simba took another bite of the peyote.

Mushroom materialized at his side. "The Indians believe that when you eat mushrooms you can see all things—the future, the present, and the past."

But Simba didn't want to see anything really. He could talk about mind expansion and how he only used hallucinogens and smoke—never anything like coke—but what he really wanted was escape from all things, even himself.

* * *

Piper and Bell lay on the salt flats of Utah, under the stars, making music. Piper could feel the heat of the day still in the brittle sheets of salt that kept breaking beneath them. She could also feel the fire in Bell lying on his back and furiously beating out an intricate new rhythm on his naked torso.

Piper thought she made out a crunch upon the salt, and Simba appeared out of the dark and stood above them.

Bell stopped drumming. "You okay, man?"

Piper stared.

Simba did not look like Simba. He didn't answer immediately but stood over them looking for all the world like a Yankee preacher from long ago, not a wild rebel from 1966. "Please, I beseech you. Do not do the thing that is wrong."

Piper couldn't believe the words had come out of Simba's mouth. She looked at Bell; it was obvious he couldn't either.

Piper looked back up at Simba. Same black hair, same youthful build, but somehow he looked old. Was it a trick of the dark, or did he look like the somewhat stuffy but accessible father figure Piper had never had? She did her best to adopt an uncharacteristic expression of reverent submission. "Would you, dear sir, be kind enough to answer a question I've been wondering about all my life? What, exactly, constitutes 'wrong'?"

Simba glanced at Bell before riveting Piper with those piercing blue eyes that didn't seem to belong to Simba anymore. "The freed woman in the field," he said with difficulty now. "Wrong."

Piper dropped her uncharacteristic pose. "What, pray tell, is wrong with a free woman in a field?"

"Her dress was hitched up. I..." Simba stopped confused.

Piper actually wondered what was wrong with the self-assured Yankee preacher.

Bell laughed. "I think I get it, man."

"I did the thing that is wrong," Simba mourned. Then he brightened. "But then I did the thing that is right!"

Bell beamed. "Made an honest woman out of her, no doubt."

Piper slapped Bell playfully but even she was touched by the odd hint of an ancient, but honest, simplicity.

Touched and chilled.

The Simba that wasn't Simba walked out across the salt flats. Piper felt their heat under her again as she turned back to Bell who again beat out an intricate rhythm on his torso. He paused to point a finger toward the Simba that wasn't even walking like Simba.

"That boy is bombed out of his ever-loving mind," Bell declared.

Piper nodded and giggled. Now Bell's shoulder and arm were pressed up against her. The fiery beat fired the muscles she felt moving against her body. Moonlight glittered off the white salt, illuminating the bulge in his jeans which she stared at until she felt a pulsing between her own legs.

She bit her lip.

He slowed dramatically and turned his head toward her. "Something wrong? You're not singing anymore."

Piper had been singing all day. Back when they'd stopped outside of Elko, Nevada, new lyrics had started to bubble out of her head. She'd been lying in the sage, loving its smell and grooving on the sight of Bell dancing in the sunlight in an effort to get Josephine's attention. Bell's skin was so dark that Josephine's yellow tint looked sunny when he stood next to her. A myriad of sensations had exploded within Piper every second of her 20 years, but she had never experienced jealousy. Nor did she then. "The sun became an Amazon princess," whispered the lyrics in her head. "The night became a man. The princess was hot but melted, when his passion began to expand." Piper rolled in the fragrant sage, laughing as Bell chased the unwilling Josephine around the bus. Then a sense that there was something odd about the vehemence of Josephine's rejection brushed Piper's consciousness, along with a sense of outrage for Bell. The only appropriate response to him she could imagine in a woman was to start ripping off her clothes, but Piper pushed it all aside to spring out of the sage and bound through the underbrush toward the road. It was wonderful just to be alive. In a moment Bell caught up with her, and they went into the town of Elko together to get supplies. They'd been together, making music, ever since.

"I wanted to wait until you were finished

drumming," she said to him now, looking up at the stars.

"Until what?"

"Until I asked you if your feelings about Josephine are such that, uh..." It wasn't embarrassment, another feeling Piper had never known, that cut her off. She was so turned on she could hardly talk, so she giggled instead.

"What, baby?"

Piper concentrated very hard and managed to speak. "Such that I shouldn't tell you that I would probably commit any crime you could name, no matter how heinous, if you would just promise in exchange to do me the small favor of ripping my clothes off and banging me into the salt flats."

His drumming came to an immediate and absolute halt. His sudden quiet was far louder than any noise. Piper turned toward him. A huge grin was slowly spreading across his face. He rolled over on top of her and grabbed her work shirt, about to rip it off. She closed her eyes.

"Open your eyes. Look at me."

She looked. The stars glittered about his dark face like an illustration out of the Arabian Nights, but what she saw was Bell. She felt him throb between her legs and knew how good what was to come would be, but she felt—perhaps for the first time in her life—that that could wait. She reached up and touched his cheek.

"What do you see?" he asked.

A multitude of images erupted within Piper. Now she saw knights, princes and movie stars. A thousand fairy tales came true, then somehow rang false and withered away under the weight of his scrutiny.

"Do you see a drummer?" he asked.

"No."

He paused. "A Negro?"

"No."

"What do you see?" Bell's look was so penetrating that it occurred to Piper that he'd have to have a cock that could be measured in feet to be able to get any deeper into her later on.

Piper concentrated. At first she thought of the music they'd been making all day, of the ripple of bare muscles when the heat drove him to yank his T-shirt off on the streets of Elko. Then she remembered the one time they had stopped making music.

They had been standing in the shade of a gas station next to the soda cooler, frosty bottles of Coke upended over their heads as they guzzled the last of it. A grotesquely plain middle-aged woman in a faded floral-print house dress, which failed to conceal the 300 pounds of oddly shaped jello that passed for her body, spat in the dust at their feet. They lowered their Coke bottles to look at her. She stood in the sun squinting back at them. Nobody moved; nobody spoke. The heat of the day sat on the silence like an old, stiff, lifeless dog. Finally a fly buzzed by. The woman said "Harumph," turned on her heel and waddled off into the dust of a sleepy side street.

Piper and Bell were left to stare at each other.

"Was it my cut-off jeans and the bra I'm not wearing?"

"It could just as easily have been the color of my skin."

They were silent for awhile. Maybe it was the heat, but Piper felt oppressed. "Are we so terrible?"

Bell looked after the 300-pound woman, still visible as she returned into the oblivion from whence she came. "When I was a little bugger my grandmother used to try and dress me up in a pin-striped three-piece suit every time we went out. I'd trip on the long pants and scuff the knees. The jacket was always askew. I was a mess. When I got older I'd rationalize that it was a dumb suit anyway, something a pimp running numbers in Harlem would wear, but that wasn't the point."

"What was the point?"

"The point was that for my grandmother that suit represented elegance. She was an ugly old woman who'd scrimped and struggled and slaved all her life. Now her life was 'bout over. She wasn't very bright, and she sure wasn't any kind of artist who could leave behind some masterpiece to commemorate her life. All she could hope for was a grandson who looked what she called 'real fine' out on the street. She didn't even get that." He stepped out into the sunlight, squinting after the obese woman who had all but disappeared. "Damn, I don't know what that lady's story is. Maybe she has kids; maybe she doesn't. All I know is she needs us to be something we're not."

Piper returned to the present, to the night and the stars and Bell above her. Now she felt his heart beating on top of hers. "I'll tell you what I see," she said. "I see you naked, but it's not necessarily sexual. You're not a drummer. You're not Negro. You're not white. You might not even be a man or a woman, but there is one thing you are. You're 'real fine.'"

Bell let go of Piper's shirt and held her face. His kiss was so leisurely and so deep that when he was through she was sure his knowledge of her mouth exceeded that of her dentist. Piper felt humble in the sudden realization that a lot of the motivation behind past sex had been thumbing her nose at her parents. "Have I answered correctly," she asked Bell softly.

"Yes, you have answered correctly." The grin came back. His hands were on her breasts, gentleness gone. He yanked at her work shirt and it flew open, buttons skittering away across the salt. "And I am about to bring new meaning to the phrase, 'pounding salt up your ass.'" The rest came very fast, but when he was through he stayed in her a long time. At last he lay back.

"I love you, Bell," Piper said. She never said those words; she'd always thought they were bullshit. "And I'll never look at salt in quite the same way, but I have to go find some place to pee."

He laughed.

Piper got up and crunched out across the salt flats, leaving brittle, broken footprints. She felt so gloriously full of Bell.

She heard the crunch of a footstep, not her own. It was darker now; night had progressed. Piper looked in the direction of the sound but could see nothing.

Another crunch.

"Bell?"

"You wish." Josephine materialized out of the dark. In the deep of night all hint of sunshine was gone from her. She was staring at Piper's exposed chest.

"Are you a Lesbian?" Piper was just curious. It was neither a challenge nor a judgement.

Josephine's eyes flashed, but she studied Piper's face for a long time before answering. "I don't rightly know. I don't understand all the things inside me." She started to walk on.

"Where are the others?"

Josephine shrugged. "Mostly in the bus. Oh, by the way, did you hear about the second Hippie Hack Murder last night? Good thing we got our asses out of Berkeley!"

Jesus! Piper didn't want to believe that such things could happen in a rational world. She found a place to pee and went back to Bell.

He wasn't where she'd left him. The newly risen moon was enough to illuminate the icelike sheets of salt which were all shattered. It looked like someone had broken a million panes of frosted glass. Piper was leaning toward the salt, mesmerized by the weird effect, when someone grabbed her from behind. With the wind half-knocked out of her, she craned her head backwards to peer into a face so ruthless it took a moment for her to recognize it as Bell's. He let her go.

"Sorry." Bell stood back, and she saw he was carrying an antique dagger. His T-shirt was tied around his shoulder. There was a dark stain in the middle of it. "You know how men are, always falling asleep after making love?" He touched the stain. "This boy has learned his lesson."

"What happened, goddammit?"

"Someone stabbed me with this dagger!"

"Who?"

"Think I know? First I was asleep, and then I couldn't see any too well in the dark."

"Holy shit, Bell." Piper removed the T-shirt, fumbled for a flashlight among their things and examined the moist red hole in his shoulder. To her Caucasian eye his dark skin made his paler insides look all the more vulnerable, but Bell didn't flinch. He was looking out over the salt flats towards the bus.

Piper cut off the flashlight and followed his gaze. Someone had turned the bus headlights on. Their beams looked stark and cold spilling across the pebbly white crust of salt. "Maybe all those frightened hippies in Berkeley are now safe."

Bell put his good arm around her and drew her close.

Parsons stretched, rubbing his paunch, and smiled. It was great to be out of pinko commie Berkeley. The diner was modern. The people were Republican. A sign behind the cash register read: "America, Love It Or Leave It." Parsons took a huge bite out of his burger, savoring the raw juices that dripped off his chin. He felt at home.

Then he remembered his daughter. He hadn't let the Berkeley police see how he felt, or they might not have entrusted him with his assignment, but he'd been glad someone murdered that goddamned gangly kid at her place. One punch, that's all he'd gotten in! Ronna had passed out, and that long-hair kid had come downstairs. Parsons had had to hide behind a door while the idiot hung over his slut daughter jabbering some heroic crap about how he wouldn't let anybody hurt her anymore. If the kid hadn't gone off to get a washrag, giving Parsons a chance to slip out the back, Parsons would probably still be behind that door.

On the other hand, he might have found out who the murderer was that way. That would have given him a hell of a jump on his present assignment of apprehending the Hippie Hack Murderer.

Parsons broke his reverie with a long, luxurious sigh. He looked around again. Not a long-hair bum to be seen in this town. All the women teased their hair. All the men had crew cuts. Utah was OK with him. The only pinkos were in that goddamned school bus he was following.

Chapter 4

Ronna had never slept with a man before. She wasn't a virgin, although she hadn't had a lot of experience, but she had never in the literal sense slept next to anybody.

The literal sense was all there was to it. For just a moment, when Simba lay down next to her and took her in his arms, she had wondered about his intentions, but he had only drawn her to him as if she were his teddy bear and had gone to sleep.

Now it was morning, and Ronna woke to find herself snugly wrapped in his powerful arms. Her head was on his bare chest, rocked gently by his breathing. A forest of black chest hairs tickled her nose and shaded her one open eye from the already bright glare of sunlight off the salt flats.

She could hear the others breathing deeply as they slept in the back of the bus where the seats had been ripped out. Chutney was on the other side of Simba, wedged in next to the mountain of black amplifiers and sound equipment piled up against the rear emergency exit. On his back atop an orange and brown plaid flannel sleeping bag, he produced an occasional, fittingly theatrical snore. The early morning sun set afire the red in his beard and the thick hair on the arms folded across his chest. Thick-set, he looked to Ronna like a kindly Papa Bear.

Ronna snuggled up in Simba's arms and turned her head in the other direction. Ursula's face was inches from hers, grey eyes open and staring at Simba with an oddly cold reptilian lust. Ursula glared at Ronna, brushed a greasy strand of her dark hair away from her face, and snapped her eyes shut. Ronna frowned with concern at the deathly pallor and premature wrinkles in Ursula's pasty skin. Lying naked on the bare floor, emaciated Ursula reminded Ronna of some medieval painting of the body of Christ.

In sharp contrast, Josephine's warm, brown, muscular body stretched out like a Nubian slave behind Ursula. Josephine slept in a yellow top and orange shorts, her long legs wrapped protectively around her bass guitar.

Behind Josephine, gnomelike Midas was curled up in the fetal position, a hand with mousy brown hairs that stuck up at strange angles resting on the pot of a wilted plant. Next to him was a clutter of plants, pots, water bags, cooking gear, and the box in which Mushroom had stowed away with an ax leaning up against it.

Mushroom was propped up against the back of the last seat, head to one side. With her inhuman mass of red hair, she looked like an abandoned doll on a child's shelf. Ronna studied the elfin face with its prominent mouth, then the waiflike body. Despite the obvious signs of womanhood, it projected an aura of childhood as if refusing to acknowledge that puberty had come. At odds with this image, the poster of ducks screwing in midair that Ronna recognized from her own front door had been used to block the light from the window closest to Mushroom.

Finally Piper and Bell had chosen, for some reason, to sleep apart from the others in the very front of the bus. They had used a black T-shirt with bright purple letters that read The Gizmo Delicious as a makeshift curtain. In spite of the wide-open window, not a breath of air disturbed the T-shirt, and Ronna could see there was a stain of some sort on it.

Piper wore cut-off jeans and a workshirt that did little to conceal a Marilyn Monroe figure that compensated for Mushroom's lack of sexuality by projecting more than enough for both. Although white, she had an Afro, but what really attracted Ronna's attention was the firm set of the jaw and the easy sprawl of her body against Bell's. This, thought Ronna, is a person who has never once in her entire life stopped to wonder if her slip was showing.

Two 18-wheelers zoomed past on the road right

next to them, jiggling even the bus. The ax next to Midas shifted, and Ronna started to leap up. She didn't like Midas much, but she didn't want to see anyone hurt and was afraid the ax handle would fall on him. Fortunately, it didn't because Ronna never got up. Simba didn't let her.

Held tight by his arms, Ronna turned back toward Simba and was surprised to find him still asleep. Amazed, she tried to move again. Again, his arms tightened about her. She looked up at his closed eyes and listened to his slow deep breaths. "Stay, Ronna," he mumbled in his sleep. "I love you."

Ronna melted. First she looked at Simba with dawning wonder, then finally the others with a gentle gratitude for taking her in. She felt a great warmth in the center of her, like a cup of coffee on a cold morning. Her frostbitten heart thawed. She put her head back on Simba's chest and closed her eyes. At last she felt safe and fell into a dreamless sleep.

"Maybe a local yokel did it."

Ronna opened her eyes. The sun was much higher. She must have slept for hours.

"Naa." It was Simba answering Chutney who had spoken first. Simba looked down at Ronna, touched her cheek, reached behind her and handed her a steaming cup of coffee. "That peyote was short but sweet, so I don't remember everything that happened last night, but look outside the bus."

Chutney did.

"Not so much as a twig to hide behind," Simba

declared. "If somebody had parked even a mile
down the road and crunched across the salt flats
to stab Bell, one of us would have noticed something."

Chutney nodded. Ronna almost spilled her coffee, then sat up gingerly to sip it, using Simba
who was already seated as a backrest. She caught
a look of terror in Josephine's face that was
quickly masked by disdain.

"My, my, my. Mr. Big Bad Wolf done figured
it all out by himself." Josephine downed the last
sip of her coffee and handed the cup through the
open window to Piper, who was cooking on an
open fire outside with Bell. Piper handed her back
two plates of eggs, one of which Josephine made
a point of handing to Ronna. "What would poor
Ronna do without you, Simba?" Josephine batted her eyes; on her it looked ridiculous.

"What's your problem, bitch?" Ronna could
feel Simba's snarl through her own body.

"Just for your information, did it ever dawn
on you that the rest of the country ain't like
Berkeley? Maybe these folks figure 'hippie' is as
bad as 'nigger.' Put 'em both together, like in
Bell's case, and it's time for a lynchin'."

"That may be true," Simba said, "but what
does it have to do with visibility across the salt
flats?"

Josephine opened her mouth, then closed it.

"And how," Simba continued, "do you explain
this?" He held out an antique dagger on a leather
thong.

Josephine, looking at the dagger, started to

shake. "It's what they used on Bell. So what?"

"It's mine," Simba said.

Chutney choked on his coffee. Midas's and Mushroom's eyes popped open, making them look even more like creatures from a child's fairy tale. Ursula, dressed now, shrugged.

"So?" Josephine answered. "Remember when you started coming on to me last night, boy?"

Ronna felt a stab of pain.

"You! No way. I'd cut it off first," Simba said.

"Like, he doesn't remember again," put in Ursula. In full daylight her pale skin looked even paler. "Happens every time he starts babbling that puritanical bullshit, man. Remember the night that guy you balled got chopped up into little pieces, Josephine?"

Wide-eyed, Josephine glared back at her.

Ursula didn't notice. "Remember Simba started in calling me Lucy, or some such shit, and going on about how I wasn't doing my chores? Remember you got pissed as hell at them both?"

"Girl, shut your mouth," Josephine said.

"Simba's slipping into another century," Ursula persisted.

"Hush!" Josephine snapped.

"Like, nobody ever believes me, man. It's the curse of my life." Ursula hung her head; her brunette hair seemed to cling to it in shame.

"Your dagger, no lie?" Josephine asked.

"My dagger," Simba answered evenly.

"Now I know you're not about to start telling us about how you been slicing people up," Josephine said, strutting down the aisle between the seats in the front, then doing an about-face. "So what we about to hear is how one of us stole your knife when you weren't looking, and this whole thing gonna' turn into one big nigger hunt, and meanwhile somebody from the outside could have slipped his ass on in here while we was all—"

"Unfucking likely. I lost it."

"That's just what I was saying," Josephine snapped. "You—"

"Lost it in Berkeley," Simba said.

"You . . ."

"Hadn't seen it since the night of the first murder."

Ronna felt ice at the back of her neck. Midas's and Mushroom's eyes opened even wider, making them look completely inhuman. Josephine backed up like a spooked horse and bolted out the front door of the bus. Mushroom scampered after her.

In the silence left behind Ronna listened to the mournful whine of a car in the distance.

"Chutney McLaughlin, Devil's Advocate of the First Water, at your service. Is it possible, Simba, that you only thought you lost the knife? That you had it with you all along, stuck in with your things somewhere? Maybe Josephine's right. Maybe it was an outsider rifling through our things."

"Perhaps." Simba looked worried and very tenderly gave Ronna's shoulder a squeeze.

* * *

The steering wheel spun free in Simba's hands. The bus's tires squealed. The sky was a pure, brilliant blue. The craggy, snow-capped Rockies rose sharply above Central City, Colorado. Simba clamped his hands back down on the wheel. Only the rear tire slipped off the side of the road, launching rocks off a 200-foot drop. Next time a sign said, "Hairpin turn, slow to 10 miles per hour," Simba was going to pay attention.

The thing to remember was that they couldn't flee from the danger, no matter how fast he drove, because they hadn't left it on the salt flats of Utah. Simba darted a glance at the other occupants of the bus, visible in the rearview mirror along with fishing rods, water bags, backpacks, lanterns, plants, pots, kettles, shovels, sleeping bags, instruments, sound equipment, mike stands, AC cords, amplifiers, and a psychedelic poster of the Jefferson Airplane. They'd brought everything, including the danger.

In a way Simba didn't care except ... He stole a look at Ronna on the seat directly behind him. Could a girl give meaning to his life, settle him down? It sure as shit hadn't worked before, but he felt the inklings of something new with Ronna—peace and completeness. Then he saw Mushroom and Josephine slide onto the seat next to Ronna. Despite the sun beating through the windshield, Simba felt a chill. One thing he was very sure of—he didn't want anyone to ever again hurt Ronna.

Simba jerked the bus off the road onto a lookout plateau and yanked on the emergency brake.

"More than enough mountain driving for me. Next?" He was out of the driver's seat before he'd finished speaking, standing over Josephine, who was sitting next to Ronna.

"Can't cut it, Mr. Show Off? I'll drive." Josephine was on her feet, strutting toward the driver's seat.

Simba slipped into the space left next to Ronna before Mushroom could move over. "Chutney," he called out. "Your turn."

Josephine wheeled, glaring at Simba. "My turn. Chutney can wait."

Simba gave her a hard look. He thought he knew where the danger was. He knew he didn't want her near Ronna. On the other hand, he didn't want her at the wheel either. He spoke evenly but bored into her with his eyes. "Chutney's turn."

The bitch stood her ground for a moment, then tried to save face with an exaggerated shrug before flopping into the seat across the aisle from Simba's. Chutney materialized at the wheel and undid the brake.

"Watch the turns, man," Simba warned. "Whatever speed the sign suggests? I'd halve it."

Chutney pulled onto the road carefully, and they started back down the mountain toward Central City.

Simba put an arm around Ronna, partially because there otherwise wasn't enough room on the seat for the two of them and Mushroom. Ronna snuggled up to him. For a moment all nobility of feeling fled as he felt Ronna's breast against his ribs. Before he could suppress it a part of him he hated wondered what it had felt like to rape her.

Then the wind shifted and Simba became aware of Mushroom on his other side. Odd, she smelled like a child although she obviously wasn't anymore. He looked down into Mushroom's impish face. She was dirty. The matted red hair reminded him of some kid's beat-up old doll, but there was nothing childlike about the liquid iridescence in those green eyes. "You into reincarnation?" she asked.

"Never gave it a thought," Simba answered. Mushroom had spooked him at first, but this line of conversation he recognized. He figured the next thing she'd want to know was his sun sign.

"Close your eyes."

Mushroom's voice was odd, both soft and loud, reminding Simba of how the dual notes on his 12-string guitar had, at first, sounded unnatural. Oh fuck, he thought, hippie parlor tricks. But then, what the hell! He was used enough to leading to know a good leader; especially he knew that one who has just won a power play should loosen up occasionally and let the followers exert some power. This was harmless. Also, it occurred to Simba that since he didn't know a soul in Central City, Colorado, he certainly didn't know anyone who dealt drugs. Simba closed his eyes.

"Relax."

Easy for you to say, bitch. You don't have a tit in your ribs.

"You are getting younger."

At least she didn't say, "You are getting sleepier."

"Relax."

Yeah, yeah. At least it seemed to be working on Ronna. Simba could feel her breathing deepen.

"You are getting younger."

You are getting repetitive, thought Simba, but he also started to feel a little strange. There was something funny about keeping his eyes closed for such a long time when he was fully conscious.

"Relax completely now. You are young."

Yeah, sure. But the sunlight playing across Simba's closed lids as the bus jostled down the mountain was beginning to form itself into images. He was sure he wasn't hypnotized but, like a kid left awake in a dark bedroom, his mind was beginning to play itself out in the void left by his missing sense of sight.

"How old are you, Simba? What do you see?"

What the hell. "I'm going to be seven on December 7th. I'm on the playground." Was his voice higher? Simba could see the playground on the back of his closed eyelids, but he still knew where he really was. He could hear the bus creak, strain and generally complain as Chutney forced it around yet another turn.

"What do you see?"

That big kid next door who would never play with him. Simba had long since forgotten his name. "I see Eddie Naumburger. You know, that big kid in the ninth grade?" Eddie was towering over him.

"What else do you see?"

"The woods at the edge of the playground. I'm not supposed to go near there."

"What about Eddie? What's Eddie doing?"

"Showin' off. In front of the others."

"What others?" Mushroom persisted.

Simba looked around. They all had greasy hair and black leather jackets. He wheeled slowly. They also had, at about his eye level, huge bulges in their tight jeans. "High school kids. Hoods. Mommy says stay away. I have to go now." But Eddie wanted him there, and Simba wanted Eddie to be his friend. Eddie smiled down at him; it was a funny smile, but it was still a smile.

A voice that seemed to be in his own mind asked Simba what happened next. There was silence now, and Simba remembered that there had been a noise of some kind just a few minutes ago, but he could no longer remember what. Then he heard Eddie's voice, something about Simba being a girl's name. Something about Simba's pretty blue eyes. Eddie started shoving him. Simba thought it was kidding around. He didn't want to be a cry baby, so Simba tried to take it and shove back a little like he was playing, too. Eddie got a funny look on his face, real determined. Suddenly Simba was looking backwards, at one of the high school kids behind him, then he was on the ground. His chin hurt. They were rolling him over onto his tummy and pulling his pants down. He heard in a moment of absolute clarity the sound of someone unbuckling a belt. Why were they going to beat him? He hadn't done anything. Someone was on top of him. Simba was very scared.

Abruptly the scene ended.

"What happened next, Simba?"

"Nothing. Nothing happened after that, Mommy."

"Something must have happened after that." Vaguely Simba realized it was Mushroom talking.

"No. Absolutely nothing."

"Relax, Simba. You are getting younger again."

Yeah, yeah.

"How old are you now, Simba? What do you see?"

"I'm big now. I'm in kindergarten."

"What do you see?"

"Mommy."

"What's Mommy doing, Simba?"

"Leaving." The classroom was huge and full of noise. Simba didn't know anybody. If Mommy went through that door, he would be all alone. Mommy wasn't always nice to him, but Mommy was Mommy. He ran as fast as he could and caught her.

"Don't leave me here!"

"All kids say that the first day." Mommy looked tired and turned to go.

"No!" Simba could feel the tears burning his cheeks.

"Simba, let me go. I have to go to the store."

"I can't, Mommy! I can't." The world was swimming through his tears. Blackboard whales lumbered about with their pilot fish escorts, the erasers and multicolored chalk. Kids with liquid screams dove after a darting school of identical chairs. Light exploded through a dense sea of desks.

"Oh, Simba, I've had enough of you. Just be someone else. Be someone who can."

"I don't understand, Mommy. I'm Simba, and I'm very scared."

"Oh, I don't know. Find someone else to be. Find someone who is never scared." Mommy stood up quickly, tearing free of Simba's hands. In an instant she was gone, slamming the door behind her. Simba screamed. It was as if she had taken part of him—his hands, maybe—with her. He could not stand the pain. Simba had to find someone else to be.

This scene also ended abruptly. Simba felt fingers touching his neck with gentleness and concern and realized they were Ronna's.

"Something must have happened after that," Mushroom insisted.

"No. Absolutely nothing."

"Relax. You are getting younger again. Much younger. Now you are a baby. Now you are getting even younger than that. Listen carefully. You are walking backwards through time. There is a long corridor with a huge door at the end. Can you see the door, Simba?"

Yes, he could see the door.

"What does the door look like?"

It was part of an old house with a funny double porch in front, but it was also a secret.

"What does the door look like, Simba?"

Mustn't tell. Shouldn't go there really except when very scared.

"Never mind. Open the door, Simba."

No. Mustn't. Shouldn't.

"Open the door."

Simba reached for the door. Abruptly the scene ended. Simba opened his eyes and looked directly into Mushroom's. "I did see a door, but there was nothing behind it."

"That's not possible." He'd forgotten how spooky Mushroom's voice was in full consciousness. "Memories, life, lives . . . They are all a continuum. Events do not cut off like a TV someone's clicked off. Something's wrong, Simba."

Josephine said, "I can't."

Simba looked at Josephine in the seat across the aisle. Her eyes were closed.

"You can't do what?" Mushroom asked.

"I can't get the door open," Josephine answered.

"What door?" Simba asked.

"The door at the end of the corridor," Josephine said. Her eyes were still closed. Her body was so relaxed that she jostled dangerously about the seat when Chutney took another turn.

"Yes, you can," Mushroom said. "What does the door look like?"

"It's just an old wood thing. Part of the shack."

"Does it have a lock?"

"Oh, no, missy. We ain't got no money for a lock."

"Why won't it open?" Mushroom asked.

"I don't rightly know, ma'am."

"Look carefully at it. Is it stuck?"

"Nails."

"Nailed shut?" Mushroom asked.

"Nailed to the one next to it."

"How many doors are there?"

"It's all doors."

"What is?"

"The shack. We didn't have nutin' else to make it with."

Mushroom studied Josephine. Simba noted that Ronna's eyes were closed, too, apparently in sleep. "I think," Mushroom said to Josephine, "you've already passed through the door I was talking to Simba about."

"There ain't no door."

"What do you mean?"

"We ain't got no money for a door."

"What do you have?" Mushroom said.

"We got us some land!"

"Who's we?"

"Pappy, Gus and me."

"Who's me?"

"I can't see that."

"Look down. What are you dressed in."

"Field clothes. It's all I got."

"Describe them," Mushroom commanded.

Josephine frowned a little, concentrating. "I can't rightly make out the colors on this old dress. It's so faded. Tattered, too. 'Specially the hem, where it touches the ground."

"Where it touches the ground?"

"Reckon the briars got it," Josephine observed.

As Chutney took another turn, Josephine fell toward the aisle. Mushroom tried to catch her, but their weight differential wouldn't allow it. Simba leaped across Josephine to pull her back towards him and away from Mushroom. The bitch was heavy, solidly built. He sat against the window on Josephine's seat, wondering who he was holding in his arms—a mass murderer? Simba turned from Josephine, craning his head to look out the window behind his back. Central City was directly below them, the drop so sheer that he could have dropped a penny into the closest chimney.

Mushroom climbed back onto the opposite seat in time to catch Ronna, who was clawing at her own neck, eyes still closed.

Ronna started to scream.

"Enough!" Simba bellowed. "Everybody wake up. Now!"

Everybody's eyes popped open. Simba turned to Mushroom. "This is crap."

"You wish." Mushroom, face half in shade, looked like an ephemeral wood nymph about to become transparent, then disappear.

"I know."

"No, Simba, there are things about yourself that you definitely do not know."

Piper, curled up with Bell a few seats behind the others, had had a great dream. She had dreamt she was a prostitute.

Then Bell gave her a hug. "Sleepy?" he asked.

"Umm . . . a little flat, perhaps," Piper answered.

Bell gave her a wide-eyed look of disbelief.

Piper yawned, then beamed broadly. "Maybe what I need is a little salt."

Bell beamed.

Chutney pulled the bus off the road in front of an old Western bar. He yanked the brake on and fell back against the seat. "Methinks I must reevaluate my intellectual's disdain for those who drive large, many-axled objects for a living." He let his hands drop off the wheel and leaned his head back, closing his eyes. "I envision a Truckdrivers' Hall of Fame for any who manage to cross the Rockies without littering the gullies with themselves and their eighteen-wheelers."

They piled into the bar, dark mellow wood relieved only once by the muted pastel face of a beautiful girl painted on the barroom floor.

Piper stretched luxuriously, noting that the bartender looked her over. To her Berkeley-oriented eye the young bartender, like the young locals in the place, looked ludicrous with his short hair and straight jeans. Had it occurred to anybody that there was life beyond Elvis?

Midas hurried over to the bar, pushing his way between two locals who eyed him with obvious hostility. "Barkeep," he demanded.

"Barkeep?" said the shorter local. He had a blonde crew cut, small pig eyes and a large fleshy jaw. "What's this weirdo think? We're back in the 1800's?"

Midas didn't seem to hear. "Barkeep, I need

about a gallon of fresh water. The stuff we've been getting isn't any good for my plants and—"

"And this ain't the local nursery," the bartender interrupted. He then leaned over the bar to look Midas over as if he were an animal at the zoo. "Where'd you come from, boy?"

"Well, actually, I guess I come from all over. I was born in Ventura, but then my parents moved all the way north to Santa Rosa when I was in the second grade and—"

"You aren't one of those beatniks, are you?" It was the taller local. He had dark hair, loaded with Brylcream. "You know, like Maynard G. Crebbs on the Dobbie Gillis show?"

"'Beatnik'? Even I know better than to use that word. You guys are really out of it."

It was said with a child's simplicity. Piper knew Midas wasn't trying to pick a fight, but there was no mistaking the sudden tension in all the locals. Piper didn't think much of Midas, but she knew he wouldn't be there, facing these people, if it weren't for her. She saw Simba, in her peripheral vision, moving toward the bar, but she made it there first.

"What it is is we're all part of a rock 'n' roll band." Piper figured she'd better specify rock 'n' roll or who knows what they would expect. She hoped they would accept this as a reasonable reason for looking very strange to their eyes and realize that Midas was not by any means alone.

"Oh, yeah?" the shorter local said. His belligerence melted somewhat when he noticed Piper's chest. "What's the name of the group?"

Piper felt someone close behind her, then heard Bell's voice. "The Gizmo Delicious."

The locals stared at Bell, then scanned the others until their gaze came to rest on Josephine. Piper decided that if she ever got any money from playing in this band, she'd send it all to Martin Luther King.

"I never heard of you," the taller local said. "You can't be any good."

"Wanna' find out?" Piper challenged.

"Now?" the shorter local asked.

"Why not?" Piper demanded.

" 'Cuz we ain't never even played together, girl," Josephine hissed in her ear.

"Where?" the bartender asked.

Piper leaned toward him a little and locked eyes. "Here." She could see him starting to melt.

"Why is it," Chutney whispered in her ear, "that straights love hippie chicks and hate hippie men?"

"Because hippie chicks put out." Piper could feel Bell stiffen. "But this one won't. Come on, everybody, out to the bus to get our stuff." She turned and found herself looking up at Simba.

He nodded.

Out by the bus the air was crisp and clear as they started to pass out the instruments and sound equipment, bucket brigade style.

Josephine tossed a huge amplifier into Simba's arms. "You sure better play that twelve string better than you drive."

Simba caught the amplifier easily. "I haven't

93

heard you on bass guitar yet either, bitch."

"Watch the Swedish Ivy!" Midas protested from inside the bus.

Piper picked up a drum and found battered Ronna at her side, helping her carry it. "Careful, Piper. That's heavy."

Chutney handed another drum out to Bell, who bounded toward the bar with it, beating out the deliciously complex rhythm he'd been beating on his thighs when Piper first met him.

Mushroom, carrying a few AC cords, sniffed at the air and watched everyone carefully.

Ursula stood apart, arms wrapped around herself in the shade of the building, and did nothing.

Back in the darkness of the bar, every cord tangled, and every mike stand managed to get knocked over. The locals reminded Piper of a restless wolf pack. Were they going to lick hands? Or leap at throats? Piper cleared her own throat. "Having gotten us into this, can I ask a real dumb question?"

The others paused.

Piper continued. "What are we going to play?"

There was a moment of silence.

"I suggest," Chutney whispered, "something patriotic."

"I suggest," Bell said, "something—if there is such a thing—that we all know."

Simba, who had been busy setting up an amplifier, stood and leveled his hypnotic blue eyes at them all. "We will start with 'This Land is Your Land.'"

"Say what?" protested both Bell and Josephine in unison.

Simba didn't flinch. "Trust me." He hefted a gorgeous Martin guitar and leaped onto the bar's small stage. Most of the others followed.

The bartender gave Piper another appreciative look, shrugged and pulled the plug on the juke box.

Chutney tested a mike by tapping it; it worked.

"Right on!" Bell exclaimed, leaping onto the stage himself.

Chutney continued to test the mike by speaking into it. "Anybody, excepting me of course, know the origin of that particular phrase?"

"What phrase?" Ursula snapped as she passed the stage in the midst of wandering around uselessly.

"Right on!" Chutney's voice boomed through the mike.

Simba stooped to adjust the volume. "Righteous Brothers?"

"No!" Chutney's voice was still a little too loud.

"Malcolm X?" Bell and Josephine asked together, as they finished setting up the drums.

"No!" Chutney's voice was about right; Simba had been busy.

"Joe Namath?" Midas guessed.

Chutney gave him a look, then cradled the mike. "Ah, the vanity of youth. All of you assume nothing hip managed to exist prior to the emergence of your own generation."

Josephine batted him with the bass guitar she was tuning. "Cut the shit and tell us the answer, fool, 'fore I wrap that mike stand 'round your head!"

Chutney drew himself up. "For I have neither wit, nor words, nor worth, action or utterance, nor the power of speech to stir men's blood; I only speak, right on!"

Even the restless locals were silenced by the timbre of Chutney's voice. Piper had goose bumps. "Shakespeare?" she asked.

Chutney nodded. "Marc Antony's funeral oration."

The crowd started to become restless again. Simba took the mike to address them. "And we only sing right on, which is why we want to start with something some might call corny, but we really feel. It's about the fact that this is a big country with lots of different kinds of things in it and lots of different kinds of people. Please help us celebrate that by singing along." He turned toward Josephine to tune his guitar to her bass and gave the final order. "Key of G."

Piper stepped up to her mike. Her first appearance singing, and the song had to be something her dumb parents would sing?

Simba leaned toward Piper, locking eyes as he finished the introduction on his 12-string. They started to sing:

"This land is your land. This land is my land. From the redwood forest, to the New York island."

Piper wasn't even sure they had the words right, but Simba's voice was rich and strong, and Bell kicked in with a beat that transcended any antiseptic grammar school quality the song might have had. The place rocked; the floorboards throbbed. Simba and Josephine faced off, battling to outdo each other on their guitars. Chutney cheered, jumping off the stage to become part of the audience.

Piper closed her eyes. At first she heard each element separately—her voice, Simba's, the two guitars still battling it out, and Bell's drums. Then Josephine and Bell started singing—as did the audience—and Piper lost all sense of her own or anyone else's individuality. They became one voice, the instruments a part of that voice. The music bloomed with its own life; the people involved were only the the now-lifeless seed from which it came.

When, at last, it was over it took Piper a moment to remember who she was and where she was. Then she spotted the wolf-pack locals, whose numbers had swelled. There was a moment of silence, then they started to clap. The shorter local with the pig eyes, who obviously wasn't paying attention to who was standing next to him, gave Midas a good-natured slap on the back.

Simba put his hand over the mike. "That's it. Let's get out of here."

"I ain't leaving after one song. Not after all the work of setting this shit up!" Josephine's eyes flashed.

Chutney stood by Simba. "Methinks it would not be wise to linger to debate, say, the relative merits of U.S. involvement in Viet Nam."

They started packing up.

* * *

Parsons was studying his notes. He'd phoned that asshole rookie earlier in the day and pumped him for information on Josephine. Seems she'd been arrested in 1964 for stabbing her own father with a knife. Under 18 at the time, she'd gotten a suspended sentence. The social worker's report said something about Josephine's claim that her father had bet her virginity in a card game when she was seven and lost. Parsons couldn't care less about that kind of stuff.

He figured the cause of all this was these people's lifestyle. Christ! He'd seen two more hippies hitchhiking a few miles back. The girl had the usual long brown hair and the stupidest look of happiness on her face he'd ever seen. Couldn't have been more than 16. Dumb kids.

Parsons looked around. Place was dark. Nobody could see so he picked his nose in peace, flicking it on the graffiti these idiots hadn't bothered to wash off the floor—some girl's face. Stupid. High altitude must have fried these cowboys' brains. If the owners of any self-respecting bar in Anaheim chose to leave a picture of a girl on the floor, it sure as hell wouldn't be a picture of her face.

This line of thinking prompted Parsons to gaze back at the now-empty stage. Again, he felt the beginnings of an erection. That goddamned frizzy-haired hippie was too much. He closed his eyes, remembering what she'd looked like as he'd watched her sing earlier from his hiding place in the back of the crowd. Then he smiled. His own daughter hadn't spotted him. Not only that, but from the looks of her some considerate soul must have finished the job he'd started on her face. True, he would have preferred to do the job himself, but he was a reasonable man. Warmed by his own kindness, he let his head fall forward and started to doze.

Just before the final drop into sleep, an odd thought jerked him awake again—something about the young girl hitchhiking and how he didn't think he'd called her when he called all the others together. Didn't make any sense so he dropped his head again and dozed.

In his dream Parsons saw that the fear he so yearned for was in all of their faces—a woman and three girls.

Chapter 5

Ronna was cold; Simba was hot. She had been out under the stars; he had been inside the bus. She stiffened at first when he drew near, triggering some subliminal memory of her recent rape, but laughed when he covered her with her Mickey Mouse rug and made a big deal of tucking it under her chin.

Simba settled in next to her and turned over to go to sleep.

Ronna's eyes closed, then popped back open. "I'm not a child."

For a moment he didn't answer, and she was afraid he'd gone to sleep. "Meaning?"

Ronna didn't know what to do. It was like the ouija board she couldn't get to work when she was a kid until she just let go. She just let go, and touched his back.

"Uh . . . Ronna . . ."

Ronna ignored the warning in his voice. She ran her fingers over his shoulder to his neck, then up his neck into his hair. Then she put both hands on his back and moved them down over his body.

Sex, the few times she'd had it, had always been something that was done to her, done to her body really. It was almost as if she just happened to be there. She half-expected the boy to look up at her in the middle of it and say, "Oh, hi, Ronna. What are you doing here?" Maybe life had always been something that was done to her.

When Simba turned toward her, Ronna started to stiffen again, acutely aware of the difference in their size, weight and musculature. Unlike the last boy, he didn't immediately get on top. He touched her face.

Ronna was puzzled, then remembered and could feel herself turn pink with shame. "I'm sorry. I forgot what I look like."

He shook his head, brushing her comment aside.

"And that you've never seen me any other way."

He stiffened, as if she'd said something wrong. Ronna couldn't figure out that one.

No sex, she thought, pulling herself away a bit, but she couldn't stop herself from asking a question she knew begged pathetically for a compliment. "How bad do I look?"

"Close your eyes," he said.

She complied.

He took a heavy breath. "You are beautiful, the sleeping princess."

She was pleased, but figured he was just being nice.

"Long thin brows arching high over deep-set eyes."

How did he know that? She knew her eyes were still swollen.

"A softly upturned nose."

Her nose wasn't its usual self yet either.

Another heavy breath. "Beautiful lips." He was having trouble speaking now. He kissed her.

She thought it was going to be a gentle kiss, the kind that says, "No, thank you, but you're sweet."

It was not.

Afterwards she lay next to him, strangely restless. She hadn't come, but then she didn't always—and there had been the rape. Certainly he had made love to her, yet it gave her an odd chill.

Ronna got up and headed toward the road. Even in the deep of night the snow glowed on top of the mountains. A car passed her, blinding her with its lights, then whining away into nothing.

"Son of a bitch!" It was the voice of a man, close by, that Ronna didn't recognize.

"Like, wow, look at the stars."

The girl's voice brought to mind Ronna's first grade teacher, a kindly fool who was determined to keep her voice soft no matter how many erasers were thrown.

"I don't give a flying fuck about the stars," the man snapped, closer now. "If someone doesn't pick us up soon, I'm going to freeze my balls off."

Ronna could make them out now as two shapes, carrying backpacks along the side of the road and getting closer.

"I love the crisp mountain air."

"Shut up, Poppy. There's only one goddamn thing you're good for."

The two hitchhikers were almost upon her now. Ronna figured she better speak soon or she'd scare them to death. "Hi! You two having trouble getting a ride?"

"We've been walking since the last town, whatever the hell it was called." The man's unnaturally thick hair fell to his shoulders. He looked Ronna over and must have decided she was cool. "Nobody'll give our kind a ride. What're you doing out here?"

"I'm traveling with a band. We've got an old school bus." Ronna didn't even think before adding, "You're welcome to join us."

"Far out!" Poppy squealed. She grabbed Ronna's hands and started jumping up and down on the pavement. Another car buzzed by, catching Poppy's long brown hair and Howdy Doody expression in its headlights.

It's a child, Ronna thought. Can't be more than 16.

Poppy was giggling and clowning pretty far out on the pavement. Another car was coming. Ronna wasn't altogether sure it would occur to Poppy to get out of the way. Ronna wrapped an

103

arm around Poppy's thin shoulders and pulled her off to the side.

"Come on," Ronna said softly. "I'll fix you something nice and warm to drink."

"Got any herbal teas?"

"Sure," Ronna said.

"I just love camomile."

"You would," the man said, trailing along behind.

"Oh . . . My name's Poppy, and this," Poppy trailed off to give the man a lovesick smile Ronna didn't think he deserved in the least, "is Siddhartha."

Siddhartha? Ronna checked him out in the light of Piper's campfire—dark hair, yes, but blue eyes and freckles?

"Nickname, from the book," he said lamely. It appeared to Ronna that he was correctly interpreting her look of disbelief.

Ronna introduced herself, then Piper and Bell who were still up. Ronna made tea. Yes, they had camomile.

Holding the warm cups, they sat around the fire. Ronna listened to its crackle and the occasional whine of a car passing. The fire's grey smoke coursed across the sky like an ever-changing rivulet, staining the inky black of night.

Poppy pulled out a deck of ordinary playing cards. "I tell fortunes," she announced. "Who's first?"

Bell, good-natured, acquiesced.

Poppy took all the twos, threes, fours, fives and

sixes out of the deck and handed what was left to Bell. "Shuffle," she said.

Bell did.

Poppy snatched the cards back eagerly, cut them, took the top card of the lower pile and the bottom card of the upper one. Those two cards she slipped inside a leather thong she tied around her forehead. The rest she divided into three equal packs.

On the opposite side of the campfire from Ronna, the dark, powerful form of Josephine materialized out of the gloom. Ronna introduced her to Poppy.

"Welcome, little girl," Josephine drawled.

"Blessed be," Poppy answered her. "Meet Siddhartha." Poppy gave Siddhartha another lovesick look.

Sparks from the fire flashed in Josephine's eyes as her gaze fell on the group's most recently acquired man.

"Hi," Siddhartha said.

There was no answer.

Siddhartha frowned.

Poppy, oblivious, turned to Bell. "This pack represents the present." She started turning up cards. "You are in love with a clever young woman."

"That let's you out," Siddhartha muttered in Poppy's direction.

Bell winked at Piper.

"But she doesn't even know you exist," Poppy continued. She put a hand on Bell's shoulder. "Sorry."

"Hey, there's nothing to be sorry about," Bell told her.

"Really?"

"Nothing personal," Piper said, snuggling up to Bell, "but the cards seem to be a little...off tonight."

Siddhartha was laughing. "Poppy's fortune-telling is very consistent. She's never right."

"The surprise cards are always right," Poppy exclaimed, undaunted. "Everybody says so."

Ronna was touched by the innocent sincerity. "What are the surprise cards?" she asked.

Poppy plucked the two cards out of her head-band. "The King and the Ace of Clubs, reversed. The king represents Bell, an honest, generous man who fails to see the lack of honesty in others. The ace signifies success—but it will be short-lived."

"Do mine," Ronna said.

Poppy did. "This band will provide you with an excellent opportunity to advance your musical career," she proclaimed.

Ronna, Bell and Piper squirmed in unison.

Siddhartha turned to Ronna. "May I ask what you do in the band?"

"Um..." Ronna was trying to think of a way to spare Poppy, but there was no helping it. "Actually, nothing."

Siddhartha broke into a gale of laughter.

"What about my surprise cards?" Ronna asked Poppy quickly.

Poppy flipped two new cards out of her head-band. "The Queen of Hearts. That's you, Ronna—

a gentle, loving mother—but it's reversed too, which means there is great danger in love for you."

"And what does my Eight of Clubs there mean?"

"It's reversed too," Poppy said. "I've never seen so many reversed cards. That means a dark person's passion, if reciprocated, will be the cause of great danger."

A knot of pine exploded in the fire. Ronna peered behind its sudden uproar into the dark where she'd left Simba. Did she imagine him standing beyond the light, his black hair coursing across the sky in ever-changing rivulets that mirrored the streams of smoke from the fire?

Josephine stepped into the circle of light around the fire. "My turn." She pushed her way between Poppy and Siddhartha.

In the firelight Poppy's cheeks took on the glow of a little girl who suddenly finds herself the center of attention in a group of adults. She shuffled happily, cut and tucked Josephine's surprise cards into her headband.

"Ah ah," Josephine said, shaking her head no.

Poppy blinked up at her.

"Just the surprise cards."

Poppy's cheeks lost some of their glow, but she obeyed quickly. "The Queen of Spades—"

"Uh huh," Josephine said, nodding her head in agreement.

"—and the Nine of Spades," Poppy continued. "Both reversed again. That means the queen is a dark, dangerous and deadly woman—"

"I'll buy the first two."

"—and that someone you care about will soon die."

"Ah ah." Josephine shook her head no again and pointed a thumb at herself. "Because there's only one person in the world this girl cares about."

"Like, wow, all my readings are real positive. I've never seen reversed surprise cards, and I've never, ever dealt a death card."

Siddhartha sneaked around Josephine to grab a handful of Poppy's rear. Poppy returned his crude grin with an innocent smile. It was Josephine who looked outraged.

"Time for you to roll out the sleeping bags, Poppy," Siddhartha said.

"Okay, but don't you want me to do your fortune first?"

Ronna could see the answer was going to be an emphatic no, until Siddhartha noticed the look on Josephine's face.

"All right, all right." Siddhartha's other hand was toying with the drawstring neck of Poppy's Indian print blouse. "But just the surprise cards."

Poppy shuffled happily, while Siddhartha slipped a hand under her blouse. Ronna studied the faces in the firelight. Piper was unperturbed, but she could see Bell's dark features tighten with disapproval. Out of the corner of her eye Ronna thought she saw Josephine reaching toward the fire.

Siddhartha let out a yelp and leaped to his feet, clawing at sparks in his long, dark hair. To Ronna's surprise, his hairline shifted dramatically.

Siddhartha's long dark hair fell into the fire. Underneath was a short red crewcut.

Piper, Bell and Poppy were rolling with laughter.

"Goddamn it! That thing cost me $29.95." Siddhartha tried half-heartedly to retrieve the wig, but it was already sizzling in the flames.

"What did you have it for, man?" Bell asked, holding his sides.

Siddhartha looked like a priest caught naked in a whorehouse. "Hey, chicks really dig long hair. Meanwhile I had this straight job that paid really well, and I'm never the one to walk away from a good thing. Poppy, shut up!"

Poppy stopped laughing, while Siddhartha gave Josephine a long, careful look.

Josephine's eyes glittered in the firelight. Next to her was a long stick, still smoking on one end.

"I did your cards," Poppy said and turned them up with the eager innocence of a dog dropping a filthy, saliva-slathered old ball in the lap of someone in his Sunday best. The firelight flickered over the Knave of Clubs and the Ace of Spades. "Like, wow, maybe you're right about my fortunetelling, Siddhartha. Like, maybe the spirits aren't with me tonight at least."

"Like, wow, imagine that."

Siddhartha's sarcasm was lost on Poppy, who was staring at the cards. Ronna suspected the expression on Poppy's face was the closest to a frown that she was capable of. "The Ace of Spades, reversed, is the worst card in the deck,"

Poppy finally said with an apologetic smile. "It means you, Siddhartha, are going to die."

Siddhartha pulled Poppy to her feet and grabbed her rear. "Nobody gets out of life alive, but of course I would never have figured that out without your help." He bumped and ground against her. "Roll out the sleeping bags, oh, brilliant one."

Simba was driving into the town of Grand Island, Nebraska, which turned out to be the home of the world's largest truck stop—nothing more. Still, he was glad of any excuse to end his turn at the wheel. He was all scratched up, especially on the back. Funny, he didn't remember Ronna getting all that carried away.

"Like, wow, that's really cool, Mushroom."

It was the new girl, Poppy, the Ultimate Flower Child. Simba eyed Josephine in the rearview mirror as he maneuvered the bus into the Grand Island Truck Stop. He didn't feel any too good about taking in any newcomers under the circumstances—especially weak and helpless ones. Unfortunately, he hadn't been around to say no, and it was a little hard to get rid of Poppy now, given her circumstances.

Then again, would physical stature make a difference? Simba remembered Ursula's description of the build of the first victim, the guy who had actually managed to get a hard on around Josephine, the Ultimate Bitch.

If only Simba could remember these things himself.

He finished parking and turned to check out Josephine again. Did he see regret in her sullen glare?

Next to her Mushroom was reading tarot cards for Poppy. "Now speak your question aloud," Mushroom said.

"Like, I want to know what happened to Siddhartha. Why he disappeared in the middle of the night," Poppy said.

"I don't need no fortunetelling cards to tell you that," Josephine snapped, leaping out of her seat like an uncaged animal.

Here it comes, Simba thought, tensing every muscle. I wonder what she did with the body.

But an expression of motherly concern took a valiant stand against the wildness in Josephine's face. "Girl, how long you known this Siddhartha?"

"Oh, like I met him yesterday."

"Uh huh. And uh, if you don't mind my asking, how many times did you two, uh, do it?"

"I don't mind. Just once." Poppy smiled dreamily. "But it was like very spiritual . . . really deep."

Piper broke out in friendly but uncontrollable giggles.

"I'll bet," Chutney snarled. He'd settled into the seat next to Poppy, knee tucked under his chin in his I'll-be-you're-unpaid-therapist pose. If this girl was in need of a friendly bear to protect her, it looked like she'd come to the right place.

"Uh huh," Josephine persisted dryly. "And when was this? Just before he took off last night?"

Poppy still looked dreamy. "Yeah."

Josephine rolled her eyes.

Then again, Simba thought, maybe the guy did just take off after taking care of business. "Poppy," Simba asked, "did he take his pack with him?"

"Oh, yeah. He said I could help him pack."

Simba breathed easier. He looked down at the last of Mushroom's tarot cards for Poppy. It was The Fool, reversed.

"Driver up," Simba called out, looking at Chutney. "Knowing how much you loved the Rockies, I've made special arrangements, sparing no expense. For you I've transformed the plains of Nebraska by installing—no, you can't see them now, but you will soon—the Italian Alps."

On the way to the driver's seat Chutney slapped both hands upon his heart. "Simba," he said in a vibrato that trembled with sincerity. "This kindness can only be repaid by lavishing a pestilence of unspeakable hideousness on your family for generations to come. Or, equally hideous, by wishing you a case of the crabs."

Poppy busted up laughing, her eyes sparkling as she actually applauded Chutney.

Simba met Chutney's big eyes, then watched him shake his head.

"Nah," Chutney said so only Simba could hear. "It would be like balling my kid sister."

"Which, depending on what your kid sister was like, might not be such a bad thing."

Chutney gave that an appreciative smirk, then pulled at his reddish beard. "It's a real stupid thing to do, I know, but I think I'm growing up."

Simba shook his head, only half-kidding. "Shame." But then Ronna appeared next to him, and the idea of getting it anywhere he could suddenly went flat for him, too.

Ronna's face was a lot better than yesterday. It was a beautiful sight, except that the true features now emerging so perfectly matched the acid flashback he kept having.

Whoever heard of a *déjà vu* acid flashback? Leave it to him to have the first.

Chutney was at the wheel, reading a small, fragile, leather-bound book of verse while he waited for the others to stretch their legs and utilize the truck stop's plumbing.

Ronna yawned, giving her an even softer, almost puppyish look.

"You've been sleeping all day," Simba said. "What're you trying to do? Put Ursula out of business?"

"That would take some doing."

Simba twirled the sound of Ronna's voice about in his mind like wine. That speech had been utterly free of either cattiness, condensation or condemnation. If anything, it was characterized by an empathy so pure it sounded as if she referred to herself, not Ursula.

"What about you?" she asked, looking up at him with eyes of true blue. "I mean after we, as Josephine would put it, did it."

Ronna looked down, but not before Simba saw her eyes fill with all those fears that seemed to plague women after sex. He put his arm around her, not knowing quite what it was to have such fears, but still not wanting anything, even himself, to hurt her.

"Did you fall right off to sleep?"

"Well, no . . ."

"Men always do," he said gently.

Should he tell her? Something in him said yes.

"But this one didn't." He sighed. "I am guilty of theft."

"Of?" she asked.

"Of a mushroom of Mushroom's."

It took Ronna a minute to process that. "Peyote?"

"Nah. This little button was mescaline, I think. Mushroom wasn't around, probably off sleeping somewhere, so I just took the first thing I could find in her stuff. Wasn't much. Don't even remember what the high was like. I went back to our sleeping bags to wait for you to come back. Must have fallen asleep before it really hit."

Ronna was looking up at him softly without condemnation. Simba was touched. If Freud was right about his mother providing the model for all the women in his life, then all women should be sources of the kind of relentless, unremitting confrontations that filled him with the determination not to ever confront anything.

"Did you dream?" Ronna asked.

"No, I never dream."

"Everyone dreams," Ronna said gently. "Maybe you just don't remember them."

Maybe.

* * *

Piper let her eyelids flutter in the breeze. She found the resulting shifts between light and shade soothed her, like the feel of the absurdly red satin sheets in the dream where she was a prostitute. She snapped her eyes open. The trees outside the window in the dream had been a little like these Iowan trees, the same odd shape she'd never seen before crossing the Mississippi.

Mousy, misshapen Midas, watering his plants with a hose at the side of the gas station, looked up at her with that unsuccessful smile of his. It reminded Piper of a double exposure of those twin theatrical masks that smiled and frowned. She gave him her warmest, sisterly smile back. Dense as Midas might be it was certainly clear to him by now that he wasn't going to get laid. Poor hobbit. Of all of them Midas seemed to have the least reason to be there. But then he probably didn't have much of a reason to be anywhere.

Chutney swung back into the phone booth, fist full of change, to scramble through the yellow pages. Whatever his fingers were doing, it certainly wasn't the walking. With the sun streaming through the phone booth to highlight his hair, beard and body hair, he looked like a chestnut bear crowded into a very small glass cage. He slammed a dime into the coin slot, dialed and started feeding in more change.

• "Hello?" Chutney inquired into the phone with his resonant actor's voice. "Yes . . . and you're located in Iowa City, by the university? Well, my friend, how would you like to have a groovy new group perform at your place tomorrow night for the truly modest sum of—"

There was a pause, during which Chutney made faces at Piper, obviously imitating some lame brain talking on the other end of the line.

"Oh, you don't," Chutney continued into the phone. "Well, maybe that's why the place is so quiet."

He stuck his chin out and gave Piper a curt, so-there nod.

"Oh," Chutney continued into the phone. "You like it quiet? What are you running? A business or a tax write-off?"

He held the phone away from his ear for a moment.

"Kidding, only kidding. Listen you can't pass this group up. We've got two dynamite singers and the lead drummer from Sabita . . . You never heard of Sabita? Come on! Go check out your juke box. Besides, forget the money. We're passing through town anyway and are willing to work in exchange for the exposure and—"

Chutney paused, then slammed a fist onto each hip.

"One soda pop each? Large size? Listen, man, one little announcement over the campus radio that you've got Bell Turner, Sabita's famous former drummer, playing in your bar tomorrow night and you'll have such a surplus of customers you'll have to—"

Chutney's face lit up. He gave Piper an excited thumbs up.

"Yes, of course you can hear us first . . ."

All right! Piper was ecstatic. She would have loved to have stayed to hear the rest, but she was so ecstatic she was about to pee in her pants. She all but flew into the lady's room.

Poppy, the new girl, was on the floor in the lotus position with her eyes closed. Her long brown hair hung over her face. Poppy wasn't breathing. Finally she inhaled saying "Raaaaaaa," and finally exhaled saying "Maaaaaaa."

Piper did what she came for, then turned on the tap, cupped her hands to collect as much water as she could, and dumped the water on Poppy's head.

For a moment Poppy blinked up at her like a half-drowned puppy, then she smiled brightly, bounded up to collect water from the still-running tap, and tossed it at Piper.

Piper stepped back. "Ya' missed."

Poppy tried again, succeeding in soaking Piper's workshirt.

"Filthy anyway." Piper peeled it off.

Poppy's eyes widened. "Like, wow, you've got a figure like what's-her-name in *Some Like It Hot* when she wears that sequined dress on that yacht?"

"Marilyn Monroe." Piper studied Poppy's innocent look of appreciation. Not a hint of malice, envy or Josephine's closet Lesbianism. It was refreshing. "Thanks."

"Look what I've got," Poppy said, digging through her pack. "Soap!"

By mutual consent they both stripped and took sponge baths, occasionally splashing each other and giggling. The sound echoed about the small rest room. Above the phony turquoise tile the dingy white walls were bathed with light from a high window. It felt great to be in the company of Poppy who, like Piper herself, smiled no matter where she was simply because she was alive.

When they were finished Poppy presented Piper with a clean, freshly ironed workshirt from her pack. "I'd lend you my cut-offs but you'd never squeeze that buxom rear of yours into them."

"True enough." Piper had to fight to get her own back on. "Who ironed this workshirt?"

"My mom."

Hmmmm. "How old are you, Poppy?"

"Sixteen."

"How long have you been on the road?"

"Oh, I ran away last weekend."

Not an ounce of deceit in this one. "Trouble at home?"

"Oh, no. I just wanted to see the world."

Piper laughed at that and leaned over with her hands on her knees to shake the water out of her hair, dog-style.

Poppy, caught in the spray, revenged herself by squirting Florida Water cologne at Piper.

Piper took a sniff of herself. "Nice."

Outside they heard a bloodcurdling scream. Piper, fully dressed, made it out the door first.

Midas, who had dropped a plant, shattering its clay pot, was staring in horror at his school bus.

Piper followed his gaze. Simba, Chutney and Bell each held huge paint brushes and cans of paint.

"Simba just got back from the hardware store," Chutney said, apologetically. "We were going to ask."

"One thing you gotta' admit, man," Bell said, accenting his dark face with a wide white grin. "It could use some paint."

"What color?" Midas asked.

Bell smoothed his already elegant goatee, while Chutney stroked his beard. They looked at each other. Simba was the one to answer Midas evenly. "Purple."

"Purple?" Midas's voice had jumped a few octaves.

"We should have discussed it with you first," Simba continued, approaching Midas. "It was a spur of the moment idea when Chutney got the gig for us tonight. It'll help the band. We couldn't have come this far without your bus, but let's face it—that peeling brown doesn't do a lot for our image." Simba clapped a hand onto Midas's slim shoulder and bored him through with his eyes. "What do you say?"

Midas looked up at Simba like a rabbit frozen by a car's headlights. "Sure, I guess."

Piper cocked a brow at Simba, wondering if he understood how incapable others were of opposing him. She was gratified by the gentle warmth she now saw as he looked at Midas.

"Thanks," Simba said. "We owe you, Midas. I won't forget."

"Far out!" Poppy yelled, rushing past Piper in a blur. "I just love to paint."

"Right on, baby," Bell answered her from atop

the bus. "How do you feel about scraping old paint off?"

"Oh, I just love that, too!" Poppy said brightly.

"All right." Bell beat out a little rhythm on the top of the bus with two paint scrapers, then handed one to Poppy. "You start on the hood. I'm doing the roof."

"Don't scrape the metal," Midas yelled, circling the bus like an expectant father.

"Fear not, faint heart," Chutney answered as Midas passed. "Here." Chutney handed Midas a teeny paint brush.

"Why so small?" Midas asked.

"Detail work." Chutney leaned close, jerking his bearded chin toward the others. "You wouldn't want to trust it to them, would you?"

Midas snatched the brush. Chutney handed him a coffee cup full of paint.

Piper stepped up to Chutney and spread her hands. He handed her a paint scraper and helped heft her onto the roof with a hand on her rear, until Bell, who was pulling her up from above, gave him a look of regal displeasure.

Josephine strutted out of the bus, bass in hand, and wheeled about until she spotted Piper on the roof.

"Hey, girl, Ronna told me about tonight." She strummed a few chords. "All right! What we gonna' play?"

Bell started to drum on the roof. Ronna appeared and signaled to Piper to hand her the scraper Bell wasn't using. Piper started to sing the songs she and Bell had worked out while shopping in Elko, Nevada, and Josephine joined in with her bass and some back-up singing.

Simba broke out his 12-string, and they were rolling. The others, even Mushroom, scraped paint to the music. Only one was missing.

"Hey!" Ursula stumbled out of the bus, rubbing her cold, reptilian eyes. "Like how the fuck am I supposed to sleep?"

"You're not," Bell bellowed.

"Oh, go do a line," Josephine said. "We need some help."

Ursula paused, then disappeared back into the bus. When she reappeared Josephine handed her a paint brush, and Ursula painted with a vengeance. Cocaine. Piper hadn't been around it much since not that many people did it. The ones that did always struck her as artificially intense and actually cold—a combination that didn't thrill her. On the other hand, Ursula had already painted the whole hood. The stuff had its uses.

Josephine and Simba were battling it out with their guitars again. Both had murder in their eyes. It made for wonderful music, but the hate Piper could see in Josephine's dark face had an intensity that could have extinguished the sun.

"Liquid sun and whisper breeze. A storybook sky that's sure to please. All I ask is to be alive. And not brought down by a bunch of jive."

Piper could feel both Bell and herself pouring everything they had into the song they'd made up when they met. Simba picked it right up with a composer's ease, harmonizing with both voice and 12-string. Even Ursula appeared with a second, albeit beat-up, bass guitar she apparently had enough ability to back Josephine with.

Poppy and Mushroom broke away from the bus to dance in the barren dirt at the back of the gas station. Poppy leaped about in the sunlight with the ingenuous asexuality of a child. Mushroom cavorted oddly in the shade, a mythical creature of dubious intent from some children's story. Mushroom's mass of thigh-length red hair formed a cloud about her inhuman face and form. Like some nymph or witch she seemed to undulate and cast a spell that was not at all sexual.

Chutney stepped back from the bus, pulling Midas back with him.

"No, wait," Midas protested. "There's a little corner I still haven't—"

"Finished!" Chutney declared. With a flourish of his paint brush, he bowed to a pair of gas station attendants who had watched all of this in horror.

Piper stood next to Bell, who was still drumming on the bus's roof. Except for the part of the roof they were on, the bus was now an outrageous purple. "How do I get down?" Piper asked.

Bell stopped his drumming.

Chutney mimed an exaggerated oops. "Could it be, fair damsel upon the roof, that unbeknownst to me they painted the other side?"

Bell looked down at the other side. "No shit, Sherlock."

Piper heard something she'd never heard; Ursula and Josephine were both laughing.

Bell backed up and then took a leap off the roof, landing like a panther on all fours.

"Lover boy," Piper said sarcastically.

Bell looked up.

"I do hope you're not expecting ole butterball here to duplicate that."

Bell held his arms out below her. "Come to Papa."

Oh, well. Piper jumped. Her mistake was not backing up first so she would clear the side of the bus. The paint felt cool and slippery on the way down. She landed by the rear tires, unhurt but half-purple.

"Oh, baby!" Bell lamented with a smile.

Oh, well.

Ronna materialized at Piper's side, trailing toilet paper from the rest room, and mopped up most of the paint single-handed. "If you would kindly step into your boudoir, madam," she purred, gesturing toward the ladies' room. "Your maidservants are most anxious to finish the job." Ronna pulled Piper to her feet, then gestured firmly at the other four females.

Poppy, Mushroom, Josephine and even Ursula trotted obediently into the ladies' room after them. Piper paused to study Ronna. A little less passive, my dear? Lessons from Simba? But then Piper remembered the way Simba controlled Ronna. Maybe it was something emerging despite Simba.

In the ladies' room they all tugged off Piper's clothing and scrubbed off the remaining paint, their voices ricocheting off the phony turquoise tile.

"Like, wow, I just love to scrub," Poppy said.

"Girl, is there anything in this whole wide world you don't just love?" Josephine asked.

Poppy was pensive.

"Like, that shut her up, man." Ursula's grey eyes were cold.

Facing the mirror, Piper could study Ronna behind her, when it was unlikely that Ronna thought anyone could see her. Piper saw the sharp stab of empathetic pain pass over Ronna's face, then saw the tenderness as Ronna approached Poppy from behind. Ronna gave Poppy's long brown hair a playful tug, then smiled brightly when Poppy turned.

"You're like sunshine," Ronna said, "and it's nothing to be ashamed of."

Heart, thought Piper as she watched Ronna through the mirror. Not stupid, but one who feels first rather than thinks. Piper preferred to think, but recognized Ronna as a person who outdistanced her in another area and admired her for it.

Ronna caught her eye in the mirror. "You are now in need of fresh clothes, madam."

Piper gave her very best helpless look. "In the bus, of course."

"I just love fetching things," Poppy said.

Josephine rolled her eyes. Ursula looked even paler.

Piper conceded she didn't have Ronna's warmth but managed to keep her voice neutral.

"Thanks, Poppy. My pack's next to Mushroom's and Josephine's."

Poppy bounded out the door.

Mushroom's green eyes glittered unnaturally as Ronna dunked her hair under the running water to wash it. "You don't understand," Mushroom protested, pouting with her prominent elfin mouth. "I'm not like other people."

"You're right. I've never seen such beautiful long red hair," Ronna said diplomatically.

Mushroom didn't seem to hear. "I was a witch in the nineteenth century in a small Long Island town."

Sure, Piper thought, but something brushed her mind for a moment and then was lost. Something about trees.

Suddenly everyone seemed down. Ronna looked vulnerable, the keeper of some dark secret. Ursula was irritable. Josephine was staring inward again at something very terrible.

Piper was actually relieved when Miss Professional Sunshine showed up with her pack.

"Hi, everybody," Poppy bubbled before turning to Piper. "Can I get your things out for you?"

"Sure," Piper said.

"Like, can I lick your ass for you?" mimicked Ursula. She seemed happier, though, with someone to insult, and Ronna was smiling softly.

Poppy was having a great time going through Piper's things. "Like, wow! 36D!" She held up Piper's one and only bra.

Ronna looked up from the arduous task of combing Mushroom's hair. "I'm outclassed."

Ursula looked up from snorting a line of coke and said something pleasant. "Not bad."

Josephine was oddly restless. "Put that thing away, girl. Now!"

Was it that closet Lesbianism? What Piper wanted to know was where the red hairs came from that she saw on her bra. They were too short to be Mushroom's.

Poppy put the bra away obediently. Keeping her eyes on Josephine, she dug further into the pack and started pulling something else out with a slightly puzzled look on her face. "This feels funny, whatever it is," she said. Poppy was still having trouble pulling it out. An odd smell filled the room.

Ronna gave Piper a friendly shrug, and they all leaned a little closer. Poppy acquired a glow and a friendly smile as she realized she was the center of attention. Piper looked at what was in Poppy's hand and saw a whole lot of red hair stuck in something grey and thick and floppy. Just as she saw the reddish brown encrusted in it, she realized it was a scalp.

Josephine started a long, unbroken scream while the thing in the hand of Poppy, who was still smiling sweetly, suddenly came free of the pack. Now they were all screaming, the sound ricocheting wildly off the phony turquoise tile, except Poppy, who turned slowly to discover what she held in her hand.

"Siddhartha?" Poppy's soft question found a break in the screams when Piper, for one, was catching a much-needed breath. Poppy was staring blankly into the eye of her lover of the night before, held loosely by a jagged slab of his now-grey face. Siddhartha's gaze seemed to drop from Poppy's face to her breasts. The eyeball appeared to bulge before falling forward out of the piece of face with a precise little slurp like a fish breaking the surface of the water to feed.

Piper watched the eyeball splat onto the tile floor trailing its moorings and the optic nerve like the umbilicus of an egg yolk. It slid a little closer, peering upwards at her nakedness, until in losing its motion it became tangled in its own moorings. The eyeball came to rest staring downwards in horror at the phony turquoise.

"Like, who needs this fucking shit, man?" Ursula's voice was an ear-splitting soprano.

Piper studied Poppy, the only one who still appeared calm, noted her shiver and decided the only reason she appeared calm was because she was so taken by surprise that she hadn't gotten it together enough to change her expression. Poppy still held the eyeless slab of face now sporting an eyehole from which red tissue drooled.

Ronna fainted as Simba barged in in time to catch her. Mushroom wailed. Ursula did another line.

Piper forced herself to stop screaming.

Suddenly Mushroom was also quiet. She got down on the floor on her hands and knees and peered at the eyeball. Piper studied her eyes and was sure she saw red reflected in their unnatural green.

Simba's mesmerizing blue eyes looked straight

at Piper's, completely disregarding her nudity. "Where's Josephine?"

Josephine was gone.

Parsons was holding a stiff dick, but it wasn't his own. He tossed it aside, and it rolled across the road next to him like a frozen sausage. Mine's bigger, he thought.

He'd gotten over the initial shock about the same time he'd figured out that the dismembered body parts he'd found by the side of the road belonged to one of the hippies he'd seen hitchhiking the day before.

Parsons rubbed his paunch. He was getting used to this. He got up and walked a little further along the ditch. The mountain air was crisp; the last of the Rockies was beautiful. Oh, look, there was the guy's ass, grey and bloody but wonderfully intact. Parsons lowered himself with a grunt so he could see it close up. The waist had been hacked through, a long and sloppy job, and the legs had been cut off. A broken thigh bone had been planted in the ground nearby.

A finger was visible protruding from the pile of feces just below the anus. Parsons reached in and pulled out a hand. It was intact but broken, and pieces of someone else's flesh were stuck under all the fingernails. The pathology department in Berkeley had told him the kid at Ronna's place had died of a dagger wound in the back before he was cut up. This guy had seen it coming and probably broke a fist trying to defend himself. After that he'd done a lot of wild clawing. Considering what was being done to him, even Parsons couldn't find anything to blame him for in that.

Parsons had some serious thinking to do. All his life he'd watched incompetents get the things he himself deserved—good grades just because they studied, girlfriends who put out just because they were nice to them. The list was endless. It included promotions at work.

Following procedure, what would happen when he reported this incident to Colorado's local yokels? They just might get gung-ho and arrest everybody in that purple bus, including his own daughter, which could be embarrassing. They just might get that nigger girl to confess, or some such thing, and then take the credit that Parsons deserved.

No. For once justice was going to be served. Parsons was going to get his. He scraped his hand against the broken edge of thigh bone to get the gunk off and leafed through the commie bastard's I.D. He wasn't under age. He'd didn't appear to be connected with anything or anyone of any importance. Who the fuck was going to miss this piece of shit?

And if anyone knew how to conceal a body, it was a cop.

Parsons smiled; he felt smug. Stretching, he slapped the victim's rear, just to see if it would bounce. Nice ass. Firm. Parsons was starting to feel really good. Maybe he would bury that part last.

Chapter 6

Ronna is with Mommy again, the Mommy with the long cotton skirt. Mommy is boiling clothes outside in the big silver tub again. Ronna's two sisters are playing in the dirt with Ronna. Ronna is happy until she just happens to look up at Mommy.

Ronna can see through the steam that Mommy's hands are bright pink. Ronna remembers how rough they feel when Mommy touches her and how ugly the burns on them are.

Funny, Mommy isn't working. Mommy always works, but now she's looking up at the sky with her face all twisted up. Sweat is pouring off her face, but the water from her eyes must be tears. Poor Mommy.

Ronna gets up from her play and runs to

Twisted

Mommy. She puts her arm around Mommy. Mommy puts her scratchy, ugly hot hands on Ronna, but Ronna doesn't mind. She kisses Mommy's hands. She even kisses the scabs on Mommy's hands.

Now Daddy's coming with his hunched back and his hate. Uh oh. Trouble. Daddy always yells at Mommy for not working even when she's working. What will he do now that Mommy really isn't working?

Ronna's sisters, Lucia and Portia, join them. They all look up at Mommy. Mommy has such fear in her face. Now Mommy's looking at Daddy and so are the three girls, and they all have fear in their faces.

Ronna is so scared, scared for Mommy. She doesn't understand what's happening or why big people do what they do, but there is one thing she understands perfectly—emotion. She can see it. She can smell it. She can taste it on the insides of her cheeks.

Daddy is mad, but there is something else. He is looking at the fear in all their faces, the woman and three girls, with yearning.

He likes it.

He is starting to smile and raise his hand. Mommy is pushing the three girls aside. Funny, Mommy doesn't look scared any more, just very hurt and maybe just a little angry.

Daddy hits Mommy. Spit and blood are spraying out of Mommy's mouth in a long stream. Something little and white lands in the dirt—

131

Mommy's tooth. Will Mommy be like big brother Eb and grow another?

Laughter. Through the trees. A horse whinnying. Someone coming along the road in a great big open carriage with a lot of horses and a lot of dust. Daddy lowers his hand to look. Ronna snatches the tooth off the ground and runs to Mommy. She thinks she better stick it back in where it belongs just in case Mommy isn't like Eb, but Mommy is looking at the carriage, too, and won't lean over. Now there's yearning in Mommy's face and a painful, faraway look. Ronna holds Mommy's hand gently in both of hers and turns to look, too.

In the carriage is a very colorful lady. She's wearing bright red rouge on her lips and a shiny purple dress. Ronna can see she has boobies that are even bigger than Mommy's. She's drinking something from a bottle; Ronna doesn't know what. She's laughing with the other people in the carriage. They're all men.

The carriage is going slowly over the rough road. The lady is opening boxes wrapped in colored paper. Ronna has never seen such things. Just as the carriage is closest, the lady pulls some shiny red material out of one of the boxes.

"I say, Edward," one of the men says, "she already has red satin sheets. More than one set, I'll wager."

"And you'd win that wager," the lady says. "For once."

The men laugh.

The lady's smile is rich and happy; her voice

is raspy and low. "My enemies say I've a set for every man I've ever had."

Edward, who hadn't laughed, speaks with difficulty. "Accept my abject apology, light of my life."

"That I will not do, dear Edward."

"Because?" Edward is very upset.

"Because I always pride myself in living up to the things my enemies say about me. So you see I'll be needing many more sets." The carriage is about to drop from sight over the next ridge, but Ronna can see the twinkle in the lady's eye. "As 'tis, I've only three closets full."

The men burst out laughing as the carriage disappears over the ridge. Ronna remembers the tooth still in her hand and tries to reach Mommy's mouth to put it back in again. She stops when she sees the look on Mommy's face.

Mommy is staring at Daddy with something more than hurt. Daddy is staring after the lady in the carriage with something more than hunger.

"Where is she?"

Simba's voice.

"I don't know, man."

Chutney—warm and concerned.

Ronna opened her eyes and saw she was in the bus. How did she get in the . . . ? She remembered the ladies' room, started to feel faint again, but decided she was not going to spend her life being a gothic heroine no matter what happened.

And this was certainly "no matter what."

"Who are you looking for?" she asked Simba.

"Josephine," he answered.

Ronna took a deep breath. "I'll find her."

Simba's arms tightened about her. "No."

Ronna wanted to snuggle up in his arms and close her eyes again. Instead she forced herself to think, not feel. "I'm the wrong sex to be at risk. Think about it."

"She's got you there," Chutney said.

Simba leveled his electric blue eyes at the others huddled about them. "We're in a very dangerous situation. We have to think very carefully about what we do."

"I see her," Midas said, looking out the other side of the bus.

They all scrambled to get a look. Across the highway was a softly lit, exquisitely pastoral field that could have been painted by Boucher except that even that romantic soul would have rejected its perfection as too unrealistic. In the middle atop a gentle green knoll was a huge, perfectly rounded tree. Its only defect was its lack of the requisite flower-bedecked swing with its rosy-cheeked cherubs swarming naked over the seat. Instead the incongruously Amazonian Josephine sat awkwardly at its base, her clothing askew, her dark arms clutching the trunk. She was crying.

Ronna bolted for the bus door; Simba clapped a hand around her wrist.

"Like, Simba, let her go play with the dike, man," Ursula said. "I'll keep you warm nights."

"What are we going to do?" Piper asked.

"Stay together," Simba said.

"When are we going to call the police?" Midas asked.

Ronna, frozen in her aborted exit stance, saw Simba and Chutney exchange a look. It was obvious who was second in command.

"Never," Simba answered.

"What do you mean ne—"

"Midas, this is Middle America," Simba patiently explained. "Compared to the two coasts, it's a completely different country. For starters, I know two people who were arrested in Joplin, Missouri, on suspicion of looking like beatniks. Can you imagine what they would do with a bus load of hippies who show up with part of a corpse?"

"Like, wow!" Even this prospect seemed to trigger Poppy's inexhaustible sense of wonder.

Ursula nervously fingered the pocket where Ronna knew she kept her cocaine. Chutney stroked his beard, then folded his burly arms across his chest. Mushroom shivered, shaking water from the long red strands of her still-wet hair.

Piper sandwiched Bell's dark hand between both of hers. "They probably publicize KKK meeting times in the local paper."

Ronna looked at Josephine and pulled at Simba's hand.

Bell asked, "What are we going to do with the bitch? Leave her here?"

"She could follow us, hitchhiking," Simba said. "Show up in the middle of the night when we least expect her. She could go to the police."

He looked out the window at Josephine. "They might not listen to her because she's colored, but then again her clothes are pretty straight. She's the least hippie-fied of any of us, and they might just listen to whatever tale she decides to tell."

"A situation fraught with possibilities," Chutney injected.

"All of them unpleasant," Simba agreed. "Even if she doesn't do anything to us, what might she do to others?"

Chutney was on his feet. "Sterling point! If we decide, intelligently I think, not to turn this over to the proper authorities, then it becomes our responsibility to protect even these middle Americans from any harm that might result from that decision. What's right is right."

Ronna forced herself to confront the others. "You're talking as if this country consists of two entirely separate worlds—us hippies, if I can include myself in that—"

Ursula interrupted her. "Like, not really, but you do look the part."

"And what you all call the straight people." Ronna stopped to collect her thoughts, then stopped altogether when she realized by looking at all of their faces that what she had stated was—in their minds, at least—a foregone conclusion.

"Come on, everybody," Simba said, nodding toward Josephine. "We gotta' take care of our own."

They filed out of the bus and across the highway. The field smelled vaguely of flowers and long ago. Ronna didn't want to be part of a group of nine descending on a disheveled woman crying piteously at the base of a tree. She wanted them all to be children, playing and laughing and skipping in the sparkling sunshine.

Maybe they could play tag.

Maybe they could roll in the grass.

Maybe they could look for four-leaf clovers.

Josephine saw them coming and got to her feet.

Ronna looked up at a grim-looking Simba beside her. "With all of you here, I'll be safe," she said. "Let me talk to her alone." She could see the no in his eyes. "Just for a moment," she added, and then with all her heart, "please!"

Simba's eyes blazed, but he took a deep breath and waved the others back, looking miserable. Ronna went on ahead.

Walking those few steps to Josephine took forever. Squish, squish, went Ronna's feet in the grass. One, two, buckle my shoe.

Josephine's stormy face was getting closer.

Three, four, shut the door. Shut all the doors. Windows, too. Batten down the hatches.

Ronna was scared.

Josephine grabbed her, arms tight around Ronna's neck, wet cheek pressed against Ronna's cheek. Into Ronna's ear Josephine whispered, "I'm scared."

It was the voice of a very little girl.

A wild-looking Simba pulled them apart.

Ronna signaled him back, but he wouldn't budge. Ronna felt a tear slide down her own cheek. "I'm okay, Simba. Please?" Ronna didn't know if the tear was hers or Josephine's.

Simba backed away slowly.

"You're scared, too?" Ronna asked Josephine. "Is that why you ran away?"

"Girl, why else would I run away?" Josephine looked down. "Remember when Simba tole' us the knife that was used on Bell was his, and then that he hadn't seen it since that boy I did it with got all cut up in Berkeley?"

"Yeah?" Ronna prompted.

"Way that chump boyfriend of yours was looking at me I thought he thought I did it."

"And?" Ronna asked.

"And I knew I didn't do it. And I knew Simba didn't do it or he wouldn't have told us about the knife being his, but, honey, that's when I knew that one of us in this group did it. And I was scared." Josephine looked up at her with eyes that were starting to tear again. "Ronna, seems like I been scared all my life, and I hate being scared."

"I know what you mean."

"It's all because of men." Josephine's face hardened, her voice dropping to a whisper. "I hate them."

Ronna felt a chill, although the sun was perfectly hot. "Even that boy that you...uh...did it with?"

"I don't rightly know. I don't understand all the things inside me."

"What things?"

"Oh Ronna, honey, don't ask." Josephine buried her head in her hands and started to cry hard.

"Tell me," Ronna said.

"No...well, maybe just a little bit, or I'll go crazy. Something funny happens to me when I have sex."

"What?"

"All of a sudden like, I love all the things I hate, and I hate all the things I love."

"I don't understand," Ronna said.

"I know. I don't either. I don't want to talk about it anymore."

They both stared down at the grass.

"Do you know," Josephine said, "that I used to be better than any other girl on the block at skipping rope?"

Looking into each other's eyes, they almost smiled.

"What happens now?" Josephine asked.

"I guess we go back to the bus."

Simba was parking in the back of the Cross Roads Truck Stop in Des Moines. A pudgy dishwasher got right in his way to watch. Simba was about to call him an idiot when he finally got a good look at the guy's face and saw he was Mongoloid.

I'm the idiot, Simba thought. I will never let Ronna have her way about anything ever again.

Standing back while Josephine was within striking distance of Ronna had all but killed him. Little had been said since then, no direct confrontations. Simba had been keeping tabs on them all in the rearview mirror. He had noticed that everyone except Poppy had looked over at the big box at least once. The ax that was leaning against it was no longer there.

The problem was that Simba didn't know where it was.

"I've only three closets full." It was, at once, Piper's voice and not Piper's voice. The others giggled. Simba checked the mirror. Piper was asleep.

"Pit stop!" Simba bellowed. "Up and out! Those remaining in the bus will be charged an extra fare—or asked to cut their hair." Nobody laughed.

They descended on the coffee shop in silence. Ronna started to sit next to Josephine, but Bell slipped in before her, then met Simba's eyes.

Simba nodded. Good man.

Midas and Poppy slid in opposite Josephine, Bell and Ronna.

Someone clapped a hand on Simba's shoulder, and he turned to find warmth in the golden-brown of Chutney's eyes. There was an empty booth next to the one where Josephine sat, but Simba directed the remainder of the group to a booth a little further away.

Chutney and Simba sat on one side. Piper, Mushroom and Ursula sat on the other.

Chutney and Simba could see the other booth.

"How long are we going to keep this up?" Chutney asked.

"Until we reach the east coast," Simba said. "We'll turn her over to the proper authorities in New York City."

"Can I ask a real dumb question?" Piper said.

"You're on," Chutney answered.

"Have any of us stopped to consider the possibility that Josephine may not be the killer?"

"Josephine isn't the killer," Ursula stated.

"Shuddup, Ursula," Simba said.

"Like, nobody ever believes me, man. It's the curse of my life," Ursula lamented.

Simba glared at Ursula's wan face and dark, stringy hair. It occurred to him to wonder how Ronna would feel if she knew he'd had sex with her. Someday he'd have to tell Ronna.

Ursula managed to misconstrue Simba's glare and gave him a macabre attempt at a come-hither look in return. Women! They all thought they were so damn irresistible.

"It's Josephine," Simba said. "It's gotta' be. Think about it, as Ronna would say."

Simba made a point of looking at Ursula when he mentioned Ronna. Ursula looked hurt.

It had to be Josephine. Bad as the situation was, it would be unendurable if he had to imagine the worst every time any one of them got close to Ronna.

"Do we go ahead with the performance tonight?" Chutney asked.

"Sure," Simba answered. "Keeps us all together, keeps her hands busy with the bass, and provides an audience to discourage and/or stop any trouble. What could be safer?"

Mushroom's green eyes sparkled. "It would be safer, Simba, if you knew the things inside you."

Oh, crap, here we go again. The holy roller side of hippie life. Simba fought down the temptation to answer with a very sarcastic, "Like, wow ... heavy!"

"What happens when we all go to sleep nights?" Chutney asked.

At least somebody had his feet on the ground. "You and Bell and I take turns guarding her." Simba sighed heavily. He hated to say it but ... "I think we're also going to have to tie her down. Otherwise, if one of us gets a little sleepy and looks the other way for a moment, the consequences are just too great."

"Oh, no!" Piper said. Miss Free Spirit. Probably couldn't stand the thought of tying anything down, not even an idea. Still, Simba had to agree with her. Really Piper was an all right person. She was just a bit too strong-willed for a woman.

"Relax," Mushroom said to Piper. "Close your eyes."

Better her than me. Simba watched Piper smile and comply. Mushroom pointed her fingers at Piper like a witch, then started to massage her face and temples. Light from the diner's window streamed across her elfin face, playing in the unnatural red of her hair.

"You are getting younger."

There was that odd quality to Mushroom's voice again, loud yet soft. A young boy and his mother with a bouffant hairstyle seated themselves warily at the next booth. The waitress showed up. Simba ordered a round of hamburgers for all. He had to give credit where credit was due. It didn't seem to break anybody's concentration.

142

"Relax. You are young. How old are you, Piper?"

"I'm ten."

"Where are you?" Mushroom asked.

"Mother's kitchen," Piper answered. She sounded annoyed.

"What is Mother doing?" Mushroom asked.

"Cooking, scrubbing, wiping my brother's runny nose, ironing Father's shirts."

"What's Father doing?" Mushroom asked.

"Reading the paper, watching TV, drinking beer, belching, picking his nose and complaining about Mother's cooking."

Chutney gave Simba a thumbs up. "Sounds ideal."

"Relax," Mushroom said to Piper. "You are getting younger again."

Piper started to giggle.

"What's funny?" Mushroom asked.

"The sun."

"Because?"

" 'Cuz it's shining all over me. It's so snuggly."

Even the mother who had been frowning at them from the next booth smiled.

"How old are you, Piper?" Mushroom asked.

"I'm five."

"Relax," Mushroom said. "You are getting younger again. Much younger. You are a baby. Now you are getting even younger than that. Listen carefully. You are floating backwards through time. There is a long corridor with a bright, pure light at the end. You are walking through the light to the other side. At the end is a huge, heavy door. Can you see the door, Piper?"

"Yes, but my name is not Piper, my treasure, and I'd much rather stay here with you than go anywhere in heaven or earth."

Mushroom paused, then asked, "Who am I?"

Piper's voice was raspy and low. "The only one I've ever loved."

"What do I look like?" Mushroom asked.

"Just as I saw you last." Piper fought to steady her voice and smile despite tears. "Hair soft as sunbeams, eyes as vast and pure as the sky. I loved you so much that I listened to my enemies, who I never listen to. They said I was no good for you, but you do not belong to this other woman with her pursed lips and dead eyes, or this big house with its furniture no one can sit on. You are and always will be my dearest, my treasure, my child."

As if the Blue Fairy from *Pinocchio* had just granted her life, Mushroom suddenly looked human. She asked her next question with glistening eyes and a tremble in her lower lip. "What happened?"

Piper's whole body jerked and when her eyes fluttered open for a heartbeat, she looked like a torture victim whose captor had just delivered the master blow. "After you were born I never let them spend the night, no matter how much they paid." Her smile was soft. "Instead I'd crawl into bed with you, of a winter night, and make a nest for you in the bedclothes right next to my heart. You'd tuck your toes in under my legs to

144

keep them warm, and we'd cuddle and giggle and make up stories and look through the frosty windows at the stars."

The young boy in the next booth rested his head against the backrest next to Piper and smiled up at her. His mother frowned and whisked him away.

Piper knit her brow. "When the man and his wife with the pursed lips took you away, they gave you tutors and riding lessons and trips abroad. They took you to church, and they gave you a huge bedroom with a canopy bed. Not able to have children of their own, I suppose they did love you in their own funny, hollow, distant way, but I know you told me once that they never ever came into your room at night."

The waitress served the hamburgers, but Simba noticed that nobody moved.

The Piper that didn't sound like Piper continued. "It wasn't until after you were gone that they took pity on me and allowed me into their house so I could sit in your room and touch your things. It was only then, alone in that drafty cold room night after night, that I began to understand how it was that what started as a chest cold managed to kill you."

The others sat frozen in the sunlight and watched the untouched hamburgers turn equally cold.

Another sensation Piper had never experienced in her 20 years was sorrow. She did now. It twisted her, mixed as it was with an almost exquisite yearning to be with Star again.

Shit! She was doing it again. Making herself miserable, pining after a dead child she had presumably named Star who may or may not have existed in some hypothetical past life. The performance in Iowa City had been great, life was grand, and she wasn't going to let anything bring her down. Still, she was too honest not to admit that another sensation she was feeling for the first time was that of feeling, not thinking. Ronna, step aside.

In fact, Ronna was across the campfire, standing her ground against Simba who wanted to tie Josephine up for the night. She probably wouldn't win, but Piper noted that her defense was peppered with words like "logical" and "rational."

Actually, Piper thought, if I'm changing, so is she—in the opposite direction. They were two souls, whose mission in this lifetime was to switch places. Piper gave Ronna, who would never see it, what felt like her extra-special, all-time warmest smile.

Piper stuck another marshmallow on the end of her stick and found a good coal to toast it over. Another Ronna touch, that and the hot chocolate at her side. It seemed to work, or perhaps they were all still high from the thunderous applause their performance had earned them in the bar. Whatever the cause, as Piper studied the faces circling the fire, they seemed to belong more to the participants of a scout camping trip than a band of social outcasts harboring a murderer.

Twisted

Chutney's marshmallow had reached the pinnacle of perfection—a uniform golden brown without a hint of black. The group ooh-ed as he pulled it from the fire with a flourish, then aw-ed as he presented it ceremoniously to Poppy who clapped her hands in delight.

Miss Professional Sunshine popped the marshmallow into her mouth and beamed up at Chutney, who settled in next to her with a knee tucked in under his chin.

"Tell me, oh radiant one, have you lived in Vancouver all your life?" Piper studied Chutney's face as he spoke to Poppy. His warmth was far more than a reflection of the firelight, but it looked like Poppy had come to the wrong place if she was in need of getting laid.

"Vancouver?" Poppy answered. "Like, yeah, all my life. I just love it."

"Hmmm." Chutney stroked his beard, which was glistening red in the firelight. "And do you just love your parents?"

"Like, yeah."

"Do they know where you are?"

"No," Poppy answered brightly.

"Because?"

"Because I didn't tell them."

Snickers erupted from across the fire. Both Chutney and Ronna glared at Ursula.

"Why didn't you tell them?" Chutney asked.

"They think it's dangerous to hitchhike. I didn't want to bring them down."

"Don't you think not knowing where you are at all might bring them down?" Chutney asked.

147

"Like, wow, I never thought of that."

Chutney reached into the pockets of his somewhat baggy, very faded, brown corduroy trousers. "My purse is heavy with coin, fair Poppy. Ripe for a phone call to Vancouver." He angled his watch toward the fire. "Eleven minus two hours ... Might your parents be home at nine o'clock of a Saturday evening?"

"Like, yeah, but I don't want to call them."

"Because?" Chutney asked gently. Ronna looked concerned.

"I'd be interrupting 'Gunsmoke.'"

"Oh." Chutney chuckled. Even Ronna shook her head. "No problem," Chutney continued. "We'll just wait till 'Gunsmoke' is over."

"Like, yeah, we could do that," Poppy said.

Chutney glanced at Josephine, who sat as far apart from the others as Simba would allow, staring fixedly into the fire. "Simba, my man, think you can take the first watch while Poppy and I take a walk to the nearest pay phone?"

"Sure," Simba said and then turned back to Ronna, who sat closer to Josephine than anyone else. "But that settles the arguement. Josephine, I'm going to have to tie—"

"I'll tell her, and I'll do it," Ronna interrupted. Josephine regarded Ronna with a combination of pathos and gratitude. They talked quietly among themselves.

Poppy pulled out her playing cards.

"Like, please do my surprise cards, Poppy," Ursula said. "I'd be lost without you."

148

Ursula's sarcasm was wasted so Poppy complied.

"Far out," Poppy said. "My cards are still coming up negative. You're the Queen of Diamonds, Ursula, which indicates poor breeding and a love of the tawdry side of life."

"Right on!" Bell called from across the fire, but it was good-natured.

"And your other card is the Seven of Hearts," Poppy continued. "Right side up it means serenity, grooving on things, but yours is reversed. That means a kind of tired soul. I don't really understand it."

"You wouldn't," Ursula said, her eyes as cold as a snake's. "Do Josephine's."

Again, Poppy complied. Josephine's eyes, showing white with the fire's light, had the dull sheen of a caged panther's suppressed savagery. Piper, studying the two of them, wondered if two more opposite extremes had ever sat facing each other.

Poppy flipped up the first card. "The Queen of Spades, reversed again," she said brightly. "A dark, dangerous and deadly woman. Wow, that's really accurate."

Groans were heard around the fire. Josephine's jaw tightened.

Poppy blithely flipped up the second card, but this appeared to daunt even her spirits. It was the Ace of Spades, upside down.

* * *

Parsons came, then rolled heavily onto his back. Good, he thought, but he had to admit that it wasn't as much fun as yesterday.

"That'll be five dollars extra, mister," the girl said. "You came inside me."

Yeah, yeah. The bit about the thighs. Parsons knew the rules.

"Wasn't I supposed to?" he asked innocently. "Gee, I'm sorry. That's what I thought I paid the fifteen dollars for, not to mention all those drinks I bought you. Gosh, I'm a little tapped out. Could I mail you the extra five?"

The girl studied him. "I've never done this before, but I'll trust you for it. You're a real nice guy. I've never met one nicer." She wasn't very bright.

While she was in the bathroom, Parsons pulled out his money roll and counted. $493. He was doing just fine except that he kept breaking fifties so the roll was getting too big. He'd have to remember to get rid of some of those fives and tens.

The girl came back out.

"Don't forget to leave your address, now, so I can mail you that five as soon as I get it," Parsons said.

The girl scribbled something on some motel stationary she found next to the ice bucket and the Gideon Bible. On his way back from locking the motel door behind her, Parsons threw it out.

The bed was too soft, made incorrectly by some incompetent, but Parsons fell asleep pretty easily. He had the strangest dream. It started with the woman and the three girls looking up at him with fear in their faces.

He enjoyed that.

Then the children were gone, and he was in bed with the woman.

He couldn't get it up.

Next he was with a whore. It was then he realized that this was all taking place in the 19th Century. The whore, a very colorful lady with bright red lips, was dressed in a low-cut, shiny floor-length, purple dress.

She was refusing him, even though he had the money. Parsons didn't like that at all.

Next he was still with the whore, but it must have been a different day because she was wearing a different dress, though equally low-cut.

Parsons was carrying a harpoon.

After that he woke up. Some incompetent in the next room was walking around. Parsons checked his watch. 10:00 A.M. Some people had no consideration at all.

Parsons wanted some coffee, the kind Ronna used to make for him before she went bad. He also wanted to forget about those goddamn dreams and get on with the day. The problem was those goddamn dreams were hard to forget about. They seemed so real.

Chapter 7

A girl scout is clean in thought, word and deed. This land is your land.

Ronna was trying to be brave. The truth was she was scared to death of going to sleep without Simba at her side. Far from the bus, where he'd be keeping watch over Josephine, he'd wrapped her Mickey Mouse rug around Ronna by the side of an old barn. All the others he'd somehow managed to arrange in a semicircle around her. Nobody could get to Ronna without stepping over the bodies of what looked like a pretty sleepless group.

A yard or two from her toes, Midas kept fidgeting in his sleeping bag, banging against the barn in his perpetual search for the perfect position. A flurry of grunts and annoyed tongue clickings composed Midas's lullaby. It failed to lull him, or anyone else, to sleep.

Against the barn beyond Ronna's head, moonlight accentuated Ursula's pallor as she brushed a dark strand of stringy hair aside so she could snort another line of cocaine. It wasn't likely that she'd be caught sleeping anytime soon.

Piper lay out on the grass, the firm set of her jaw visible even at Ronna's distance and in the light of a half moon. Piper was staring at a star.

At a slight distance Bell sat perfectly still, exuding dignity and calm. With his red headband, dark satin skin and elegant goatee, he reminded Ronna of one of the wise men in an old Sunday school illustration.

Only Mushroom looked like she might be sleeping. Ronna couldn't tell because her face was turned in the opposite direction and all Ronna could see was the mass of hair that lay on the grass like some amazingly red fox curled up by Mushroom's head.

A tinge of resentment pricked Ronna. She had to search for the cause. Then she remembered that Simba had stopped to talk to Mushroom just before standing guard at the bus so that Chutney and Poppy could walk into town and call Vancouver. Ronna had been impressed with Simba's candor in admitting he'd stolen some drugs from Mushroom the night before. What this positive feeling had masked until now was Ronna's fears over what had followed. Far from being angry, Mushroom had given Simba another mushroom. Ronna, though working on being aggressive, hadn't quite had it in her to leap up and tell Simba no. Surprisingly, it was Simba who had said no. Mushroom had persisted, and now Ronna realized she resented this because, in the end, Simba took the mushroom.

Did he eat it? Ronna herself had tied up Josephine, but even so . . . What would happen if Simba blacked out again?

The problem was that Luke did know where it was.

An ax should always be kept in a dry place, close at hand. There was a lot of wood to be chopped in this life, and Father suggested that Luke didn't work as hard as his brother Eb, that what he had learned whaling was of no use, that he was of no use. The only people Father thought were of less use were women.

There was a woman in front of Luke now.

She was wearing funny clothes again, but Luke still knew who she was. Luke had known her when he first saw her after waking up in this funny time. His witch sister Lucy had called her another name, but Luke knew. She was the freed woman from the field, the one that had made him do the thing that was wrong.

He hadn't known his own sister Lucy right away. That was the first time he'd woken up in this funny time, and that was why his witch sister had been able to make him touch her in that wrong place.

He'd been lost. He hadn't known where he was. Now, each time he woke up in this funny time, he could feel himself getting stronger and stronger. He knew who they were, he could recognize them all, and he knew what he was there for.

He was going to do the thing that was right.

First, the ax needed sharpening again. The woman wasn't going anywhere. After all, she was tied up. Luke looked for the sharpening stone which was right where he'd left it.

The woman's eyes were big as saucers. What was the matter? Hadn't she ever seen someone sharpen an ax before? Luke remembered what Father had told him about women once. Father had said, "Of what use is a person whose arms are so weak that they cannot chop the wood needed to keep them warm at night. Such a person has no right to live."

They had all been chopping wood—Father, Eb, Zak, the hired hand, and Alex, the slave. "Masa Carnes?" Alex had said with a broad smile on his black face. "There's one thing womenfolk is good for."

Luke had watched Father's twisted back stiffen. "That's the most evil thing of all," he had said. "It makes more people—little weak ones whose fireplaces have to burn hot with wood they themselves cannot chop."

The woman started to moan, bringing Luke back to the present for a moment. She had moaned in the past, in the field when they did the wrong thing. Father had said it was her fault, not Luke's, and that she should be punished.

Luke had done as his father had told him to,

but here she was again, forcing him to concentrate on the here and now. Luke would have to do it again, or Father might get angry. Father was terrible when he got angry.

What if she screamed? Luke looked out the window. In the light of the half moon, he could just see the barn where the others slept. Zak, the hired hand, would be next to the barn still. Alex, the slave, would be near the town whore. The town witch would be alone, casting her spells. His sister Lucy would complete the half-circle around the most evil one of all—his headstrong sister Rachel.

But they were far enough away. As long as they stayed put, no one would hear, and Luke had to admit something to himself—he liked the screams.

He put the ax down and backhanded the woman. She did as she was supposed to. Luke was pleased by the scream and the way her breasts jiggled from the impact. Maybe he wouldn't need the ax this time.

He had needed the ax with the man who had done the wrong thing with Luke's sweet sister Portia. Even with the ax that monster had scratched Luke's back terribly before Luke managed to whack him in the face.

That had been funny. The man had looked cross-eyed at the ax buried between his eyes before he'd died. The man before that, Luke felt a little bad about.

It had been a boy, thin and useless as a woman Father would have said. Luke had done it because the boy was stopping him from punishing his sister Rachel. Rachel was being lazy again and sleeping instead of doing her chores, but Rachel was even more of a witch than Lucy. In her sleep she had cast a spell on Luke, making him do the wrong thing just like he'd done in the field with this woman before him now. Father would be angry with him again. Maybe if he hadn't killed the boy it wouldn't have happened.

Luke touched the dark woman's breast. She squirmed around a lot and then did the right thing and bit his arm. Their eyes met, and for a moment they were perfectly still. Luke looked into her soul, the same way he could look into all of their souls and see who they had been. There was pain in her, an awful horrible lot of pain—just like in him. Maybe, just maybe, she would understand.

"Please," Luke said, "I beseech you. Do not let me do the wrong thing." The woman looked at the ax; Luke felt a rush of peace.

She understood! The woman knew what was right. That's why she looked at the ax. That's why she bit him when he did the wrong thing. She would help him.

Luke looked deeply into her eyes again. He could see revulsion mixed with a desperate cunning and an even more desperate hope. This he didn't understand.

"Untie me," she said. Her voice cracked.

Luke took another look at the ax. Axes were good. They represented the one thing his father had taught him to respect—hard work.

Then he looked back at the woman. She wasn't going to let him do the bad thing. He didn't need the ax. He smiled and patted her cheek in a nice way. He started to untie her, then stopped.

"Do you promise?" he asked. Luke had to be sure.

The woman squeezed her eyes shut, opened them to look behind Luke in the direction of the door, then answered in a low, flat tone. "I will do whatever you want."

Luke untied her. He felt better about things until he saw her lie down.

"You're doing as you did in the field," he accused.

For a moment the pain in her eyes was replaced by surprise. "How you know about my field dream, white boy?"

" 'Tis no dream. Oh, that it were."

"Don't matter." Her voice was flat again. Then she did it. She took his hand and put it on her breast. Before he could react she rolled on top of him, shoving her leg between his legs.

The woman tried to moan, but her voice was still cracking. She seemed to want to get to the other side of him, but most of all she wanted to do the bad thing.

Luke was going to need the ax after all.

"What's the matter, baby," she said in a phony sweet voice that sounded strange because she was so terribly nervous. "Can't you get hard?"

"Witch!" She had tricked him. He backhanded her again. He was disappointed when she suppressed her scream and tried—of all things—to smile, but he was beginning to feel better. He started to reach for the ax. He'd show her hard.

She started to roll over toward the other side of him, found his arm in the way, and quickly rolled back off him in the other direction to where she had been before.

"You can spank me if you'd like. Go ahead."

Maybe he wouldn't need the ax. Maybe . . .

No, far from helping him not to do the bad thing, she was now pulling off her funny clothes.

Luke grabbed the ax.

The woman scrambled for the other side of him again. What was over by the door that the witch wanted? The supplies for the galley, perhaps? A knife with which to hurt him? He sunk the hard head of the ax into her naked rear end. It did not matter.

Now she screamed, but it didn't sound penitent like he imagined the others' death screams to be. It sounded angry. She surprised him by turning on him; instead of trying to get away she wrenched the ax out of his hands. Strange for a woman, and not at all what she had done the last time he killed her.

"Men!" Her screech was deafening. "No pleasing them no matter what you do!" She had the ax. Naked, her muscles shown as powerful as a man's. Maybe Father was wrong about this one.

The woman swung the ax at Luke, sinking it deep into the wall next to him. Luke was impressed except for one thing. Aim!

Aim came of a lifetime of hard work. Aim came of being beaten out of bed to chop wood at the age of five while it was still dark outside. Of being beaten if he missed, even if his fingers were so cold he couldn't feel them.

The woman looked past Luke toward the door, then yanked at the ax imbedded in the wall. Her muscles bulged beautifully, but she yanked straight. Stupid.

Luke knew how to do it. He grabbed the ax handle and jerked it smartly from side to side. It came free in both of their hands.

They struggled over the ax. She was amazingly strong. Luke was having trouble and looked into her eyes again.

The woman was crying. Again their eyes locked, and Luke could see that incredible desperation. "I want to live," she said in a husky voice. "Please. I ain't never had nuthin', and I ain't never gonna' be nuthin', but I just want to live."

"So you can do the wrong thing?" Luke asked.

They were deadlocked, four hands on the ax handle. Luke could not believe the power of this woman in both will and musculature.

"I don't understand right and wrong," she forced out through clenched teeth. "I just want to feel sand between my toes." Sweat ran down the side of her face. "Listen to James Brown." A vein popped out in her forehead. "Eat Devil Dogs."

Luke did not understand about James Brown and dogs from the devil, but the mention of Satan gave him new strength.

Father always talked about Satan and women

and evil. Luke knew he must do the right thing, or Father would be angry.

One of the woman's hands was facing up on the ax handle. Luke jerked downward toward that hand, and the hand lost its grip because it couldn't pivot outward. Before the woman could recover, Luke twisted the ax handle out of her remaining hand.

"No," she whimpered. Their eyes locked again. At last he saw fear. "Help me! Please, Simba."

Simba? That's what the first one he'd had to kill in this funny time called him, the one who did the wrong thing with this very woman. Why did they all call him that?

Luke brought the ax down neatly in the center of her skull. There was a moment of hopeless horror in her eyes, a blinding explosion of pain in her soul, before her head burst open and gobs of grey and red sprayed evenly in both directions.

Aim.

Luke beamed. Once again, he had done the thing that was right.

Stars, still haunted by stars.

The sky in the middle of the night was gorgeous—rich and infinite, a glorious escape from all things trite.

There was a funny smell as the others followed Chutney into the bus. Simba was out cold and looked very tired.

Piper, mesmerized by a star, was the last one in. She looked around. The mountain of amplifiers and sound equipment against the rear emergency exit looked eerie in the half light.

That smell, what was it? Odd, since the place looked as if someone had given it a much-needed cleaning.

Her psychedelic poster of the Jefferson Airplane had been moved. Damn! Something brownish grey had splattered over a corner of it. Someone had wiped it off as well as was possible, but it would never be the same. The poster of the two ducks screwing seemed to have met with a similar fate.

Meanwhile, there was no sign whatsoever of Josephine.

Midas expressed his feelings with a long, eloquent yawn.

"I apologize most humbly for waking you all in the middle of the night," Chutney said. "I apologize even more humbly for the length of time Poppy and I were gone. There's a tale to tell behind that one, but it has, for the time being, clearly been eclipsed by a far more immediate concern." Chutney kneeled next to Simba and shook his shoulder. "Simba, Simba, old buddy, wake up!"

Simba came awake with a start, took a wild look around the bus and grabbed Chutney by the neck. "Where is she?"

Chutney, in a death grip, was having trouble speaking. "I don't know, man. You were on watch."

Simba looked confused, then released Chutney. "Oh, shit, I must have fallen asleep."

Chutney sighed heavily and sat down beside

Simba, tucking a knee under his chin. "Yes, that you must have. It was my fault, too. Poppy and I were gone way too long."

"Ronna!" Simba was on his feet. Piper could see him scan the group till he found Ronna, then relax slightly as he looked over the rest of them.

"All present and accounted for," Piper said. "Except one."

Simba walked to the front of the bus and yanked the control that closed the door behind them. "I want each of you to think carefully." He penetrated each soul with those piercing blue eyes before turning out the interior lights. Out of the utter darkness into which they were plunged came Simba's deep voice. "The question is— where is the ax?"

Piper couldn't see a thing. "Actually, the question is—why did you turn the lights out?"

"If Josephine is outside the bus with the ax, do you really want to be visible to her while she— in the dark—is invisible to you?"

Simba's voice seemed closer. It startled Piper which annoyed her. Never had she allowed herself to react to even the most skillfully told ghost story, yet she now felt a slow chill shiver its way up her spine. If this was part of her new way of feeling, she didn't want to have anything to do with it. Still, she had to ask the question once again. Piper looked around, knowing they were all there yet unable to see them. "What if the killer is not Josephine?"

"Josephine isn't the killer," Ursula said.

"Shuddup!" Simba snapped.

"Like, nobody ever believes me, man. It's the curse—"

"Shhhh." Someone cut Ursula off. Piper didn't know who.

"Bell?" Simba said. "Where are you, man?"

Piper heard a sound in the back of the bus. "Next to the amplifiers," Bell answered.

"Ursula?" Simba called.

"What is this? Fucking attendance?"

"She's up front with us," Piper said.

"Ronna?"

With no other sense to focus on except her hearing, Piper found the vulnerability in Simba's voice when he called for Ronna was too much to bear.

"I'm here, Simba," Ronna called from somewhere in the back close to Bell. Her voice was soft, yet strong.

Chutney's voice rang out from the middle of the bus. "Midas, Poppy and I are where the seats end."

"Where's Mushroom?" Simba asked.

"Here."

Piper almost jumped out of her skin, then hated herself for it. It was that peculiar quality to Mushroom's voice, soft and loud all at once. Mushroom was very close. She must have been the one to shush Ursula.

"Ursula?" Simba asked. "When did you last see the ax?"

"What is this? Perry Fucking Mason?"

Chutney boomed a perfect imitation of Raymond Burr. "Just answer the fucking question."

Ursula sighed. "I don't remember ever seeing an ax."

"Bell?" Simba called.

"Leaning up against the box Mushroom stowed away in, man. At least for the first day or two. I don't remember seeing it after that."

"Midas?" Simba asked.

"Ditto."

"Piper?"

Piper thought carefully. She would have liked to have contributed more. "Ditto."

"Ronna? Poppy? Mushroom?"

"Ditto."

"Ditto."

"Ditto."

"Chutney?" Simba called at last.

"The very same."

Piper had a question of her own. "Who brought the ax to begin with?"

"I did," Midas said.

All of which adds up to nothing, thought Piper. Damn. "I want answers," she said aloud.

"Ditto," Simba said.

Piper saw something in her peripheral vision and jumped again, hating herself. She turned her head slowly to find that her eyes had adjusted. The floor next to her was just barely visible in the cool white of moonlight. There was a dark shadow on the floor.

"Far out!" Poppy said.

"What new wonder have you discovered now?" Chutney asked. Only a trace of sarcasm marred the gentleness in his voice.

"I can see outside."

Piper heard them all shift positions.

"Can anyone see Josephine, or even the hint of a person's presence outside?" Simba asked.

They all answered in the negative.

"If she doesn't show up by morning, we'll have to brave the local pigs," Chutney said. "What's right is right. She could kill others."

There was an uncomfortable silence during which Piper sat down on the floor, propping herself up with her hands.

"It's all my fault," Ronna exclaimed. "I must not have tied her up tight enough. I did as you told me, Simba, but maybe that part of me that didn't want to do it at all somehow undermined me."

The new feeling in Piper leapt toward Ronna. In the dark, Piper leaned toward Ronna, repositioning one of her hands in the center of the dark shadow she had seen on the floor.

Her hand was wet.

Someone must have spilt something, Piper thought absently. She wiped her hand on her workshirt. "Might not have been your feelings, Ronna," Piper said. "Might have been a simple and understandable lack of expertise in the fine art of tying people up. Even if it was your feelings, those same feelings were shared by most of the rest of us."

"I thank you, Piper. That's really sweet." Piper could hear the tremble in Ronna's voice that meant she was battling tears. "But if someone out there dies, it's my fault."

Piper's fingers were still sticky. "Any more so than Chutney and Poppy's for not coming back sooner?" She cleaned them on her workshirt, doing the best she could in the dark. "Or Simba's for falling asleep?" Vaguely it occurred to Piper to wonder if whatever was on her fingers left stains.

"It's still my fault," Ronna persisted. "Even if some of the blame is shared by others."

"All right," Piper said, switching into high. "I don't buy the word 'fault' but I might buy the word 'responsibility.'" Piper, who felt she could think her way out of anything, was determined to do likewise for Miss Professional Feeling. "The problem in this society is that we're so used to delegating all the heavies to paid, disinterested professionals, that we've forgotten what it is to bear the weight of these things ourselves."

"Say what?" Bell said.

All right, it's the middle of the night, and I'm still half-asleep, Piper thought. You expect me to make sense?

"Take death," Piper said aloud. "The minute it looks like Great Aunt So-and-So is going to croak, we ship her off to either the nursing home or the hospital. That way whatever happens it was either unavoidable or, worst case, it was the hospital or nursing home or doctor's fault. We're spared the weight of looking fate in the face and realizing that the heavies are just like anything else in life. They're subject to blind fate, human foibles, and silly—unavoidable and avoidable—mistakes."

"Oo eeee, baby," Bell said. "Give it up!"

Piper laughed. Okay, back to feeling. "Ronna, you gave it your best shot. You tried to do what was right for both Josephine and the rest of the world. That's all any of us can do."

"Try telling that to the mother of her next victim," Ronna said flatly.

"Even I wouldn't try to tell anything to the mother of her next victim," Piper said. "But ask yourself this, Ronna. Is there any guarantee that things would be any different if you hadn't taken responsibility and acted in this situation? Simba, I assume, hasn't had a lot of experience in tying people up either. If, for instance, we'd turned her over to the local pigs they might very well have decided there wasn't enough to hold her on and let her go."

"Maybe," Ronna said.

Piper smiled in the dark. It wasn't so much the word spoken as the relief she heard in Ronna's voice.

"Anybody see any sign of Josephine?" Simba asked.

Again they all answered in the negative.

"Has anybody seen or heard any sign of anybody outside?" Simba asked.

Piper thought she imagined a noise under the bus and got annoyed with herself again. The rest said no.

"What happened with the phone call, Chutney?" Simba asked.

" 'Twas a sterling example of how personality traits skip a generation. Not only do Poppy's par-

168

ents lack the almost clinical serenity of their daughter, it turns out they're completely hysterical. Not only did they badger the pigs into issuing an all-points bulletin on Poppy after she'd been missing all of two hours, but they now refuse to have it removed, even with me promising to bring her home with all due haste."

Piper imagined she could see Simba's eyes flash. "Meaning that in addition to everything else we now have to worry about harboring a sixteen year-old runaway?" he asked.

"Precisely," Chutney answered. "A sixteen year-old runaway girl. How old are you, Midas?"

"Me? Well, I may not look my age in these clothes. You see my mother picked them out, and I didn't want to hurt her feelings by returning them, and I can't really afford—"

"Your age, Midas," Simba barked.

"Twenty-six," Midas answered.

Probably lying again, Piper thought.

"One candidate for arrest on a charge of statutory rape. Bell?"

"Twenty-one."

"That's two," Chutney said. "Simba?"

"Twenty-two."

"Three, and I'm twenty-two so that's all of us," Chutney said.

"Excuse me," Midas said. "What's statutory rape?"

"The pigs' major defense against premarital sex," Chutney explained. "What it comes down to is that if the chick is under age and you aren't, you can be convicted of rape even if the bitch tied you down and threatened to murder your grand-mother if you didn't cooperate."

Simba laughed. "A situation you've experienced often, Chutney?"

"It's awful," Chutney moaned. "The threats against my family, the rope burns..."

"Seriously," Simba said, "it's another argument against going to the police."

"Yes," Chutney answered, "it is. But when you consider what we're up against, I don't think it's a strong enough argument to stop us from going to the police. I don't think anything would be."

"Maybe," Simba said.

Piper was reminded of Eugene, her last one-night stand. Simba seemed to use "maybe" the way Eugene had used "perhaps." It meant he thought Chutney was wrong but was too savvy to discuss it further at this time.

"Maybe," came Mushroom's voice out of the dark, screaming and whispering all at once, "it is time to truly know ourselves.

Piper thought she heard something under the bus again, which bugged her no end.

Parsons was most uncomfortable. Just when he thought he had everything in order and was ready to nab the nigger, maybe have a little fun with her first, and then trade her in for the promotion he so richly deserved—where was the bitch? Finally Parsons had to give in again to the need to shift his weight. He'd been in some tight corners in his life but never anything as cramped as underneath a school bus.

Above Parsons was a pinprick of light he figured for a small hole in the floor of the bus. He could see a droplet of something dark forming on the axle below it. Oil? He caught it on his finger, then sucked his finger clean. Not thick enough to be oil. It tasted a little like the last time somebody'd punched him hard in the mouth, with something solid and squishy added in. He hadn't even realized there was something solid; now he ended up swallowing it before he knew what he was doing.

Just his goddamn luck. Parsons had been snooping around the bus when all of a sudden all the hippies decided to descend on it at once. There hadn't been any place else to hide. Parsons was going to wait until they all went to sleep. Instead he could hear that the redheaded witch with the weird voice was leading them in some kind of pinko subversive ritual. She kept yelling/whispering to relax. Even Parsons was beginning to feel drowsy.

"You are young," the crazy bitch said.

Parsons wished it was true. No paunch. No puffing up the stairs. Able to get his rock off five times in the same day. Parsons let his head fall forward.

Parsons was in what he figured was some kind of weird dream, carrying a harpoon. The whore in the low-cut, floor-length dress stood in front of him, shaking her head no.

"I told you before, Joshua Carnes, I've young bucks aplenty to keep me amused. I don't need your money to pay my bills. I will not do it with a married man."

"Here's the money, swine of Satan," Parsons heard himself say. "You're a whore. You have to do it."

"Yes, I am a whore, but I always pride myself on living up to what my enemies say to me. They say they might be able to forgive me had I become a whore out of pitiful desperation, but that I am unnatural because I became a whore out of choice. 'Tis true. I love being with men, lots of them, far too much to ever settle down with one. I also love sex far too much to allow anything negative like your obvious belief that it is bad to interfere. And you are married, sir, so let's have an end of it. Good day."

The whore turned her back on Parsons. He grabbed her and pulled her dress up. She fought like a wildcat, but he gouged her eyes out with his thumbs. That shut her up. Then he tied her down, but there was still a problem. He couldn't get it up.

As the whore lay whimpering something about never being able to see a star again, Parsons got an idea. He spread her legs again and reached for the harpoon.

Chapter 8

Rachel lies on the sand, half-closed eyes staring at the sky. Why won't it rain? It needs to rain; the air is so thick with water she can't breath. And Rachel can't move. All she can do is lie in the sand pit, only a small wooden bridge away from Father.

Why can't she move? There isn't anything wrong with her body. Nothing is holding her down. Rachel tries to be aware of her arms, thrown carelessly—like some rag doll's—across the damp, dirty sand. She manages to move her eyeballs; to move her head would be too much. She sees an ugly black beetle is crawling up one arm, but it isn't worth the trouble to brush it away.

Mother is dead. Why is Rachel still alive? Is

Rachel still alive? When was the last time she took a breath? It seems she must remind herself to take each laborious breath. She tries to be aware of her stomach. She tries to remember when she last ate. She thinks it's been at least a day, but she can't remember. Is she hungry? Something inside her is gurgling, but all the muscles in her abdomen are tied in knots so there doesn't seem to be enough room left to identify the emptiness of hunger. Is she tired? She doesn't remember sleeping, but she can't find anything resembling the comparatively cozy feeling of being tired in the churning maelstrom inside her. Maybe she needs to cry, but whenever she tries nothing comes out. Like the sky.

It would be better to be dead like Mother.

Why is the sky narrowing down to nothing? It must be because her eyes are closing....

Something is shaking Rachel's shoulder. Her eyes open. Kneeling at her side is a stranger, a man who is not part of her family. He isn't angry. He has gentle brown eyes with a wholesome sheen. His brown hair blows freely in the breeze off the pond. He helps Rachel sit up.

"Are you all right?"

The only other man who ever asked Rachel that was her favorite brother. But her favorite brother just ran off to sea on a whaling boat. When was that? Rachel tries to concentrate. Was that this morning? The day before? Why did he have to run away and leave Rachel?

"What can I do to help?"

What sweet words. For a split second the throbbing pain is gone, then it returns in a torrent. Rachel gasps.

"Can you speak?"

Rachel opens her mouth. Nothing comes out.

"I shan't hurt you. Honest."

A drop falls on Rachel's hand. Has it started to rain? Rachel looks up at the sky. No, that sky will never rain. But the drop . . . Now something Rachel can't identify is happening in her chest, a kind of choking as if she will vomit.

"You're safe now. Don't fight it. Go ahead and cry."

Cry? Yes, that's what it is; she doesn't have to fight it. Rachel finds herself sobbing on the stranger's shoulder, soaking his shirt with her tears. When she is finally finished it feels so odd that a giggle escapes her.

"Better?"

Maybe a little.

"My name's Rupp Hanlon, miss, from over yonder. What's yours?"

"Rachel Carnes." Had those flat, lifeless words come from her mouth? Rachel guesses they must have.

"I've something for you, Miss Carnes," Rupp says.

Warm hands press something into Rachel's hand. Rachel opens up her fingers. In her palm is the most wondrous multicolored shell ever. Why is the corner of her mouth twitching? Rachel looks up into the gentle brown eyes of the stranger.

"I had to scrape a heap of sand off it, but it

Sue Hollister Barr

was worth it just to see your smile."

Faraway someone laughed. "Unfucking likely." It was Simba's voice.

Light flared. Ronna's eyelids flickered open. She was in the back of the bus. Simba held a roaring Zippo lighter in the front of the bus. Had the tendrils of green in his eyes been electrified with jealousy? Hard to tell. His irises still appeared compressed, the pupils large. Perhaps the drug he'd taken earlier that night hadn't worn off altogether. Ronna could tell, even looking at the front of him, that his back was stiffening.

"Try," Mushroom said to Simba. "Try."

Suddenly Simba sagged, gingerly touching his arm. Was he hurt? Ronna craned forward to see, then realized even Simba wouldn't be able to see much by the flame of a lighter.

Simba looked very tired.

"You must try," Mushroom persisted.

"I can't," he said simply. He held the lighter higher and looked around at all the others.

Ronna looked, too. Everyone seemed to be slumped over with their eyes closed, although Ronna wasn't too sure about Poppy.

"Everyone else seems to be able to get into this other world," Simba said, "but me."

Mushroom, near the front, reached over to touch his arm. Ronna noticed she avoided the part that was hurt. "Sometimes it is hard to see. Even I—"

"You?"

Ronna couldn't tell if he was being sarcastic or sincere.

176

"Even I. Remember the night we first met? There are parts of it I can't remember. In the antique store."

Poppy sprang to her feet, which sent a loose pot clattering across the floor. She was doing some kind of an Egyptian-looking dance and humming to herself.

"No, don't tell me," Simba said.

This time there was no mistaking his sarcasm.

"Uh ..." he pondered, then snapped his fingers. "I've got it. Cleopatra."

Poppy squealed with delight. "That's right," she said, sounding very much like Poppy.

"This is bullshit," Simba declared. "This is not the way—"

"Jesse ..."

Simba jerked upright. Even Mushroom looked a little startled. A shiver passed through Ronna at the sound of a voice she had never heard yet recognized.

"Ah, Jesse."

The voice vibrated with sensuousness, a lively young woman in the arms of her lover. Ronna looked at Piper, slumped over on the other side of Simba. Simba must have had the same thought, because he moved the lighter so it would illuminate Piper's face, but even Ronna could see Piper's mouth was slack.

"Ummm ... Oh."

"Other side of the bus," Ronna said. "Other side of Mushroom."

Simba moved the lighter.

On Ursula's face was a huge, sensual smile,

very unlike Ursula. Her body gyrated gently. "Aw, Jess, we mustn't. Not til ..."

That voice ... The bus was narrowing down to nothing and then was gone. Rupp is before Rachel with a huge smile and his gentle brown eyes. Behind him his brother Jesse is showering her sister Lucia with kisses.

" 'Twill be a double wedding. You shan't lose your dear sister Lucia, except a little bit to my dear brother, Jesse. See, Rachel, things will work out."

Warmth swells in Rachel's heart, but the cold still inside pushes back.

"Believe, Rachel, believe."

She can't quite, but she can't bear to tell those warm brown eyes so. Nor can she lie to them. Better not to use words at all. Rachel reaches for Rupp's face, tracing its planes and angles with her fingertips. Rupp turns his face slowly to kiss each of her hands.

"Speak, Rachel. I always worry when you are silent so. 'Tis like when we first met."

"It comes over me at times," Rachel says. "Oddly 'tis when things seem most hopeful."

"Yes, I've noticed that." The muscles in his face tighten beneath her fingers.

"But I will marry you, Rupp Hanlon. I've told you so."

"When?" His face is rigid.

"When it feels safe to do so," Rachel answers.

"It may never feel safe to you," Rupp says. "It may never be completely safe, but is it safe for you and Lucia to stay?"

Twisted

"It may be horrible for Lucia and me to stay, but it is safe, I think. Why should it not be?"

"Perhaps because things do not always stay horrible in just the same way. Sometimes things get worse."

"Like when Mother died?" Rachel whispers.

Rupp opens his mouth to speak, but it appears he also decides it is better not to use words. Slowly, he nods.

The cold steals over Rachel's heart. Wary, she looks about. Jesse Hanlon is still kissing her lively younger sister, Lucia. Behind them the yellow grass rustles furiously in the breeze near the water, like a rattler's tail issuing its warning. The waves roil about dangerously out on the sound. Rachel scrutinizes the sand pit between Jesse and Lucia and Rupp and herself, then turns to find the wooden bridge leading back to her father's property far closer than she thought.

"What if they find out?" Rupp asks gently.

Rachel shivers. Why is it, living with fear and Father all her life, that she isn't the one thinking of this? She looks back at Rupp and feels herself caught by his warm brown eyes. Again she reaches out to touch him, all thoughts of Father gone.

Rupp smiles, then looks inquiringly at her. Rachel has trouble remembering what he asked at first, then shivers again as it comes back to her. "Father? The ever-stern Joshua Carnes? Who believes all women are evil except my utterly and completely sweet sister Portia? Our crazy brother Eb? Who is forever telling Alex—"

"The slave?"

"Yes, or Zak—remember I told you he's the hired hand?—about the witches Eb sees right here in the pit, boiling potions in their cauldrons and casting their spells?"

"Yes," Rupp says, wrapping his arms around her. "What then?"

"They already think Lucia and I are evil. If they knew we wanted to marry..." Rachel cannot stop shuddering.

"Because it is the Hanlon brothers, poor tenant farmers, you wish to wed?"

"No, there's naught wrong with you or Jesse," Rachel protests, touching Rupp's cheek again. "It's because marriage brings..." she stops to pull back from him a bit. "Children."

Rupp lets go of Rachel, seeming to respect her sensitive feelings on such a subject. "Dear Rachel," he says in his softest voice, "I shan't hurry you about that. Only when you're ready. But once you're wed, surely even your father cannot be anything but happy to have grandchildren."

Rachel wraps her arms around Rupp. "You think there is a way in which I would not want you to touch me? And yet, thinking thus, all that you do and say is designed purely to comfort me?" She squeezes him. "Not so, though Father thinks it's evil. I am sure that with you, at least, it must not be, though the truth is it's hard for me to imagine what it's like."

Rupp holds her close, resting his head on top

of hers. "Your father will forgive you at the sight of his first grandson."

At that Rachel pulls away. "No, you don't understand. For Father babies are evil."

"How could this be?"

"Because they represent the biggest, largest evil of all," Rachel says sadly.

"Go on."

"Work."

"Work is evil?"

"No. Work is good, says Father. But anyone who makes more work necessary and cannot do it himself—"

"Or herself?"

"Yes, or herself, is evil."

"That's crazy," Rupp muses.

"Yes, I know, and because Father can see in my eyes that I do not believe every word he says, like Portia does, I am the most evil person of all."

Rupp grabs Rachel almost roughly. "Then we must get you and Lucia away to safety as soon as possible."

"But how? And how will we ever marry? Father will never consent." Rachel wrings her hands.

"You must run away. Jesse and I have an uncle in Princeton, New Jersey. He's a preacher. He'll perform the double wedding with or without your father's consent."

In the deepest cellars of Rachel's heart something stirs, a sign of things to come. But Rachel can't determine whether the thing stirring within her is hope or fear.

Fire is flaring, flared. Ronna's eyes fluttered open.

Simba turned toward her, the muscles of his back stiffening, his hair and beard raven black, his blue eyes filled with tendrils of electric green that hypnotized her.

You must . . . must run away . . .

"Have you seen Chutney's leather-bound book of verse?" Simba asked Ronna, digging through Chutney's pack.

"No," Ronna answered mechanically.

"Unfucking believable." Simba sagged, gingerly touching his head. "I'm so sick of this bullshit, I was ready to read anything."

"I saw someone's Shakespeare, *Richard II*, around," Ronna mused. "Ever read it?"

"Shakespeare?" Simba smirked. "Like a brother to me."

"Thrice," muttered a voice from the middle of the bus. "Thrice the brindled cat hath mew'd."

Simba moved forward with the lighter. Chutney's head, slumped to one side, bobbed as he spoke. "Double, double, toil and trouble; fire burn and cauldron bubble."

"Who are you?" Mushroom asked from the front. "Try to see."

"I am Eb," Chutney said. "I see witches in the sand pit. Witches, witches, everywhere, and no end to our work."

Fear shivered through Ronna, but just then Simba turned toward her again, leveling her with his eyes. What was on his face? Ronna couldn't make it out in the flickering light. Was it a smirk or a smile?

"You," Chutney said to Mushroom. "You are

the town witch. Everybody knows. Two of my sisters have caught your evil. They do not do their work. They must learn."

Ronna had decided it was a smile. Simba flipped the top of his Zippo lighter closed, extinguishing all light.

"They do not do their work. They must learn."

Ronna's eyes closed.

Rachel is watching Eb, twisted just like Father, trying to push past Luke, but Luke stops him. "They will learn, Eb. Don't be so rough. Lucia and Rachel are still young." And Luke turns toward her with a smile and a wink.

The thing stirring within Rachel is hope.

Fire is flaring, flared. Ronna's eyes fluttered open. Simba kneeled before her, smiling. He touched Ronna's face.

"You are so pure," Simba said, caressing Ronna's cheek. "You don't deserve this bullshit. You deserve nothing but the truth." But then he frowned and pulled his hand back to touch his own head.

Rachel! Inches from Luke's face. Reaching for Luke's face. Concentrating and caressing. Luke could see her casting her spell this time, trying to make him do the thing that was wrong with her again.

"Simba? What's wrong?"

That name again. Why? It did not matter. That is what Father would say. What mattered was that his headstrong sister Rachel was before him, the most evil one of all. Fast as a serpent, her hand darted toward something at his side, but Luke caught it.

"Ouch! Careful, Simba, that hurt. Look, I found Chutney's leather-bound book of verse for you."

In the witch's hand was a book that looked more natural than most things in this funny time, but must have aged unnaturally because of her wicked witch's touch. Luke held his tiny torch closer to the book. Yes, machine-made, far too recently to look that old. Despite himself, the hand holding the torch shook.

"I'll read," the witch said, flipping through the pages. "Oh, look, Yeats!

"O love is the crooked thing,
There is nobody wise enough
To find out all that is in it,
For he would be thinking of love
Till the stars had run away
And the shadows eaten the moon.

I wonder if that's true," mused the witch, flipping more pages. "Remember the one about the cat and the moon?" she asked.

Luke was remembering where the ax was.

Rachel was running her finger down a page, then wrinkling her brow. "Here at the end is the really strange part:

"Does Minnaloushe know that his pupils
Will pass from change to change,
And that from round to crescent,
From crescent to round they range?
Minnaloushe creeps through the grass
Alone, important, and wise,
And lifts to the changing moon

His changing eyes.

"Wow ... Simba?"

Luke was edging toward the ax.

The witch was answered by the town witch's whispered scream. "Rachel, now Ronna, will you never see? People never see what's right in front of them. It's the easiest way to trick them if that's what you want to do, but you, Ronna, you must see!"

"What are you talking about, Mushroom?"

Mushroom? Why did Rachel call the town witch ...! Never mind. It did not matter.

"In order to survive, Ronna, you must see. In order to help us all bring this to a close one way or another, you must guide us there. You must go deeper, much deeper. So deep that you not only tap into random memory but into the mind itself that stores basic information like road directions."

"Huh?"

"Close your eyes, Ronna. I'm going to take you and everyone else except Simba, the uncooperative, deeper than you've ever been before, so deep you'll remember nothing I say, only the mind of Rachel who I shall immerse you in."

But Luke was getting bored with all this. He had more important things to think about, like how he was going to get at the ax with two sleeping people in the way. The town witch babbled on a bit. Luke looked at the two sleeping people. Like animals slaughtered in their sleep their muscles kept slackening. Luke glared at Zak, the hired hand. Zak's hand, with brown hairs that stuck up at odd angles, fell sideways until it came to rest against the cheek of Luke's sweet sister Portia. Luke knew about Zak, had seen the looks he gave Portia when he thought Father wasn't looking. Zak wanted to do the thing that was wrong with Portia.

Luke wanted to do the thing that was right with Zak.

Even the smile that was always on Portia's face slackened until her lips hung open and some spittle dribbled down her chin. She was seated on the floor with her back to a seat. Her head fell to the side; Zak's hand fell to her chest.

Luke shook with rage. He wanted to rip Zak's hand apart, but he knew he had to be careful. There were a lot of people who might be hard to handle all at once. He would at least have to wait until he got the ax. Instead he pushed Zak's hand away from Portia, careful not to touch Portia's chest himself. Then he stared hard at Zak's fat belly, considering some interesting possibilities. Again, he shook with rage.

"Simba?"

That name again. It was the town witch behind him. He must hurry. Get the ax. Luke shoved his arm between Portia and Zak.

"Luke?"

Luke jerked to a standstill, knocking against Portia.

"Luke!"

Luke heard the recognition in her whisper-scream with such a spooky mixture of fear and bitter triumph that it even made him shudder.

See . . . she wanted everyone to see. Luke wanted to make sure that this witch, at least, would never again see.

Luke heard the witch get up behind him, moving toward him.

Portia was falling sideways. She might be hurt. Luke threw his arms around her, cradling her gently. Full of tenderness, he was peering into her face just as the witch kneeled down to peer into his own eyes.

"Luke?"

Luke didn't care about the witch just now; he was worried about Portia. Still, he could tell there was doubt in her voice now.

"Hard to tell with the only source of light being Ronna."

She seemed to be musing. He set Portia to rights.

"But the tenderness . . . And the fact that your pupils, even in this poor light, are no longer large might mean that the drug must be all—or very near all—worn off. Oh, come on, speak to me, Simba. You scared me to death. Yes, I want you to try and go back, but I want to know when you've done it."

Luke stalked away silently, past his brother Eb and the town whore, to the closed door. He wasn't going to make a grab for the ax with the witch right there. With luck she would follow.

"Oh, be like that. Damn you, Simba. I'm tired. I'm so tired."

But she didn't follow. She sat where she was, brazenly leaning her back against Zak.

Zak stirred and mumbled something Luke could not understand.

"Ah, Midas, you weren't very articulate as Zak either, were you?" the town witch said. "Poor dear." Sinning more, she leaned her head back against Zak's shoulder and closed her eyes. The hired hand's head flopped forward on top of the witch's head, so that their foreheads almost touched.

The witch's eyes popped open. "No, Zak," she said, "I wish I could tell you otherwise, but it would not be telling you the truth. Portia did not think of you that way."

She did not, she does not, and she will not, thought Luke. Sweet Portia could not possibly think in a way that would lead her to do the thing that is wrong. But something bothered Luke. Something was wrong.

"I speak in past tense because in our separate state, which allows us to be separate and talk to each other, one of the separators is a thing called time. According to the thing called time the Zak who once loved Portia without ever being loved back is separate from the Midas now who has decided it is safer to love plants that cannot either respond or fail to respond to him."

The first thing that was wrong was that the side of Zak's mouth was just visible in the light of the moon. Like Portia's it was slack. Like Portia's it was not moving.

The second thing that was wrong was that the town witch was no longer whisper-screaming. Her voice was clear and pure.

"How do I know this, Zak? I know this because I was once one of those stubborn seekers of the ultimate truth. I broke down all the walls. I stared so hard and ruthlessly at the world that it finally melted before my gaze. Anxiously I awaited my first glimpse of what would be left after all pretense and artifice was gone. Anxiously I awaited my first glimpse of the ultimate truth."

For the first time, Luke found himself just a little bit interested in what a witch had to say.

"Zak, your impatience to hear the rest reveals the seeker in us all, but I fear you will not like the answer. More and more of the world was vanishing faster and faster. Just before the end I anticipated the first shock. The first truth was that everything that ever was, could have been, should have been, is, will be, or might be—well, it all was, is, and will be pretense and artifice."

"That is not true," Luke stormed. "Good and bad are not pretense or whatever that other word you said is."

"Yes, they are," the town witch answered, staring at Luke with such an unwavering gaze that he began to fear he himself would vanish.

Luke was beginning to feel weak anyway.

"Everything you or anyone else perceives as reality is pretense and artifice. What was that, Zak? Why? Because the only way anything can exist—be it an idea or a blade of grass—is by denying the possibility that something else might exist in its place. And this is never true, not really."

Luke was completely confused. It was time to

get back to more important things before he went to sleep.

"That's right, Zak. Reality is infinity minus one. The one becomes reality simply because we all agree to see a lake where a forest or a field or a desert might just as easily exist. Why was my world vanishing? Because suddenly I began to see not just the lake, but also the forest and the field and the desert and every other thing that could possibly exist in that same space until they all started canceling each other out. It was like algebra gone mad. You can do anything as long as you do it on both sides of the equal sign, so I just kept on doing it until nothing whatsoever was left on either side of the equal sign. Then the equal sign itself had no reason to exist so it disappeared along with separators like space and time."

Halfway back to the ax the torch by Rachel finally went out. At first Luke could not see a thing. He sat where he was, so his eyes could adjust, and considered for a moment. "So, you never did see the ultimate truth, did you?"

"Yes I did, Simba," came the town witch's clear new voice.

Luke got his bearings and moved a little closer. "What was it?"

"It was nothing."

Reaching across the floor in the witch's direction, Luke found a foot so floppy he wondered if the person was dead, though still warm. "Like I said, you never did see the ultimate truth."

"Yes I did. The ultimate truth is nothing."

"What does nothing look like?" Luke asked the dark, inching closer.

"Imagine a clear transparency with nothing behind it."

Luke paused; he was very tired. "I do not understand, but there is something I would like to understand."

"*Who* would like to understand?"

Cautious, he stopped and remembered the sound of the town witch's voice earlier—Simba? Luke? Luke! He was too tired to think it through but sensed that as long as he was unarmed, unable to see and so terribly tired, it would somehow be safer if the witch called him Simba. "Simba. That is who. And what is your name, town witch?"

"Who am I now? The town witch? Mushroom? No. Those and all those many, many others I have been are like clothes through which my shape— if you know what you're looking for—can just barely be seen. No, just now I am myself without the clothes of whatever lifetime I happen to be living. I am just a small portion of the oneness."

"The oneness?" Luke asked.

"We, all life from a plant to an an ant to a human, are all one. Failure to recognize this, far beyond spiritual poverty, results in faulty decision making. For instance, the mistaken impression that you can solve the problems of a relationship by leaving the other person. The problem is that the other person is not really another person but a dormant part of yourself that you have become aware of and will then have to spend a lifetime trying to deny."

"Again, I do not understand, but—"

The witch cut Luke off. "Forgive me for rambling. You had a question."

"Yes," Luke said. He was so tired. "Why are we all together again? How did it happen? How is it possible?" Why, he thought to himself as he rubbed a sore muscle, do I have to do the thing that is right with all of you again when it is such hard work and I have already done it?

"It has to do with not letting go."

"How?" Luke persisted sleepily.

"Equilibrium. Lack of equilibrium. Each portion of the oneness travels through time living many lives, that is to say being separate many times so that one may have the company of other separate beings. The purpose is to get ready for that oneness, which exists in the place beyond time where there are no separators, which means, oddly enough, being alone because there are no others."

Damnation, Luke thought. If I reach behind her and get the ax, will I have enough energy to use it?

"I'm not ready to be alone yet though my soul is old," the witch continued, "so that is what I must accomplish in this lifetime. I'm not even close yet."

Luke stretched out upon the floor. "My question?"

"Sorry. We are all together again because what happened last lifetime was so horrible we can't let go and move onto another lifetime and another lesson."

Luke's eyes were closing. "How did we find each other?"

"By dropping a few of the separators on the way to the ultimate truth."

Luke yawned. "How?"

"This illusion called reality that we've concocted? It's not as solid as you would think. There are times, particularly in sleep and dreams, when you can see through it a bit. At those times you can see through the people to their souls, their parts of the oneness. At those times you can—well, it's a sixth sense—let's say hear and speak to them over hundreds and hundreds of miles like humpback whales."

"Who called us all together?" Luke asked.

There was a noise under the floor behind Luke and to his left.

"That I do not know," the witch said.

Luke thought he knew. Who else would be under the floor, behind him and to the left? Satan. Still, Luke was so tired that even that thought didn't rouse him at first. Half-asleep, he turned and found the floppy foot again, and then he knew. It was his witch sister Lucia. The town witch was right. Half-asleep, he had been able to "hear" her.

His witch sister Lucia was even more asleep.

Luke ran his hands up over her body.

His witch sister Lucia did not react.

Luke found his hands on her breasts and pulled them away quickly. He felt bad. He did not want to do a wrong thing. This was Satan's work, all of this, trying to undo the right he already had done before.

On the other hand, it should be easy—at least with this one—to do the thing that was right again. All he had to do was find her neck.

Thrashing.
Piper couldn't wake up.
More thrashing.
Piper still couldn't wake up. It was even worse than the time someone woke her up an hour after she'd fallen asleep after staying up for 48 hours straight, cramming for a final. It was deeper than the deepest level of sleep. What could possibly be that deep? Death?

Panic pulled Piper slowly upward. Someone or something was moving close to her. Under her bed? Her worst childhood fear? She fought to open her eyes and look around. Was she still asleep, or was the slimy tentacle that had just slapped itself up over the bottom edge of her bed real? The tentacle was sprouting other tentacles which were creeping across the dumb eyelet bedspread her mother bought her, coating it with slime on the way to her foot.

But the foot was small; Piper remembered she'd grown up. She must still be asleep. She tried to open her eyes again.

This time it was the closet door. Naturally she'd forgotten to close it again. Something darted from the closet to underneath her bed. Piper had no idea what it was except that it was dark and huge and she'd caught a glimpse of a highly arched, furry back. Now she could hear it breathing. It seemed to be suffering some sort of respiratory distress. This apparently did little to improve its disposition. Now it was snarling, chattering some irritated gibberish to itself, and had started to gnaw at the mattress springs directly underneath Piper's shoulders. Springs snapped at a rate similar to popcorn popping. Whatever this thing lacked in pulmonary prowess, it more than made up for in dentition. When it paused to pant and slobber a bit, all Piper could do was lift her head and look down at herself.

No boobs.

Piper tried to open her eyes again.

Something banged Piper's shoulder blade from underneath the floor of the bus, but she still couldn't open her eyes.

Thrashing, thrashing, and more thrashing.

Piper opened her eyes. It didn't help; she couldn't see a thing. She sat up anyway and immediately put her hand in something wet again.

Whatever was underneath the bus stopped moving. Piper was cleaning her hand off on her workshirt again when she realized the thrashing was still going on—inside the bus.

Piper's mother would have screamed. Piper's father would have pushed Piper aside and called the police. Piper wasn't going to let anything bring them all down again.

Piper pounced.

It had to be Simba, since no other guy was that big, but he wasn't the one doing the thrashing. It was someone underneath him jerking around as if in the midst of an epileptic attack. It was a woman.

"Oh shit," Piper said aloud. She could hear Simba rolling off the top. "Ronna? Simba? Look, guys, I'm really sorry. You know I'd be the last to break a couple apart, but I was having all these scary dreams and I thought—"

The lights went on.

Simba lay on his back, covered in sweat as his eyes closed in sleep. Typical man, Piper thought, but as she looked Simba over a slow chill went up her spine. Sure got his jeans zipped and buttoned fast, she thought. Piper continued to contemplate that part of his anatomy. Either Simba's got a dick the size of a peanut, she thought, or he sure got soft fast.

"Luke?" came a whisper-scream behind Piper.

Piper turned to see a wild-eyed Mushroom standing next to the light switch. Piper turned back to Simba in time to see his eyes flutter open.

"Who?" Simba asked. He looked thoroughly annoyed, then panicked. "Where is she?"

"Where is who?" Piper asked.

"Jos—" He broke off confused.

"Go back to sleep, Simba," Mushroom said. "Everything's okay now."

Piper shook off another shiver, irritated. Feeling, she thought, too much feeling.

It was then that Piper caught motion in her peripheral vision and noticed the woman lying next to Simba. It wasn't Ronna; it was Ursula who was rubbing her neck. Her breathing was labored. Her normally unhealthy-looking skin looked even worse. The pallid grey seemed to have given way to a hint of blue.

"What happened to you?" Piper asked, almost annoyed, feeling for Ronna.

"Simba tried to strangle me," Ursula said.

"Oh, come on, you were dreaming," Piper said, standing.

"Like, nobody ever believes me, man."

"It's the curse of my life," Piper finished dryly. Still, she had to shake off another shiver. Feeling, she thought, too much feeling. Piper almost jumped out of her skin when she felt a hand on her shoulder and turned to find Mushroom behind her.

"You jumped on Lu—uh, Simba?" Mushroom asked.

"Yeah," Piper admitted. "Stupid of me, but you see I was having these dreams and—"

"Good of you," Mushroom interrupted. "Yours is a spirit that soars, that isn't afraid to change things."

Piper studied Mushroom's warm smile and the fire she saw clearly in Mushroom's eyes. Piper was puzzled.

Parsons was still catching his breath. "Who called us all together?" his son had asked. And Parsons, decent individual that he was, had wanted to step forward and identify himself. He, Parsons—Joshua Carnes—whoever—had called them all together. Hey, it had been fun the first time, so far be it from him to pass up sloppy seconds.

So he'd banged and banged on the floor of the bus, but not one of those commies had in any way responded. Incompetents, nothing but incompetents.

Parsons, Carnes...It was getting confusing. Weird, weird dreams like the one about the whore and the harpoon. He'd used a little too much force. The harpoon went between her legs all too easily. She screeched and shuddered like she was really enjoying it, but the harpoon kept right on going. Bitch went limp before the point busted through her upper ribs and came to rest parallel to her neck. Died too quickly for his taste. He would have liked to have gotten in a few more thrusts.

Confusing, very confusing. Parsons didn't like things he couldn't control.

"Methinks we have all had quite enough, Mushroom," Parsons heard Chutney—Eb—whoever say.

An eerily unfamiliar sentiment shivered its way up Parsons spine. It was agreement.

Chapter 9

Ronna knew.

Simba was driving like a maniac, barreling down the highway toward Chicago. The old bus creaked and moaned. An amplifier tumbled off the mountain of sound equipment in the back. One of Midas's plants fell over. A ballpoint pen rolled across the floor. A fragment of what looked like some bloody bone their nonexistent dog had dragged in rolled across the floor after it.

Ronna knew she had been sleeping with her own brother, Luke.

Mushroom was sitting next to Ronna. Intermittent sunlight, escaping from behind telephone poles zooming by, flickered over the teeny chips of red in her green eyes. Like a surreal vision from a hopelessly unrealistic dream, Mush-

Sue Hollister Barr

room slowly turned her elfin face toward Ronna. "We learned a lot last night," she said.

Yes, witch, thought Ronna. I know. Things only the town witch could have shown us.

They looked into each other's eyes. Ronna saw the white house with the double porch in the front in her mind's eye. Next she imagined Mushroom's blazing red hair darkening to a sooty black. Her dress was floor-length.

"Are you a good witch or a bad witch?" Ronna asked.

"Neither," Mushroom said. "The spiritual world is neither good nor bad. It just is."

"Did you have anything to do with the murders?" Ronna asked.

"Which murders?" Mushroom asked. "The ones in this century or the ones in the last?"

"Either," Ronna said.

"Neither," Mushroom said. "I did not spill blood. My blood was not spilled. I did nothing to bring about the spilling of blood. Those in the spiritual world only see and attempt to get others to see."

Ronna looked into the apparently inhuman eyes, still green. "Is that ever hard for you? Do you ever wish you could change things?"

The eyes misted and became human, the otherworldly quality gone. They were just two girls in an old bus in 1966.

"Yes," Mushroom said simply.

Poppy, seated behind them, poked her head between them. "Like, wow, I always knew I was someone famous in some past life. Cleopatra! Far out!"

No, Ronna thought, I know my sweet sister Portia was never an Egyptian queen.

"No," Mushroom said aloud. "You weren't Cleopatra, dear Poppy. You got into that before you were hypnotized. I could hear it in your voice."

Poppy didn't seem to hear. "And then I was Marc Antony's wife in the next lifetime, and then—"

"Marc Antony's wife was alive at the same time Cleopatra was," Mushroom said gently.

"Much to Cleopatra's distress," put in Chutney on his way up the aisle.

Ronna looked after him. Of all of them, brother Eb seemed the most different in this lifetime, she thought.

Chutney put a hand on Simba's shoulder.

The older brother's affection for the younger, Ronna thought, was still there a century and a lifetime later.

Ronna could see Simba preparing for a power play, that stiffening of muscles across his back. Strong-willed. Of all of them he was the only one Mushroom hadn't been able to bring back into 19th Century Long Island the night before.

Long Island? How did she know they had all lived on Long Island? Ronna knew she wasn't hypnotized anymore, and she certainly wasn't dreaming. Yet she felt sure she could have—had they been on Long Island—given Simba all the directions he would have needed to drive to the old house with the double porch.

Chutney's voice was gentle. "Simba, what's right is right. Josephine never showed up, and you and I looked high and low before leaving this morning. Innocent people are at risk. With all due and fully appropriate respect for pig paranoia, we must—"

"Be sure to get to a place where we stand some chance of being believed as soon as possible," Simba said, stepping on the gas.

"Methinks you've been drag racing fate all your life, my friend," Chutney boomed, "but I fear you have finally come up against something even your long legs can't outrun."

The silence that followed was interrupted as Ursula, stirred from sleep on a seat near the front, looked out the window, and read a road sign in the flattest of monotones. "Joliet, Illinois."

Ronna knew. In sorrow she looked at the lifeless shell of a person who had once been Lucia, her lively younger sister.

"Joliet, Illinois!" Midas screeched. "That's where those people got arrested on suspicion of looking like beatniks."

Zak, the hired hand. He had loved Portia last lifetime but didn't seem to have noticed her, in the form of Poppy, in this lifetime.

"Joplin, Missouri," Chutney corrected.

"Same difference," Simba said.

Chutney cleared his throat. "I say we check out the Joliet cop shop."

"And I say we don't," Simba said. Somehow

he managed to make it sound final without sounding nasty. "Because if we do, those innocent people will be even more at risk."

"Because?" Chutney queried.

"Because we might get arrested on suspicion of looking like beatniks—"

"In our case, I'll grant it would be more than suspicion," Chutney interrupted.

"—and then we wouldn't be able to get to New York City and report this to someone who might be able to forget about long hair long enough to take this situation seriously," Simba finished.

Chutney paused, then shook his head no. "Simba, what's right is right and—"

Simba cut him off. "What do you think, Midas?"

Deft, Ronna thought. She was in love with Simba, but she was beginning to see things.

"Well," Midas said, "I think it's very important that we don't get arrested, and it seems to me—"

"Do we visit the cop shop in Joliet, yes or no?" Simba interrupted.

"Well, no," Midas mumbled.

Ronna knew. Zak hadn't been any too articulate in the last century either.

"Bell?" Simba queried.

Alex, Ronna thought, the slave. Unlike Poppy, Bell really did have royal blood in his background. A prince in his own country, he never lost his regal bearing—even a lifetime later.

Right now Ronna sensed he was, for some reason, trying to project a certain lightness. "Dig it," Bell said. "We're between a rock and a hard place." He drummed out an introductory flourish on his thigh. "So here, my man, is what we are going to do. Y'all cruise on by the cop shop, drop this boy off and keep on truckin'. It's the have-your-cake-and-eat-it-too option. If the cops don't mess with me, we could save lives. If they do mess with me, the rest of you are still free to give the heat in New York City a try."

They were fast approaching the exit for the town of Joliet. Bell slid to a stop by the bus's front door. "Uh, 'scuse me, mistuh bus drivuh, sir, but I believe this is mah stop."

Simba pushed the gas pedal to the floor. "Unfucking likely." They zipped past the exit. Simba's voice softened. "But a nice, in fact a noble, try."

Noble. The word repeated on Ronna like something deep fried in rancid oil. Once she had thought her father, the police officer, was noble—the valiant upholder of truth, justice and the American way. She had, in fact, believed in truth, justice and the American way until the day she came home early and found her mother alone in the house with a strange and beautiful young man.

They were sitting at the kitchen table, their conversation confidential and close. Ronna's mother had been crying; the young man had an arm about her. Both fell into an awkward silence at the sight of Ronna.

Ronna's faith in the world in general and her parents specifically was such that she wouldn't have thought a thing of it except that her mother, as soon as the young man was gone, had begged her not to tell her father about him. Ronna assumed her mother was having an affair and traumatized for months over which constituted the greater moral crime—ratting on her mother or not telling her poor upstanding father. In the end she discovered that the young man was not her mother's lover, but rather an idealistic young rookie who felt no human being should be allowed to waste away her life being tricked and lied to by another.

During the months Ronna had been traumatizing, the young rookie had been busy. He was an excellent photographer. Ronna had looked at the pictures that dropped through her mother's numb fingers onto the impeccably maintained front lawn—her father in bed with another woman, her father in bed with another man, her father in bed with a very scared looking young child.

At last her mother had known. Now Ronna knew even more. This fraud who had led her to believe in Santa Claus, the Tooth Fairy, and himself—all equally unreal—had tormented her by being her father more than once.

Ronna looked at each of her companions in the bus. Poppy, once her sweet sister Portia, would probably leave undisturbed a mosquito found biting her arm. Piper, once a laughing lady in a shiny purple dress, had far too much positive energy in both lifetimes to harm a fellow being. Ursula, lively and nervous as Lucia, was now too lifeless and nervous to do anything except cling to the artificial life supplied by cocaine.

Mushroom, once reputed to be a black-haired witch, was strange, but Ronna had peered into her eyes and did not feel she was the one. Mushroom's desire to reveal everything to the others through hypnosis and her simply and sincerely revealed desire to change things were convincing enough. Besides, according to the police, Josephine was probably the only woman with the physical strength to hack people apart.

Ronna knew it wasn't Josephine, but she also knew she didn't know why.

Midas, once an equally inarticulate but far more heroic being as Zak, would have been first choice in a 1950's psychodrama but again lacked the psychic energy. His focus was plants and other generally inanimate obsessions.

Bell, once called Alex in lieu of an imperial sounding African name nobody could pronounce, had far too righteous a soul to be chopping people up. Chutney, formerly Ronna's eldest brother Eb, might have been a possibility—Eb had been unstable, obsessed with evil that was solely the product of his own paranoid imagination—except that Chutney was too unlike Eb to warrant consideration.

That brought Ronna to Simba. She looked up at him, still driving like a maniac. Did he really think he could outrun it? Suddenly he yanked his right hand off the steering wheel and held it in front of him. He stared in amazement at what looked like a bite on his arm. Poor baby. Ronna hadn't known much about her brother Luke except that he used to always protect her. Then he ran off to sea, whaling, perhaps thinking in that lifetime also that life was something he could outrun. Father, of course, had been angry again.

Ronna knew. As Josephine had pointed out, Simba would never have admitted that the knife that had been used to stab Bell was his if he was guilty. Simba couldn't be the one.

Goose flesh broke out on Ronna's arms. Lions and tigers and bears. Oh my. She wasn't sure how or where he was, but Ronna knew.

It must be Father again.

Simba was so horrified by what he had done that he was in a state of shock. He had been trying to gear himself up for what he knew he must tell Ronna.

How could he? He who was so concerned for everybody else's safety. He who was so adamant about avoiding any kind of contact with the local heat. He'd been distracted, thinking of Ronna. That was his only excuse, and it was a piss poor one for not spotting the cop in time to slow down.

The cop was busy writing up the ticket. Simba fought back the fear-induced numbness and his rebellious tendencies to continue to search for the words with which to tell Ronna about his once balling Ursula, rather than concentrating on the situation at hand. This was his opportunity to check the cop out.

The guy was stocky and short. Simba had the advantage over him there, psychologically as well as if it actually came down to a fight. On the other hand this cop was so straight Simba was sure his badge would melt at the sight of all the hippy paraphernalia inside the bus. And Simba was sure it was only a matter of time before this upstanding protector of Middle American Mediocrity got around to searching the inside of the bus.

The cop moved around to the back to get the license plate number, temporarily out of earshot.

Simba leaned toward Chutney. "When you called Vancouver last night, did you tell Poppy's parents where you were calling from?"

"Before establishing that they'd call off the heat until I brought her home to them—which, of course, never got established? Do I look stupid?"

"In other words, no?" Simba asked.

"In other words no," Chutney answered.

There was still the all-points bulletin to worry about, but Simba started to breathe a little easier.

"Like, that's okay," Poppy said brightly. "I told them."

Simba's breathing became labored again. Poppy looked about serenely and went back inside the bus. Simba noticed Chutney staring off into space, smiling. "What the hell are you smiling about?" Simba asked.

"A thousand pardons. It's the trees. Remember my telling you about the nightmares I had when I was a kid and how my grandfather told me that the trees I described from them came from the north shore of Long Island?"

"Yeah," Simba said, but he was really watching the cop who was starting to head back.

"Well," Chutney continued, apparently quite pleased, "these trees aren't quite the ones I dreamed about, but they're getting there."

Simba gave Chutney a quick glance. He had that otherworldly look again. It reminded Simba of that regression-to-past-lives shit Mushroom had kept them all up with last night. It annoyed and concerned him that he was the only one of them that didn't eventually get sucked into it. Goddamn hippy parlor tricks. He'd figured it was harmless at first. Now he wasn't so sure. If these people wanted mind expansion, he'd have to show them how to do it right—drugs.

Which reminded him of two other things as he watched the cop head back toward him. One was uncomfortable. The acid flashback he kept having of Ronna's face turned out to be a completely accurate vision of what she looked like, but it wasn't the least bit psychedelic. The other was comforting. Whatever Mushroom's faults he was sure that when the cop first pulled him over and he had turned to mouth the word "drugs" to her that she had understood perfectly. She had stayed in the bus and probably managed to get her stash out the opposite windows by now.

The cop pulled up short in front of Simba and gave him a look of hate and contempt that Simba knew all too well.

"Listen, freak," the cop said, "even if you'd

been going fifteen miles an hour I would have written your ass up. And I'm not through." The cop swaggered a bit. "Let's take a look inside the bus. See how many drugs you've got."

See how many drugs you got, Simba thought to himself. This guy's as hip as my long-dead Great Aunt Petunia. If he knew anything he sure as hell wouldn't have wasted so much time outside writing up the speeding ticket.

The cop banged on the bus's front door and trotted in smartly when Poppy opened it.

"Like, peace, officer," Poppy said with what Ronna so accurately described as her Howdy Doody smile.

Like, imprisonment, Poppy, Simba thought. Long years of it for any guy over twenty-one whose misfortune it is to know you. Why don't you draw a little more attention to yourself? Show the nice officer a profile in case the front shot that came over the wire as part of the all-points bulletin was a little fuzzy. Talk a little more.

"Isn't it a pretty day?" Poppy asked the cop, looking sideways out the window.

I knew I could count on you, Simba thought.

The cop was looking at Poppy as if she were crazy, taking a good long look.

Shit! Simba had to do something. "Excuse me, officer, I don't in any way mean to rush you, but since we know how the people of your fair state feel about people like us, we were kind of hoping to be across the state line by nightfall." Bad, real bad, but it was better than the bit about rushing to see someone's dying grandmother, which was the only other one that would come to mind. "Anyway, we don't use drugs. You see my brother, well, he died because of drugs." Ah, warming up. "Well, we learned our lesson, officer. The hard way."

"Oh yeah? Why don't you cut your hair?"

What a breathtakingly original line, Simba thought. The cop looked real proud of himself.

"It's for the sake of the band, sir," Simba said, giving the officer his ultrasincere look. "So far the only places that have given us jobs playing expect it, both on the east coast and the west coast. You know how that is."

"Oh, yeah? Why don't you get normal jobs?"

"Well, you see, sir, the band was the only thing that was important to ..." Simba was trying as hard as he could to produce a misty-eyed look. A tear would have made him ecstatic. How did women do it? And what the hell was his mythical brother's name? "Well, to Ricky."

"Your brother?"

Brilliant, Simba thought, what a mind. He nodded slowly. "So go ahead, please, and see how many drugs we got. I swear on Ricky's grave you won't find any."

The pig's partner stood outside. The rest of them were inside. Simba caught Piper's eye, then Bell's, and started to hum, then sing:

"This land is your land. This land is my land. From the redwood forest, to the New York island."

The cop was digging through their stuff, but

Simba saw he was slowing down. Meanwhile, Mushroom, calm as anything, was quietly arranging something on the floor.

All must be well.

"Whatcha got there, girlie?" the cop said to Mushroom.

"Mushrooms," she said.

Mushrooms! Simba's breathing became labored again. It occurred to him that he might, now, be capable of producing a tear on cue.

"I collect them," Mushroom said. "I got bored with stamps."

The cop squatted in front of Mushroom, who handed him a button of peyote.

"Gee, I've never seen anything like it," the cop said.

Simba arrived in time to see that Mushroom was proudly displaying every mushroom she had. She smiled up at Simba, then winked. "No, I didn't think you had," she said to the cop. "I'm into the really exotic ones."

The cop took a sniff. "Any good to eat?"

Simba felt dizzy.

Even Mushroom looked a little nervous. "It's an acquired taste," she said.

The pig's partner poked his head in the front door. "Find anything?" he asked eagerly. Simba figured him for the kind of guy who would jump at the opportunity to be part of a firing squad.

The cop turned away from Mushroom, still holding the peyote. "Nah, let's get outta' here." He started to leave, then paused to look at Mushroom carefully. Suddenly he looked very serious. "Why don't you take a bath?"

Mushroom appeared to consider this. "Good point," she said. "I think I will."

The cop handed Simba the ticket, started out the door, then poked his head back in and tossed the button of peyote at Mushroom. "Almost forgot," he said and was gone.

They watched in unison as the patrol car pulled back out onto the highway, then all broke out laughing.

Bell gave Simba five. "Right on," he roared. "I'll relieve you at the wheel, brother, but everybody needs to stretch a little first, and this calls for a...How would you put it, Chutney, my man?"

Chutney clapped a hand to his heart, a character in a Wagnerian opera about to deliver his final aria before succumbing to mortal wounds. "A gesture, my man, a gesture. Something for poor Ricky." Bell grabbed a fistful of small paint brushes; Chutney was holding little cans of paint. They both disappeared outside.

Simba needed to catch his breath; so he threw himself into the nearest seat.

Ronna appeared by his side. "Are you all right?"

Simba looked down into her face. Purity. All sweetness, openess and complete vulnerability. The others had all trickled outside. They were alone.

"Ronna, I have something unpleasant to tell you, but I want to be the one to tell you for two reasons. Most important reason is because I want to tell you everything. Second reason is because if I don't tell you now that bitch Ursula is liable to hurt you by telling you at the worst possible time and in the worst possible way."

Ronna frowned. "You . . . and Ursula?"

"You're sweet, Ronna, but you're not dumb. Look, there's no such thing as bad sex, but if there was, that one time I did it with her would have been a contender. I'm not going to hand you a bunch of platitudes, but I want you to know there wouldn't have been a second time, even if I hadn't met you."

"Did . . . did you love her?"

Jesus, Simba thought, I'll never understand women and sex. "No. Not for a second did I love her. And I do love you."

"Then why did you do it?"

Goddamn bitch! Simba thought. I tell a woman I love her for the first time, and what do I get back? A fly-paper confrontation that convinces me not to ever confront anything. Freud was right. "I did it," he said aloud with as much nastiness as he could muster, "because it feels good to get my rocks off."

Simba's patience had snapped, possibly because he was feeling bad about himself and what he did and how he really measured up to this shorter member of the presumably weaker sex who was looking up at him. Then there was the close call with the cops he'd just weathered. Worse, there was a murderer on the loose, and there was a strange, uneasy feeling this gave him about himself which he couldn't understand at all.

Simba was seething and afraid of what he would say or do if he stayed around Ronna. This provided convenient support for what he really wanted to do, which was run off to the nearest bar and get blind drunk.

Instead he confronted Ronna. Simba wasn't sure what he was expecting—a slap, maybe—but it certainly wasn't the sight of Ronna breaking out in giggles and giving him a brotherly punch in the arm. She swaggered up the aisle and back, a damn good imitation of the cop, and finally flopped down on top of him, cuddly as a tired puppy.

Simba could feel the muscles in his back loosen. Ronna looked up at him with a huge smile that reeked of the unconditional acceptance Simba had never seen in his own mother. "It's okay, Simba. Really it is. Everything's fine."

Bam! Simba was simultaneously knocked off his feet by two opposing feelings.

"What's wrong?" Ronna asked.

To his own amazement, Simba found himself speaking his thoughts aloud, completely unedited. "You bowl me over with a sense of peace and completeness I've been looking for all my life. That's because I've been looking for you all my life, Ronna." He yanked her into his arms for a rough and somewhat clumsy hug. The tear that would have made him ecstatic earlier with the cop rolled unbidden down his cheek. "But something equally strong is very wrong."

She smiled, a mother's tolerance for a little kid afraid of the dark, and wiped the tear from his cheek. "Nothing's wrong. What you're feeling is wonderful. Sometimes those kinds of feelings can be scary because they're so intense. That's all."

"No. Something's off. Something's horribly off. It's deep inside me, and I can't see what it is."

Ronna snuggled up tight, wrapping her arms around him. "I think you're imagining things, suffering perhaps from a bad case of it's-too-good-to-be-true."

"I don't want to hurt you, and I'm afraid I will."

"That's silly," she said, rubbing noses.

"When I said I've been looking for you all my life, something whispered that I had been looking for you all right, but for the wrong reasons."

Ronna gave him a tough-guy look. "Maybe it was so you could get your rocks off."

Simba met her eyes and could see her lightness evaporate. He thought fear might replace it, and this somehow made him afraid of what he would do if it did. Instead it was replaced by concern. She said nothing, but in her gaze was the solemnity of a young soldier willing to give her life in order to execute whatever might be his next command. Her skin glowed with a warm blush of determination. She was beautiful.

"You're beautiful," he said, "but even that sets alarms off in my head."

"Because?"

"Because when I first set eyes on you, you were

a bloody, puffy mess, and yet I knew exactly what you really looked like."

"How?" she asked, determined to understand.

"I hallucinated it. At first I thought it was an acid flashback, but it wasn't at all psychedelic and it turned out to be competely accurate."

"I wish I could understand that better, but I've never done acid."

"We'll have to correct that," Simba said.

"I've never wanted to."

"You might be able to help me if you did," he said. "Actually, it might help all of us get to the truth of what's been going on around here."

"How so?"

"Let me explain how LSD works. Normally we humans only use ten percent of our brains at any given time. That leaves ninety percent of our brain power dormant, untapped. What LSD does is turn on that other ninety percent."

"Why the hallucinations?" she asked.

"Because they aren't really hallucinations. They're distortions resulting from seeing better than you've ever seen in your life but not being able to process and interpret it correctly. If you sit next to somebody who's tripping when you are not and ask them to explain what they're seeing, you'll find that if you concentrate you can see it all, too. Nobody actually hallucinates three-dimensional fire-breathing dragons sitting in the middle of the floor that have no basis whatsoever in reality."

"Interesting," she said, but he sensed it was for his benefit. Maybe she was one of those people who could find happiness in the world as it was and wasn't searching for something more.

Simba had always been searching, but since he had found Ronna he had the eerie feeling that perhaps he was not the one who had been doing the searching. Maybe something or someone else had been doing the searching.

Simba wanted answers. Where was the ax? Where was Josephine? He sensed he should know. It was beginning to tickle like something on the tip of his tongue.

A knock on the window next to him sent a shock of fear through Simba. He shoved Ronna behind him before realizing it was Poppy, a wide smile on her face. "Come on out and see," she called through the glass.

They did. Gizmo Delicious had been painted all over the bus in a glorious psychedelic multicolor. Chutney struck a melodramatic pose and said, "For Ricky!" Everyone laughed and clapped and hooted, except for Midas who appeared to be suffering a heart attack at an early age.

Simba studied his arm. It looked like someone had bitten him, but he was absolutely sure no one had. Dread became an albatross hanging heavily about his neck.

Piper was staring at the stars. She was curled up against the window atop somebody's sleeping bag, gently jostled by Bell's driving. Whenever she looked at the rearview mirror he stuck out his tongue.

Inside the bus everyone looked cozy. Simba

and Ronna were entwined in each other's arms, clinging to each other like terrified children. In sleep, though, their faces pressed together had found peace.

Chutney, still awake with a knee tucked under his chin, kept watch over the sleeping Poppy, Miss Professional Sunshine.

Midas slept alone, awkward even in sleep as he turned over only to get his legs caught in his sleeping bag.

Ursula was all the way in the back against the sound equipment, practicing Josephine's bass. She would pause to do a line of coke, do pretty well for awhile, and then fall into a pattern of continually interrupting herself to curse over nonexistent mistakes just before doing the next line.

Someone was tickling Piper's toes.

Piper looked down into Mushroom's elfin face, animated for once by an innocent sense of fun. Mushroom gestured for silence with a finger to her lips, then brought two closed fists out from behind her back, indicating that Piper should pick one.

Enchanted, Piper smiled, and picked though she was afraid the choice might be between peyote and mescaline, and she didn't particularly want either.

Mushroom opened her fist with a flourish; Piper imagined a sprinkling of Tinker Bell's fairy dust. Inside Mushroom's fist was an antique rose quartz ring.

"A gift for the one with the spirit that soars,"

Mushroom whispered. "This witch wants to change things and hopes this will protect you."

Piper tried the ring on. "Thank you. It's beautiful. Where did you get it?"

"It belonged to a woman who you treated with honor when you refused to sleep with her husband."

Piper was confused. "Was this anything recent?"

"No, You probably don't remember." Suddenly she grabbed Piper's workshirt. "You're hurt!"

Piper looked down to discover a bloodstain on her shirt. They both checked her skin underneath. Piper noted that Mushroom's touch was pure concern. "I'm fine," Piper announced at the end of their investigation.

"Then where did this come from?" Mushroom asked.

"I don't remember," Piper answered, but there was something that bothered her about that, something that reminded her of the odd smell she still couldn't identify in the bus.

Parsons was pissed. How dare that idiot Simba bring some other cop into this? Speeding. Didn't he know that hippies, if anything, had a habit of driving far too slowly just to annoy people? Were the kind of tight-asses that would reinforce a perfectly operational turn signal with a hand signal? Oh, why did he have to put up with this?

They were all a bunch of no-good freaks, of course, but Parsons far preferred Chutney. If the idiot would just get rid of all that hair, he could be an all right guy, the kind of son a person such as himself might have had if he'd had the good fortune to take a wife who was capable of bearing sons.

Parsons polished off his coffee, while keeping his eye on the road and the bus in front of him. Gizmo Delicious. He had to give them credit. Personally, it would have taken him centuries to think up an equally stupid name.

Meanwhile this night driving was killing him.

Chapter 10

Why didn't Daddy love her? It was a funny thought that popped out of nowhere, especially since neither Officer Parsons nor Joshua Carnes were people whose love was of any value. Still, Ronna found herself clinging even tighter to Simba's arm. At least Simba loved her.

It was night, and they were somewhere in eastern Pennsylvania. They'd be in New York the following day.

Mushroom was shaking.

"Oh, pooh," Piper told Mushroom softly, a hand with a beautiful rose quartz ring Ronna had never seen before on Mushroom's thin, elfin shoulder. "Don't pay any attention to Poppy's fortunetelling."

Mushroom looked up, and Ronna saw a wild

but somehow elegant insanity in her eyes. "That night in the antique store," she said. "I didn't remember before, but now it comes back to me—unreal as a carpet flying toward me out of an Arabian fantasy."

Simba yawned. "What antique store? What night?"

"Where and when the first murder took place," Mushroom said.

"You were there?" Simba asked.

"Yes. And I saw you."

Simba sat up. "Really? Where? What was I doing?"

"Making strange firewood."

"Firewood?" Simba smiled and shook his head at Ronna. "Unfucking likely. Too much work."

Mushroom stared at him.

"By the way," Simba said, "what was strange about the firewood?"

"It bled," Mushroom said.

The wind cried; the bus shook. Simba was on his feet. "Are you saying that I'm the killer?"

But Mushroom was screaming, an eerie, unnatural explosion of sound that set her hair in motion. Then she hugged herself and was suddenly quiet. Ronna watched in wonder, finding it hard to believe that the gradual stretching of that prominent mouth was actually a smile. "My parlor," Mushroom said.

"Answer me!" Simba's voice was enough to shake the bus.

Mushroom continued to smile. "Most of the women folks wear calico and linsey-woolsey, and their little girls wear sunbonnets and shakers, but not in my parlor. In my parlor they all wear black."

Simba took a giant step toward Mushroom.

Chutney appeared between them. "Don't take her seriously, man. Look at her. She's insane."

Mushroom continued, oblivious, and Ronna noticed for the first time that her pupils were so big it was hard to determine her eye color. "When the time comes to turn up new soil and they all get ague—chills and fever—they have nothing to do with the goose grease and turpentine I try to give them to help. Nor the herbs and the teas I have that could save them from all and everything."

Ursula picked up Josephine's bass guitar and picked out the theme from *The Twilight Zone*. She gave Mushroom a hard look. "Like, she's stoned out of her mind, man. I guess some people just can't handle getting high."

Simba's back muscles relaxed. He took a step closer to Mushroom, his face concerned.

Mushroom handed him a mushroom. "Eat it. Eat it now, Luke. I tire of watching and waiting while none of you come to me till 'tis far too late."

Simba put the mushroom to his mouth.

"No, Simba, don't!"

It was only when he turned to her that Ronna realized she was the one who had spoken.

"Don't what?" Simba asked her.

Ronna could feel herself melting before his hypnotic blue eyes. She didn't want to face him like this. All she wanted was to curl up in his

224

arms and be lulled to sleep, but she resisted. "Don't eat the mushroom," she said.

Emotions flickered across his face like a slide show—surprise, fear, anger. The anger was scary, but he suppressed it quickly. "Anything wrong with relaxing a little after all the tension around here?" he asked evenly.

Ronna started to answer; she was going to say something about the blackouts, but Simba popped the mushroom into his mouth rendering academic any further discussion.

Ursula laughed, and Ronna felt foolish. Simba turned back to Mushroom.

"Too late to do what?" Simba asked Mushroom.

"Too late to change things. Always too late. None of you folks will traffic with a witch until 'tis far too late. That is why in my parlor they all wear black. Then, only then, when your fear and disdain are lost in your pain do you come to the witch and ask what is now impossible, for even I cannot bring back your dead.

"I know this because this witch wants to help. This witch wants to be able to open her heart and feel happiness in the world. But you always come too late. I've studied and listened to the spirits who have told me that in the face of death one can only see and attempt to get others to see.

"The dead have gone on. A dead husband has already become the baby in a neighbor woman's womb. A dead daughter may be the egg of the goose you'll slaughter and feast on next Christmas."

Mushroom started to laugh but then sank into tears and a low, tender wailing of pure despair.

Luke. Who the fuck was Luke? Cool Hand Luke? Paul Newman? Some girl once told him he had his eyes. Not a bad comparison.

Simba looked around. Everyone else except Mushroom was outside the bus. Colors were becoming brighter, primary. He was seeing patterns where he knew none existed. Triangles flowed over the ceiling. Trapezoids marched across the floor. The edges of things became zigzagged.

He was looking at the poster of the Jefferson Airplane. It lay half against the wall and half on the floor, its edge a diagonal which appeared to be a progression of multicolored miniature steps. He checked the rest of the bus. Not a straight line to be found. The world had acquired the geometric distortions of a Navajo rug. That button of Mushroom's he ate must have been mescaline.

"Hey, Mushroom," he called. She'd been quiet for a long time, and it wasn't until she looked up that Simba remembered how upset she'd been earlier. Still, he was into it, excited by the drug, and continued. Maybe it would keep her mind off whatever personal demons she fought. "Mescaline, right?"

Mushroom nodded. Her hair, set in motion, was almost painful to behold as it shifted from triangles to squares and then hexagons.

"Wasn't till I did this shit for the first time,"

Simba said, "that I realized the Navajo artists were such realists."

Mushroom was staring into his eyes.

"Triangles? Squares? Parallelograms?" Simba asked.

"I am beyond the patterns," came the whisper-scream, mysterious as a voice invading his own mind. "I see those charismatic blue irises folded back out of the way to reveal a vast and infinitely deep black sea."

All right. What the hell. Go with it. It might keep her mind off other things. "And what lurks in the depths of this deep black sea?" Oops, a little heavy on the sarcasm. Would she notice?

"The first day of kindergarten."

"Mushroom, you disappoint me. I was expecting the mysteries of the universe, not the mediocrity of middle-class Americana. Here we are hallucinating our brains out and you're into kindergarten?"

Mushroom leaned closer, her eyes twin whirlpools out of a geometry teacher's nightmare. "Walls," she said.

"Slightly more interesting," Simba conceded. "Where did these walls come from?"

"The first day of kindergarten."

"Could we talk about something else?"

"Please, Simba." There was a gurgle in her voice, and he was afraid she might cry. "Talk about this. I see now. We have all been so anxious to put the uncool, unhip 1950's behind us that we hardly ever talk about our own childhoods. Simba, you—of all people—must."

Simba sighed. "The Navajos wouldn't be caught dead in our company, but ... You want to hear about Walnut Creek?"

"Yes," Mushroom intoned. It was as if she had both spoken aloud and whispered inside Simba's own mind.

Suddenly his head hurt, and he remembered it hurting just before he fell asleep the night Josephine disappeared. "What would you like to hear about first? My little red wagon?" For a strobelike moment the patterns vanished and Simba saw Mushroom's hair as black.

The next thing Simba knew Chutney appeared out of nowhere—in the flesh, three-dimensional, not a hallucination, and no puff of smoke. He was in the middle of a sentence. "—dear brother Luke, and pleased to see that Mushroom has finally succeeded in reducing you to the same reincarnation silliness she has so skillfully reduced all the rest of us to. Although, I must say, she doesn't look any too pleased about it."

Reading people's facial expressions while under the influence of hallucinogenic drugs wasn't easy, but Simba could see through the torrents of geometric shapes that suddenly Mushroom was as faraway from him as she could get with her back to the wall and her arms outstretched against it.

Simba himself was so unbalanced by Chutney's sudden appearance that he fell off his seat.

"Whoa! Careful, man," Chutney said.

Mushroom was still staring at Simba. She started to scream.

Twisted

"All right, already!" Ursula snapped.

Where the fuck did she come from?

"So he called you a witch," Ursula continued. "You should hear what he calls his own dear sisters, so like, shut up!"

Mushroom ran out of the bus.

Poppy was there, too, looking up at Chutney wide-eyed. "Like, wow, Chutney, do you believe all this reincarnation stuff?"

"No. It's the power of suggestion."

"Agreed," Piper said, bounding in the open door. "Not rational—though it is, sometimes, remarkably compelling." She curled up in a seat by a window and peered out at a star-studded sky.

"Not as compelling as a good lay," Ursula said, slithering into the seat next to Simba.

"Where's Ronna?" Simba asked Chutney.

"Safe, man. With the others. But I better go get Mushroom."

"I will," Simba said.

"That'll be the death of her," Ursula hissed.

"Shut up," Simba ordered.

"Like, nobody ever believes me, man. It's the—"

"Curse of my life," Simba finished for her, getting up.

"Methinks Mushroom might respond a touch better to me just now though," Chutney said. "No offense."

Simba was too bombed for all this anyway. "Fair enough. I'll check on the others." The floor was oscillating wildly. He couldn't tell if the

229

stairs were stairs or rectangular hallucinations. He stumbled out into the night.

Two sideways ovals materialized under a long red rectangle. Something hard and cold was pressed into Simba's hand.

"It's yours anyway, and who knows who's out there," Bell said before disappearing into the bus.

Simba was alone.

At first the black of night provided a welcome dampening of both the colors and shapes, but it soon became a hideously malleable backdrop fraught with hallucinogenic possibilities. Drawn by the occasional illumination of headlights, Simba headed for the road.

The field he'd pulled the bus off onto was uneven. It felt like he was walking across a mountain range in the dark. The air smelled of growing things that seemed to twist into dark, ominous shapes as he passed by. Simba looked toward the road.

Two figures were by the side of the road. Real or imagined? Human? Demon? Simba drew closer. One of the figures popped a third dimension. Simba decided it was real and clung to that reality, stumbling over the last of the field to get closer still.

The other figure was too distant to be sure about.

Simba came out onto the shoulder of the road next to the first figure, a male hitchhiker who greeted him with an open smile.

"Hey, man! What's happening? I just got out."

Of? Simba thought to himself. He squinted at

the man through the veil of brightly colored triangles that separated them when a car's headlights swept past. The military, he answered himself.

"Wow, dude, is your hair ever long," the soldier said.

Uh oh, Simba thought, here comes trouble. And this fucker's taller than I am.

But the soldier clucked appreciatively. "You make me feel like something out of the last century."

Whew, Simba thought. Hate fighting under the influence of hallucinogens; don't know what to punch.

But the phrase "last century" ricocheted around inside Simba's head, somehow unsettling. A hint of a headache brushed past Simba again, along with the headlights from the next car.

The soldier followed the car with his thumb till it was past. "Don't know why I bother." He nodded toward the second figure, further down the road but apparently headed their way now. "Anyone passing up a female hitchhiker sure as shit isn't going to stop for me. Although it doesn't look like she's hitching anymore. You OK, man?"

"Yeah," Simba managed, incapable of anything but the basics. He stuck his hand out. "Simba, man. What's your name?"

"Roscoe," the soldier said.

A truck roared by. Simba was surprised to discover how well he could make out Roscoe's brown eyes and short hair through some extraordinarily anemic hallucinations. "Where you headed?"

"Don't know." Roscoe's quick, bright smile caught the last of the truck's headlights. "Looking for adventure, to catch up on all I've lost. As it is, man, I feel like I'm in the 1800's. What about you?"

Pain ricocheted around Simba's head.

"Where are you headed?" the soldier asked.

Suddenly there appeared to be a complete cessation in the hallucinations. It might just have been the dampening caused by the initial return to blackness after the truck passed.

Then again, Roscoe was gone.

The second figure was suddenly much closer.

Simba turned at the sound of dirt, kicked up by a car's tires, to find a car behind him that he hadn't seen stop. It was pulling back out onto the road, while someone closed a back door. Simba turned back to face the second figure, visible in the dark as little more than an unlit silhouette. Still, he could make out the shape of the hair.

It was Mushroom.

"Luke?" she asked. He noticed she was keeping her distance.

"One, I don't know who the fuck Luke is. Two, you look as if I'm going to eat you, which is ridiculous considering we're right next to a public highway with about a million eyewitnesses. Three, Chutney's looking for you."

Mushroom came closer. "I was hitching. I was running. I was protecting myself. A witch is good at that."

232

Twisted

"So why did you stop?" Simba asked.

"I want to change things." She stood very still, looking at him for a moment, while the next car passed. The hallucinations were back in full force so Simba couldn't read her expression. "Simba?"

"Yes."

"You're stoned now. That makes transitions easier," she said as another car whipped by and then left them in darkness. "For better or worse—"

"Let's go back to the others, Mushroom."

"Let's go back to the first day of kindergarten, Simba."

"Whatever makes you happy. I come from the inglorious suburb of Walnut Creek, a place with about as much character and sense of history as the plastic town that went with my electric trains."

"Very glib, Simba, but let's not be glib. Let's feel. I feel cold and vulnerable and scared to death. It's as if my life is an eggshell cup tottering on the edge of a shelf too high for me to reach. I have never felt such an agonizing sense of loneliness. But it's time for you to feel, Simba. Walnut Creek may be Plasticville, but it was real enough that first day of kindergarten. What did you feel?"

Simba felt the erosion of his protective cynicism. He took his shirt off and gently draped it about Mushroom's thin shoulders.

She watched him carefully while another car passed, then looked up into his eyes just as he was about to step back. "Well?"

"That first day of kindergarten? When my

233

mother left? I felt—" He cut himself off as pain cut through his brain. "I don't know what I felt."

"Yes, you do," Mushroom insisted. "And you must look at what you feel, and what you don't or won't feel, or you will never see through the walls."

"What walls?"

"The walls inside of you. The walls that explain not the blackouts, but rather the times when you aren't you. Or rather the times when you are another you."

Now Simba felt cold. The pain was worse. He felt like he couldn't even see straight, let alone hallucinate. "What the fuck are you talking about?"

"What do you think happens when you black out?"

Simba felt dizzy. He lowered himself to the road's shoulder, pulling Mushroom down with him so that they both sat facing each other. A car's headlights made long shadows of them that circled slowly as the car passed.

Simba forced himself to think. Why was he always avoiding things? Because when he was little people were always accusing him of doing things he had no memory of doing anyway? So he figured he didn't have a chance to begin with and might as well avoid it all? The pain was blinding. He couldn't think anymore.

"I don't know," he said at last. "But I know that you're trying to help me, and I thank you."

But Mushroom was gone, and the world was suddenly silent. The car that had just passed must have stalled. At least the pain was gone.

Simba looked up. The stars were beautiful and basically normal, which meant he must be coming down off the mescaline. For once he was glad.

He could hear a car in the distance. He looked down, not that he could see anything, and put a hand down to the road's shoulder to steady himself so he could stand.

The car was getting closer.

Simba's hand hit something hard. In the absence of light, he identified it by feel. It was the handle of his knife that Bell had made him bring along. Must have slipped out of his pocket.

The car's light began as a soft glow across the pavement. The knife was stuck in a low lump of ground. Simba yanked it out and stuck it back in his pocket. Just then the car whizzed by, and Simba could have sworn he caught a glimpse of Mushroom's hair out of the corner of his eye.

"Mushroom?" he called.

Darkness. He felt around. Her arm. She wasn't kidding about being cold. "Wake up, Mushroom. You're freezing!" He shook her arm a bit, then couldn't find it again. Another car was coming. Simba reached for the place where he thought he saw her hair. He found her face, but it was wet. The car was coming fast. The headlights caught his hand. His little finger rested in a pool of blood in her empty eye socket. Her nose had been laboriously hacked off. He jerked his hand away. Her head turned toward him, revealing a latticework of knife slashes. Just before the light swept past, he saw the agony in her remaining eye.

Darkness. Then a final whisper-scream. "My soul is old. It was my last life. I will now spend all eternity alone." Simba found her mutilated chest and thrust his ear against it. A single beat; no more.

The situation was now unendurable. Simba skittered away from the corpse, then stopped, realizing the utter impossibility of running away. He puked, but it did nothing to diminish the agony. Simba looked up at the stars and screamed as long and as hard as he could.

He now knew who the fuck Luke was.

Midas was wearing a pair of flannel pajamas with pictures of Fess Parker as Davey Crockett all over them. Piper would ordinarily have assumed that the only explanation for pajamas that proclaimed "King of the Wild Frontier" all over them was a doting grandmother, but she wasn't sure in the case of Midas. She watched him arrange his plants about his sleeping bag, then crawl in to do battle with it, eternally in search of some perfect position that didn't exist. Poor hobbit.

Bell twirled her about, stroked her face, then grinned and ran a leisurely hand over her rear. "Oo eeee, baby," he said. "This boy wishes we hadn't decided, like everybody else, not to sleep outside tonight."

Piper closed her eyes, put her head back and

bit her lip when she felt his lips on her chest. "Me, too."

"Where's Ronna?"

It was Simba who must have slipped back into the bus while she had her eyes closed. He looked terrible.

"Right here," Ronna called from the back. She was rolling out sleeping bags for herself and Simba next to the mountain of amplifiers. "All I have to do is go back out and get our clothes."

Simba had his eyes closed, a smile of relief on his face. Piper noticed he'd changed his clothes and was holding his and Ronna's backpacks. "Don't bother. I've got them." Then his eyes snapped open again to look from one to another of them.

"All present and accounted for," Piper said. "Except Chutney. And, of course, Mushroom."

Simba collapsed into a seat, shaking, to hold his head in his hands. Even Midas looked worried.

Piper watched the others, slowly drawn to Simba like children stunned to see a parent cry for the first time. Bell put a hand on his shoulder. Ursula put an arm around him so she could rub up against his side. Poppy stood at his shoulder, her expression serene as a panting dog who would wait an eternity for her master's next command. Even Midas struggled back out of his sleeping bag to stand before Simba and fidget compulsively with his pajamas. Finally Ronna knelt by his knee.

Piper joined them, though there wasn't room left to be too close.

"Don't worry," Ronna said. "Chutney will find her."

"I sincerely hope, for his sake, that he does not," Simba said.

"You don't mean that," Bell said. "I know you don't. You're too good."

Simba's bitter laugh gave even Piper a chill. She found herself playing absently with the stains on her workshirt.

Simba looked up. Never had those hypnotizing blue eyes glittered so brightly, nor had his black hair and beard seemed so dark in comparison. "I have something I must tell you all, warn you all about," he said.

Oh, shit, Piper thought, he found Mushroom dead! She ran her thumb over the antique ring Mushroom had given her, as if, perhaps, she could call up a genie who would make it not so. She then circled the group encircling Simba. Their faces were ashen.

Ronna, crying, clutched at Simba's knee and turned her face up to peer at him with quivering chin.

"Please, Simba, we can't take anymore—especially if it looks like you can't take anymore. The only thing that keeps us going is our belief in you."

Simba looked at Ronna as if she had just sentenced him to death. He sighed heavily, and Piper saw all the luster drain from his eyes.

"All right, Ronna. You win," he said.

They all looked confused.

"Don't think about it. Everything's going to be all right. I promise."

Everyone started to regain some color. This was the Simba they were used to.

"Mushroom's gone." Simba paused a long time before continuing. "I saw her hitchhiking."

"Just as well," put in Ursula. "That chick was weird."

"No," Simba said sadly. "Mushroom was not what she appeared to be. Underneath all that spooky stuff was a soft heart and a noble soul that wanted to change things."

Piper found herself studying Simba very carefully. Perhaps the great Simba was not quite what he appeared to be either.

Parsons ran his flashlight over the shoulder of the road until he found a low lump of something. It was a nose that looked like it had been stabbed through with a knife.

Parsons stretched, rubbing his paunch, and smiled. Hadn't been hard to find the spot. Hell, he'd seen the crime. There he'd been barreling along, wondering what the hell had become of that bus and cursing the waitress in the last diner he'd stopped in for taking so damn long to give him a simple blow job. Then his headlights had given him a quick glimpse of Simba stabbing Mushroom. He'd driven a bit further, then pulled off to wait till it was over, sweating bullets every time another vehicle passed for fear some dumb-ass Good Samaritan would interrupt things.

If Parsons was going to get that promotion, he couldn't afford to have his record smudged with anything as undramatic as an arrest for assault with a deadly weapon.

Fortunately he got to laugh as the few vehicles that passed did so without even slowing. Idiots were probably all asleep at the wheel.

Speaking of idiots, Parsons's revenge against that idiot Simba for trying to mess him up by bringing another cop in on things was going to be sweet indeed.

Chapter 11

Ronna woke up with a start. It was the middle of the night, but Simba was standing over her, staring down at her.

"Oh, Simba, I had another dream," she said.

"Who's Simba?" he asked, curiously.

"What do you mean?" Ronna asked, rubbing her eyes. She felt scared and small and somewhat foolish again, mostly scared. She grabbed his hand and pulled him down to her. It wasn't like her to do such a thing. It seemed almost sexual, but it wasn't. She wasn't reaching for a man; she was reaching for a father.

"I mean I don't know who the fuck I am," he said.

Ronna peered up at him. She wanted to understand, to help him, but she was shaking from the dream. They had chopped her head off by the big house again, and it had taken monumental effort on her part not to scream as she woke up. She needed something, anything, to cling to. She threw her arms around Simba and squeezed him so tight she was afraid that despite his big frame she might actually hurt him.

"I know who the fuck you are," Ronna said, although the word fuck sounded awkward when she said it, like she was a little kid trying to be adult. "You're Simba, who takes care of us. You're our strength."

A shudder went through him, but then he seemed to gather himself together. She looked up at the set of his jaw and sensed a new resolve that pleased her, until she looked into his eyes and saw the pain.

He grabbed her roughly and held her away from him. Then he folded her into his arms and held her just the way she needed to be held. "You win. I'd do anything for you, Ronna. I'll be your strength. Everything will be okay."

Ronna laid her head down on his broad shoulder and started to close her eyes. Suddenly he held her away from him again. "Just one thing," he bellowed. "You were right tonight when you tried to stand up to me. Don't forget it. And, no matter what, don't let me get high."

With that they curled up in each other's arms and fell asleep.

When Ronna woke, Simba was driving like a maniac again.

Midas was close at hand, rocking himself and

looking cross. "First you paint her purple, then you splatter a dumb name all over the sides, and now you're going to drive her to an early grave," he muttered.

Chutney, who was passing by, slapped a hand to his chest. "All for Ricky." But when he stood by Simba he asked, "What's your hurry, man?"

"I've got to get across the George Washington Bridge," Simba answered.

"Methinks you may be overreacting just a bit, my friend. We haven't seen hide nor hair of Josephine."

Simba jumped. The bus's tires kicked up dirt off the shoulder.

Midas clucked.

Simba regained control.

"What's on the other side of the George Washington Bridge?" Chutney persisted.

"Safety for all of you," Simba answered.

"And for you?" Chutney asked.

Simba looked at Ronna in the rearview mirror, his expression unbelievably sad. "The end of the line."

"No," Bell said. "The beginning. We can put all this jive behind us and get back to the band and get it on! Right, baby?"

Bell turned to Piper for support, but Piper was so busy staring at Simba that she didn't respond.

"You still haven't told me what the hurry is," Chutney said.

Simba let the bus drift over the center line for a moment, then cut the wheel to correct himself.

"I've got to get to the closest cop shop before I lose my nerve."

Midas marched up the aisle. "That does it," he hollered with a cracking voice. "I've had enough. It's my bus, and I say we are not going to go to the police and tell them we've all been involved with some murders. I don't care what you say about New York City. I'll get in trouble, and Mother will be furious."

Ronna smiled, finding an odd comfort in their bickering, and found herself drifting back into sleep, only to bolt back awake again.

She had seen the big house.

"He's got some kind of point," Bell was saying. "What if they kind of like take exception to the fact that we didn't exactly report all this shit in a timely fashion?"

Simba took his eyes off the road just long enough to look Bell in the eye. "Believe me, after I've finished saying what I have to say, it's not going to matter." He swerved again, then corrected again.

"What if they don't believe you?" Midas asked.

"Simba, man?" Bell asked Midas. "You're jiving me. Simba can make anybody believe anything."

Ronna started to drift off again, but opened her eyes when she heard Simba sigh. She imagined she detected fear and confusion in the rearview mirror, although Simba's eyes were on the road.

Simba cleared his throat. "I don't know, man. This is going to be the ultimate challenge."

Something new in his voice cut through Ronna.

It was vulnerability. But Chutney patted Simba on the shoulder and told him he could do it, and Ronna, who apparently hadn't slept at all well due to her dreams, found her eyes closing on her again.

"Methinks we should all get a firm grip on what exactly we're going to say," Chutney declared. "The worst of this is that none of us really understand what happened."

Ronna's eyes were closed. She could hear the others talking, but she could also see the house. She was scared, but she was getting sick of being scared. She took a good look at the house. "If you want to know what happened," she said aloud, "don't stop in Manhattan. Continue to Long Island.

"Far out!" Poppy cried.

"Welcome, my dear," Chutney said, "to the legendary Gold Coast of Long Island, immortalized—should you be interested—in F. Scott Fitzgerald's *The Great Gatsby*."

"Like, wow, look at the size of that mansion," Poppy squealed.

"They say the true gems can't be seen from the road," Chutney said.

"I just love mansions," Poppy said.

Simba finally gave in and pulled over to the side of the road. For a fraction of a moment freedom from the struggle to concentrate on driving furnished what he mistook for a relief from the pain. He looked back at the pretty heart-shape of

Ronna's face, glowing softly as the afternoon's last light slanted through the bus.

Then he remembered the last time he'd seen Mushroom's face.

He had to tell himself to take the next breath, then to exhale it, then to inhale again. No air in the bus. How could the others stand it? He tripped down the stairs and found himself outside.

The same slanting light that lit Ronna's face lay like golden snow atop an infinity of gently rolling green hills. Not a blade of crab grass nor a single dandelion disturbed the meticulously cut grass. The split rail fences gave the scene a sense of airiness and endless space. Two horses stood whisking their tails serenely, their long shadows stretched out forever across the verdant green.

Simba ached, driven mad by an aura of peace he would never enjoy.

"Come on, big man," Bell called from the bus.

Simba had never felt less big. If he had anything like the strength Ronna thought he had, the last thing he'd do would be to get back into a bus full of people he cared about. He turned slowly, listening to the horses behind him graze.

Ronna stood in the doorway, her honey hair stirred by a languid breeze. Simba closed his eyes, begging for a strength he knew he'd never find. He got back into the bus, weakly attempting to convince himself that he did so because it would help them all to go to this house Ronna saw and try to find some answers.

Chutney, at the wheel, smiled up at Simba.

"My grandfather's trees," he said reverently.

"What road are we on?" Bell asked.

"It's called 25A," Simba managed. "How much longer, Ronna?"

"I don't know," Ronna answered. "I just know I'll know it when I see it."

"Like, this is what you stopped me from getting some more coke in Manhattan for?" It was Ursula blocking Simba's way. "After you took the time to score some worthless goddamn acid for yourself?"

No, Simba thought. For once, not for myself. For everyone else. Answers. We're going to get ourselves some goddamn answers.

"Nice ring," Simba said absently as he passed Piper.

Piper's only response was an almost imperceptible nod. Paranoia hit. Could she know?

Simba looked past her into Poppy's face.

"Like, I just have to ask you a question, Simba," Poppy said. She had never looked more serious.

Could Poppy know? "What is it, Poppy?" Simba managed.

"What's your sun sign?" she said.

Simba almost laughed. "Aries."

"Far out! And your planets?"

"Crossed, all crossed," Simba said. "Even my moon crosses my sun." And he passed her by, and even passed Ronna by, to throw himself down alone on the floor in the very back of the bus.

Sitting made him aware of the capsules of LSD

in his back pocket. He wanted one bad. The desire to escape reached orgasmic intensity, yet he knew he must live the rest of his life without as much as a sip of beer.

Piper poked her head out the bus window, closed her eyes and flared her nostrils. A briny wind whipped her hair about. Intermittent sunlight, far weaker than California's, flickered across her eyelids. The engine stalled again, Midas clucked again, sand crunched under the tires, and in the background Piper could hear the surf of Long Island Sound.

"'The time has come,' the Walrus said, 'to think of many things.'" It was Ronna, her voice sounding like that of a child rather than a woman.

"My grandfather's trees," Chutney proclaimed, an actor's resonance in his voice.

Piper opened her eyes. A series of twisted cedar trees explained the intermittent light. They had no leaves and appeared gnarled from the unrelenting bombardment of wind and sand. The sky was mottled, fast becoming white. The land was drab. When Piper caught her first glimpse of the water between the gnarled trees, even its blue seemed anemic. Piper caught a last whiff of the salt air and pulled her head back in to take another long look at Simba.

She sniffed again, hoping for a last scent of the sea, but had forgotten she had pulled her head back into the bus. What she got was that odd smell she'd wondered about the night Josephine disappeared.

The bus stalled again.

Midas stomped his foot. "She needs a rest. Pull over right now. It's my bus."

"True," Bell said at the wheel, slowing down. "Ronna?"

Ronna opened her eyes, sighing heavily. "We're so close, and suddenly I'm stuck. I can't see anymore. May as well stop."

Bell signaled for the first left, toward the water.

Piper spotted a male hitchhiker, very tall, on the right. "Oo ee, baby!" she called, imitating Bell.

Bell looked at her in the rearview mirror. Piper jerked her head toward the hitchhiker. Bell cocked a brow, frowned, pointed the bus at the man and stepped on the gas. At the last moment he grinned, winked at Piper, and swung the bus left into what turned out to be a beach parking lot.

"Whoa!" Chutney said.

Bell obeyed, jerking them all off their seats.

Chutney pointed to a poster on a telephone pole.

Poppy read it aloud. "Nyland Heights Rock Festival, featuring The Who."

"All right!" Bell said.

"Saigon U," Poppy continued, "A Thousand Flushes, No Free Lunch, Earth Mothers, Flexers, and Pack It and Go."

Chutney was digging through his baggy trousers pockets. He came up with a Magic Marker and a grin. Then he leaned out the window to add, "and The Gizmo Delicious." Amidst the general applause, he struck a solemn pose. With an actor's sense of timing he waited for the din to subside before adding, "For Ricky."

"Right on," Bell said.

"Know anybody in The Who?" Chutney asked him as they continued into the parking lot. "Any possibility of a connection we could use to get a few minutes on stage?"

Bell pulled to a halt and looked up at Chutney. "Sure."

Piper was excited, and even Ursula looked happy, but something caught the corner of Piper's eye. She turned to discover the sky had progressed to a chalky white so thick it appeared solid. Where once the blue of the sound had seemed anemic, it was now dark, powerful and angry. A storm was brewing. Piper turned back to Simba. Even his eyes, once a piercing blue, now seemed dark.

"Ronna," he called, "close your eyes."

Ronna obeyed.

"What do you see?" Simba queried.

"Nothing," Ronna answered. "I'm trying, but it's gone."

"Time for some help," Simba said, digging into his rear pocket.

"How?" Ronna asked.

Simba held out a closed fist, then opened it to reveal a handful of LSD capsules. "You must release your mind from the shackles of this myopic society we live in. Discover the full power dormant in your brain."

Ronna stood, wide-eyed, staring at the capsules. In one of them the powder was blue. "And you, Simba? Will you take it, too?"

Piper saw the hand that held the drugs tremble, then the storm in his eyes, but he answered steadily enough. "No. But I want all the rest of you to." He dragged himself to his feet and started handing out capsules. Ronna got the blue one. "It wouldn't do any good if I took it," Simba said, apparently more in answer to some internal argument than to any of them. "I seem not to be able to see into this otherworld like all the rest of you can."

Ursula gave her capsule the contemptuous look of a gourmet contemplating a hot dog, shrugged and downed it without water. That done, she picked up Josephine's bass and practiced calmly.

The rest stared at theirs.

Ronna looked up at Simba. "I guess I'm not much of a hippie, but I've never done this before."

"I know," he said softly. "Trust me." He found a canteen, unscrewed it and held it out to her.

Midas was turning his capsule over and over, poking at it every which way. "I have. I mean I've done this plenty of times."

Only Poppy, and perhaps Bell, appeared to believe him.

Midas continued to poke. "Doesn't look very high quality . . . as dope goes," he proclaimed.

Ronna took the canteen and washed down her capsule, a fearful eye on Simba throughout. She handed the canteen to Midas, who choked on his but got it down.

Piper was last, which gave her the opportunity to hesitate since no one was waiting on her. "New to me, too," she said, more to herself than anyone else. She'd smoked some pretty hallucinogenic grass, said to be almost equal to acid, but nothing more.

No matter.

She wasn't going to let anybody or anything bring her down, and since there had been some threats of late in that direction, this might be fun. Just what she needed. "How long does it take to take effect?" she asked Simba.

"Something less than an hour, depending on when you last ate," he answered. "We'll give the bus a rest and wait," Simba said to them all. "And then we'll get some answers."

Piper frowned. If Simba was the answer would he be working so hard to expand everyone else's consciousness? She looked back out toward the sea. It was wild, but she was determined to get off on it. She grabbed Bell's hand, grinning as she very intentionally brushed it across her rear, and dragged him out of the bus. "Come on, let's see if that groovy-looking hitchhiker is still there."

Outside the wind was fierce. Bell hefted her over his head, which set Piper to giggling, and twirled her about like a baton.

"You sure you want to do anything to displease me, woman?" he asked.

A flashing red light must have caught both of

their eyes because he put her down suddenly.

Piper looked back through the twisted trees that bordered the road. A cop car sat before the hitchhiker like some hideous beetle that had just cornered its prey. The silly part was that the cop, though a touch shorter, looked like a carbon copy of the hitchhiker himself. Both had the same brown short hair.

"Baby," Bell breathed into her ear. "Would you explain to this poor dumb boy why that cop is hassling what is obviously his own soul mate?"

Piper shrugged. "Something must have the pigs in this town in a real uproar."

"In light of their reaction to an individual who is clearly as straight as the day is long," Chutney whispered from behind, "has it occurred to either of you to contemplate what the local heat's reaction may be to us?"

Bell shuddered. "I wonder what's rattled their chains?"

As if in answer, a second cop materialized out of nowhere on their side of the road and ripped the rock festival poster off the telephone pole. "Saigon U," he snarled. "Perverted punks. They ought to be there."

"Uh oh," Bell said.

"Could it be," Chutney asked, "that there existed just a wee bit of local opposition to the choice of this particular town for a rock festival?"

"Naaa," Bell said. "And listen, man. If you'd like to go on over there and tell that nice police officer that you personally object to his ripping that poster down after you went to all the trouble of adding our name to the list, I'd be glad to back you—from a distance of about ten miles."

The nice police officer looked to Piper like the kind who was always looking for trouble. Bell put an arm around her, and the three of them backed up a few steps, then turned quietly and headed for the beach.

They passed a series of twisted cedar trees near the top of a slope which gave the parking lot an eerie look. The others joined them silently as they passed sand dunes, beach grass, and trees devoid of leaves. Piper took her sandals off at the water's edge but the sand was hard and rocky, the water bitter cold. This was not California.

"I know I said to give the bus a rest, but what are we doing here?" Midas asked, his cracking voice an awkward intrusion on an awkward silence.

Piper could smell the anticipation in the air. She studied the drab stretch of lonely beach from which no houses were visible, the dark water, and the white sky.

Simba answered Midas. "We, like the blank sky waiting for the storm, are blank pages waiting to be written upon when the drug takes effect and our consciousness expands."

The others huddled closer.

"We'll get some answers," Simba reassured. "We're on the verge."

"Of our deaths!" Ursula snapped. "This storm will kill us all." She cuddled up to Simba and glared defiantly at Ronna. "Except maybe you, you bitch." The look of desperation in Ursula's eye prompted Piper to wonder how long she could go without cocaine. "We've got to leave this place and go back to Manhattan. Please, listen to me for once." Simba shook Ursula off, but where Piper expected to see disgust in his face, she was surprised to see a look of desperation and fear even greater than Ursula's.

Chutney cocked a brow at Ursula. "Your credibility would improve tenfold, dearest, in the absence of such an obvious ulterior motive."

Ursula grabbed at Chutney's arm, but he pivoted out of reach with an actor's mobility. "I'm feeling a tad claustrophobic, dearest. In no mood to be clung to by someone so very nervous and so very negative. I'm in need, in fact, of the exact opposite. Poppy, what do you think of this beach?"

"Oh, I just love beaches," Poppy answered brightly.

"Oh, stop with that love everything shit, Poppy," Ursula screeched. "You make me sick."

"But I do love everything, Ursula," Poppy answered immediately with undaunted good nature.

Piper found herself questioning more than the girl's attitude; Piper found herself wondering if Poppy was all there.

Ronna looked up at Poppy with her little girl eyes. "Even this old, ugly, dreary beach?"

"Even things old, ugly and dreary," Poppy said.

Even Simba appeared to lighten at that, smiling despite himself.

Sue Hollister Barr

Chutney's eyes managed a warm golden glow despite the bleakness of the scene. "Behold," he said, addressing them all in a rich bass. "Beyond brilliance and insight is something far nobler—simplicity. Come, child." He wrapped a burly arm about Poppy's thin shoulders and lead her down the beach, pausing to present her with a large sea shell.

"Far out," Poppy said, all smiles.

Piper followed them with her ears, soothed by the musical contrast between Poppy's voice, high and light, and Chutney's, deep and substantial.

"Did you know, O Spirit Of All Things Bright And Pure," Chutney said to Poppy, "that the Montauk and Shinnecock Indians supplied all of the Northeastern tribes with wampum from this place?"

"Wow!"

"Make that 'how!'" Chutney handed Poppy more shells. "Observe, we are stubbing our toes on the damn mint, the Indian Federal Reserve as it were."

"Chutney, what's wampum?"

"Money the Indians made by breaking sea shells, drilling holes in them and stringing them together."

They were almost out of earshot, but Piper thought she caught a final "Far out!" She smiled, then looked out over the raging waters of the sound and remembered the storm coming.

"Anybody feel the LSD coming on yet?" Simba asked.

Piper looked around. She wasn't at all sure

256

what the famed hallucinations would turn out like, but she figured anything could improve the dreary scene before her. "Not me," she said.

The others also answered in the negative.

"Come on, people," Simba said, an ugly and uncharacteristic edge of impatience in his voice. "Turn on! Ronna, close your eyes."

"But, Simba, I'm not feeling anything yet." Ronna sounded just a little surprised.

"Please, Ronna."

Simba did not say it at all evenly. Piper thought she saw an adult's bald look of disillusionment in Ronna's eyes, but Ronna did finally close her eyes.

Simba relaxed the muscles in his back. "Concentrate on the house, Ronna. Clear your mind of all else. Can you see it?"

"No."

"The dope isn't any good," Midas stated. "If it was any good, I'd know it by now. I mean, the fellow you bought it from ... You didn't even know the guy. Mother used to always say—"

"Shut up!" Simba yelled, then caught himself. "Sorry, man. It's just that I'm trying to get Ronna to concentrate, and this is important. The dope is good; trust me. I got all but one cap from a very good source. That one might be cut with a bit too much speed, fewer hallucinations, but it should be OK. Just give it time."

Ronna opened her eyes, and Piper recognized the conflict there when she looked at Simba. It was the beginning of love dying. Meanwhile, there it was again—the beginning of Piper feeling.

Ronna's voice was gentle. "Maybe, Simba, it doesn't matter whether this stuff works or not. Maybe drugs aren't the answer."

Simba's eyes flashed. "What would you recommend? Suburbia?"

Ronna stood her ground. "I, for one, can think of worse fates."

Bell stepped between them, grabbed each of their hands and propelled them playfully into the surf. "Hang loose, you two. It's the weather that's getting you down. The sky—it's constipated."

Simba snatched back his hand.

Bell made a joke of it. "Well," he mumbled, "you can't blame a guy for trying."

Ronna awarded him with a smile.

"Come on, Ronna, Piper," Bell said, grinning broadly. "I'll race you both. Twenty yards head start since you are members of the weaker sex."

Piper and Ronna exchanged a look of outrage and started down the beach, struggling to run in the sand. At first each sinking step reminded Piper of trying to get away from a monster in a dream where she couldn't move. But they persisted, side by side, panting and stumbling, until Piper felt the first delicious hint of the power of momentum. Turning sideways, she saw the victory mirrored in Ronna's satisfied smile. They laughed as the momentum grew until it felt like they could run forever, as strong and free as the roaring surf beside them.

Just then, when Piper was sure she and Ronna

were about to break the sound barrier, a dark shadow streaked by. Piper looked ahead of them to see a whirl of sand and a blinding grin as Bell halted before them. Ronna pouted, then cast herself dramatically into the water. Piper let her momentum carry her right into Bell, who she knocked over.

"Jesus, woman," Bell protested, "you pack quite a punch."

"Care to retract that obviously unfounded statement about the weaker sex?"

They lay facing each other. Bell dusted the sand off a prominent bicep and held out an open hand. "Care to arm wrestle?"

"Ronna!" Piper screamed. "Help!"

Ronna landed on Bell with a slimy piece of seaweed she attempted to wrap around his neck despite its continual efforts to squirm out of her hands. "I was going to kill myself in despair over our defeat, but I've decided to follow your example, Piper, and be active instead of passive. So I'm going to strangle him."

They laughed, splashed and fought, coating themselves with the briny sand. Piper watched the light off the water twinkle in Bell's and Ronna's eyes and thought to herself that this was the very best of life.

It had only begun to occur to Piper to wonder why she had never noticed the remarkably intricate patterns in Ronna's irises, when the first unmistakable change—telling her the drug was taking effect—took place in Piper's hearing. Ronna's laughter slowed abruptly, deepening and dividing into a myriad of individual elements Piper never knew existed. The roar of the surf did likewise until she was sure she could hear the individual crash of each drop of water. It was as if Piper had spent her whole life listening to what she thought were single instruments but were actually full orchestras.

Startled, Piper looked up at the once white sky which now threatened, any minute, to rain every color known to man. Even Bell's perfectly white teeth had sprouted gradations of yellow and gold. "Holy shit, Bell," she said, marveling at the sound of her own voice and the elaborate tapestry of Bell's irises.

It took her awhile to recognize the low rumble as his laughter. "Outrageous," he said, and his hands were on her face, leaving electric tingles as he traced her features. They turned together to watch Ronna, staring in fascination at a drop of water on the tip of her finger.

"Whoa," Bell said. "We better get back to the others while we can still figure out what's sky, what's water, and where to step."

The walk back took forever, every repetitive detail almost painfully acute and drawn out. Dizzy from the relentless rhythm of each footstep and crash of surf, Piper threw herself down in the sand at Simba's feet, closed her eyes, and covered her ears.

It was then, in the relative absence of sensory input, that she got the first hint of what was happening to her mind. She sprang to her feet to stare up into Simba's painfully electric blue eyes. He was questioning Ronna, who still couldn't answer, about the house. Piper interrupted. "Simba, stop looking for your answers in other places and other people. Let's talk about the first day of kindergarten."

"You, too?" Simba said softly.

Another low rumble turned out to be Chutney's laugh. "That sounded like 'Et tu, Brute?'" Chutney said.

"Like what?" Poppy asked.

"Reputed to be Julius Caesar's exact last words when he observed that the next person in line to stab him with a knife was his best friend, Brutus," Chutney answered.

Piper whirled, facing them all. "This is important. Help me." She returned her attention to Simba, and there it was again. Even her new feelings were exaggerated and electrified. Breathing, living things like the heretofore lifeless shells at her feet had developed a pulse and started to move. "There was sorrow in your voice when you asked, 'You, too?' Were you thinking of Mushroom?"

"Yes," Simba said softly.

"Of the time in the bus in Colorado when she asked you about kindergarten and discovered the walls?"

"No," he answered simply and immediately. "Of the last time she asked me about those walls."

"When was that?"

At that something flashed in the eyes Piper studied so intently, something she was sure wasn't a hallucination. "The last time I saw her," Simba answered.

"Where?"

"By the road."

"Doing what?"

At that he turned his back on her, looking out at the coming storm. "When I first found her she was hitchhiking."

"First found her? What was she doing when you last saw her?" Piper found her hand on Simba's shoulder, turning him to face her.

Pain screamed in Simba's eyes. Piper touched the drop of water she saw upon his cheek, then put her finger to her mouth. Salty. It could have been the surf, but Piper decided it was a tear.

Piper repeated her question. "What was Mushroom doing the last time you saw her?"

Simba opened his mouth to answer, and Piper knew the storm brewing overhead was nothing compared to the storm within Simba. She watched in seeming slow motion as his mouth shaped itself to the word he was about to say, hearing it in her mind even before he said it. His answer? Dying. But he never said it.

Ronna interrupted, her child's voice having returned. "Simba, I'm scared. It's all so electric, so jarring." Ronna took Simba's arm and wrapped it about her. She looked up at him, shaking.

Simba continued to look into Piper's eyes as he spoke to Ronna, so Piper saw the helplessness flooding him. But his voice was firm. "You'll be okay, Ronna." He tried to smile down at her. "Even Ursula says so. LSD is like that. It's not a calming drug, especially if cut with speed. Not something for the mindless masses to anesthetize themselves with like booze. On the other hand, why spend tens of thousands of dollars on years of psychoanalysis when a five dollar trip can show you everything inside you?"

Ronna tried to smile, then frowned. "But I'm not hallucinating."

Chutney clapped a hand to Piper's shoulder. "*If* you can stand to see everything inside you all at once. Speaking of which, methinks this dear lady asked you a question before and requested all of our assistance in keeping you on the subject. While we're on the subject of psychoanalysis, Simba, for once and for all let's have it out about that first day of kindergarten."

Obediently, Simba sat down, the storm to his back. The others formed a circle around him. "Safety in numbers," he muttered.

"Bait not taken. I ain't askin' what that means," Chutney drawled, before giving his voice its full, resonate strength. "Close your eyes, Simba. Relax."

Simba did.

"Listen to me," Chutney said. "Your brain is like half a walnut, with two separate hemispheres. Concentrate. Everything that is Simba is in the left hemisphere—all the hopes, all the fears, all the memories, the entirety of you. Now concentrate harder. Like salad dressing, everything that is Simba is separating into its individual components, so you can identify each component clearly. Can you see it, Simba?"

"Yes," Piper heard Simba say, then realized as she heard herself and everyone else echo that yes that her eyes were closed, too.

"Concentrate on the memories, Simba," Chutney said, his voice majestic. "Can you see them?"

Piper sure could. Things she hadn't thought about in years, like when Timmy Holden played with her brand-new breasts in the back of fifth grade chorus and her mother took her to a psychiatrist because she admitted she enjoyed it. Or, far more remarkable, a time when she was very young—two, at most. A huge St. Bernard puppy gave her a tongue bath she thoroughly enjoyed but which disgusted Mother. What was remarkable was that Piper had never before this had any memory of this incident, or any memory of anyone mentioning this incident.

"I can see them," Simba said.

Piper forced her eyes open. Damn, if Mushroom's hypnotic regressions to past lives had been effective before, this was 100 times as effective. Whatever else the characteristics of this drug were, a very high degree of suggestibility was right up there at the top of the list.

"Now watch them," Chutney said. "They are pouring out of the left hemisphere of your brain into the right hemisphere of your brain, slowly— very slowly. You can see it all. Each little memory. Starting with the present and going backwards, like sand sifting through your fingers so slowly that you can see each individual grain. Can you see it, Simba?"

"Yes."

"Backwards. Slower and slower until you finally stop at the first day of kindergarten. Everything freezes at the first day of kindergarten, so that you can see everything that happened that day, every second. Got it?"

"Here I come to save the day."

"What are you talking about, Simba?"

"I'm not Simba."

"Who are you?"

"Mighty Mouse."

"Mighty Mouse? What happened to Simba?"

"Who's Simba?"

Chutney tucked a knee up under his beard and leaned in toward Simba. "Don't give me that, man. You're Simba. I told you you can see it all. Each individual element like grains of sand. Every second. Look at it. Look at it all. What happened to Simba?"

Piper watched the storm brewing over the water behind Simba. It appeared to merge with him, the turbulence whirling about inside his eyes. "Simba can't," he said. "Mommy said to find someone who can."

"Who can what?" Chutney asked.

"Who is never scared."

"And Mighty Mouse is never scared?"

"Mommy said to find someone else to be. Someone who is never scared."

"The teacher, the other kids, they didn't think it was strange, your suddenly becoming Mighty Mouse?"

"They liked it. The teacher thought it was cute and said I was a good boy now and not a cry baby. The kids laughed and played with me and asked me to do more."

Chutney stroked his beard. The wind kicked up, blowing a riot of red hallucinations through the thick hair on his arm. "And did Mighty Mouse know about Simba?"

"No."

"Where was Simba while Mighty Mouse was there?"

"Simba wasn't."

"When did Simba come back?"

"On the way home. When the other kids left to go to their houses."

"And did Simba know about Mighty Mouse?"

"No."

"Far out," Poppy interrupted. "Simba's a multiple personality."

Ursula gave Poppy a chilling look that reminded Piper of a snake contemplating its prey. Piper's hallucinations took the suggestion, immediately dressing Ursula's greyish skin with the diamond-scaled patterns of a rattler.

"An astute command of the obvious, Poppy," Ursula quipped. "It's such a shame that you'll be the first girl to go, since I can't imagine what we'll do without you."

"Shut up, Ursula," said a few voices Piper couldn't identify through the distortions.

"Now concentrate again, Simba—and whoever else you might be," Chutney said. "Look at each little memory, yours and whoever else's. We're going to switch direction now. The memories are unfreezing and starting to pour slowly from one hemisphere of your brain into the other, but this time they're pouring from the right back into the left and we're moving forwards in time. Slowly. Can you see it, whoever you are?"

"Yes," said the corny, somewhat silly voice of Mighty Mouse. Piper could distinguish it now, even through the distortions. "Yes," said a voice that sounded like a much younger version of Simba himself.

"So who goes to kindergarten?"

"Mighty Mouse," said Mighty Mouse.

"And who goes home to Mommy?"

"Simba," said young Simba.

"And is there anyone else?"

"No," answered each. Then Mighty Mouse added an eerie, "Except..."

"Freeze the memories, Mighty Mouse. How old is Simba now?"

"Six, almost seven," answered the mouse.

"Where are you?"

"The playground."

"The playground!" Chutney was excited. "Is Eddie Naumburger there with you?"

"Yes," Mighty Mouse said. He sounded wounded, morally more than anything else. Piper envisioned the unimaginable—Mighty Mouse being raped by a bunch of high school kids.

"And is even Mighty Mouse scared?"

There was a long silence. Finally the mouse answered softly. "It isn't working."

"What isn't working?"

"Being Mighty Mouse. It only makes them

laugh harder, and it's not a nice laugh, not a nice laugh at all."

"And is even Mighty Mouse scared?"

"Yes."

The sorrow, the defeat, the loss of innocence was unbearable. For the first time in her life, Piper found herself hating boys.

"I'm sorry about what's happening, Mighty Mouse, but this is very important," Chutney said. "What happened then?"

"Mighty Mouse can't." It was young Simba talking. "Have to find someone who can."

Chutney gripped Simba's shoulders, the storm seeming to swirl about them both. "Who?" Chutney demanded, his voice so deep it seemed to rumble forth from the earth itself.

"No one," young Simba said softly. "But Mighty Mouse stayed there for me, although he was scared and he never came into me again after that. He didn't work anymore."

"Mighty Mouse," Chutney roared, "what did you mean when you said 'except'?"

"Except when very scared," answered the defeated mouse.

"Then what?"

"Mustn't tell."

"Mighty Mouse? Keep a secret?"

"An old house with a funny double porch in front," recited the mouse with something of his old aplomb.

Ronna's eyes snapped open.

"Forget the house," Chutney said. "We're not

interested right now in touring your old home-
town of Walnut Creek, California."

Ronna's eyes snapped shut again.

"What we want to know is if there was anyone
else besides you and Simba on the playground
with Eddie and his friends that day."

Another long pause. Finally the mouse said,
"No, not that day."

"Not that day? Go forward. Slowly. The next
day?"

"No," young Simba answered.

"Where's Mighty Mouse?"

"Gone," young Simba answered sadly.

"And the next day?"

"The same."

"The day after that?"

"The same."

"The year after that?"

"The same." The loneliness in young Simba's
voice was wrenching.

"Let me get this straight," Chutney said gently.
"Mighty Mouse never came back after that time
with Eddie on the playground?"

"Mighty Mouse never came back." Simba's
voice was deeper now.

"And there was no one else? Just Simba?"

"That's right." Simba's voice was almost normal now.

"How old are you now?"

"Twenty-one," answered the Simba they all
knew.

Chutney turned to the rest of the group. "How
old is he now? Anybody know?"

"Twenty-two," Ronna answered.

"Good enough," Chutney concluded, turning to Piper. "I concur with the distinguished Dr. Poppy's brilliant diagnosis," he said in obvious support of Poppy. "Simba didn't know about Mighty Mouse, and Mighty Mouse didn't even know about Simba, which equals a clear cut case of the exceedingly uncommon condition known as multiple personality. What's even weirder, though, is that a subsequent trauma, the unspeakable incident with Eddie on the playground, apparently cured the condition. I therefore conclude that the time has come to put the question of Simba's first day of kindergarten to rest and return to Ronna and the question of where our shelter for the night is. While it is true that I'm hallucinating like a crazy person, I do believe that storm gathering over the water has some basis in reality."

They all stood amidst a dizzying cacophony of sound distortion, then headed for the bus like a pack of obedient scouts.

Piper held back, despite the drug's suggestibility, and stood for a moment alone on the beach watching Simba. Turning, she confronted the storm. Too easy, she told herself before joining the others.

The bus wouldn't start.

Ursula, of all people, was at the wheel. When Bell slammed the hood open with imperious dispatch, Ronna and Poppy jumped like startled rabbits.

Piper smiled wanly. She wasn't the only one suffering from sound distortions.

"Again, sweetheart," Bell called to Ursula.

Ursula ground away at the starter; Midas and Chutney ground their teeth. Bell tore open the carburetor. When he tossed the cover on the asphalt, where it rattled like a top before settling, everyone but Simba covered their ears, and Piper had to turn away.

The engine turned over, scattering the crowd, then cut out.

"It's the gas. You got water in the lines."

Who the hell was that, Piper thought. Distortions aside, she figured she knew everyone's voice.

"Are you sure," Bell asked.

Piper turned back in time to see the hitchhiker she'd kidded Bell about earlier take a screwdriver out of a tool kit in his pack. Bell looked at the dime he'd been using as a screwdriver and put it back in his pocket.

"You gotta have the tools if you wanna do the job," the hitchhiker said.

Bell picked up the rhythm, beating it out on the fender, then breaking into song. "You gotta have the tools if you wanna do the job." The hitchhiker grinned and went to work on the carburetor. Piper joined Bell, laughing her way through the next repetition of the song's only words. It all sounded so strange and took forever.

Piper was happy again, her determination not to let anything get her down just renewing itself, when she noticed Simba. He was backing away from the group, looking at the hitchhiker in horror.

Ursula stormed out of the bus to confront Bell, hands on hips. "Stop that fucking noise now," she hissed.

"Something wrong?" the hitchhiker asked.

Ursula slithered over to him. "Hey, I like a man who's well prepared. What else you got in that pack? Got any coke?"

"Coke? Well, yeah, but—".

"What's your sign?" Poppy interrupted brightly.

"Oh, I know that," the hitchhiker replied, obviously a little at sea amidst them all. "Aquarius, the water bearer."

"You can carry my jugs anytime," Ursula slipped in. "You said you had some coke but...?"

"It's a little warm," the hitchhiker said, digging a bottle out of his pack.

Ursula screeched in horror, knocking the bottle he held out to her out of his hand. It clattered across the pavement until Midas snatched it up, staring at the riot of carbonated bubbles in unabashed fascination.

"Cocaine, you idiot!" Ursula snapped at the hitchhiker.

"I don't smoke or drink, and I never did drugs," he said. "I'm as straight as a Joe Namath pass."

Ursula was shaking. "That's all we need. A goddamn stupid-ass drug virgin."

"Maybe it *is* all we need," Ronna said, sud-

denly appearing at the hitchhiker's side. "This
stuff's scary."

"What stuff?" the hitchhiker asked, returning
his attention to the carburetor.

"LSD," Ronna answered him. "We're all tripping except—"

"Really?" the hitchhiker interrupted, resting
his elbow on the air filter for a moment so he
could grin up at her. "Is that what everybody's
doing these days? I'm really out of it."

Piper saw Simba's eyes close, but didn't understand why. He was hanging back, out of the
hitchhiker's line of vision.

Midas, however, sauntered over to the hitchhiker as if on cue. "Yeah, man, everybody does
acid all the time. Welcome to the counter-
culture."

"Counter-culture?"

Midas puffed himself up. "Revolution, man. A
break from everything that came before."

"Why give up everything that came before?"
The hitchhiker didn't sound judgmental, just curious. He was out of it all right, but Piper liked
his open smile.

By contrast Midas, who was struggling to look
cool despite his apparent inability to think of an
answer, looked ridiculous. Piper started to giggle.
Chutney came to his aid.

"Because that is always the way to a higher
consciousness," Chutney said, putting a hand on
Midas' shoulder.

"Though drugs?" the hitchhiker asked.

"What is this? Twenty fucking questions?" Ursula asked. "Drugs are where it's at, numb nuts. Behold," she continued with a flourish of the hand that introduced the whole group of them. "The new family. Far fucking cry from Mama and Papa and Baby Bear. Step a-goddamn-side, Donna Reed."

Poppy stepped forward, a bright-eyed student about to recite. "To achieve this peak of awareness, one has to strip oneself of worldly things and use drugs to release the mind from the shackles of this total materialistic society. Otherwise it's an ugly trap. Without drugs we could never find peace and awareness."

"Yeah," Ursula said, actually agreeing. "Give peace a chance, dig?" She gave the hitchhiker a vicious jab in the ribs.

"I thought drugs could twist you out of shape," the hitchhiker said.

"No way," Ursula answered. "It's like everything else. You've got to know what you're doing."

Meanwhile Ursula started to shake again.

"Which reminds me," the hitchhiker said as he went back to work on the engine.

Bell surged up the bus stairs, landing in the driver's seat with a grin. "This cat has got it licked," he called out the window.

"Start it up. I think I got it."

Bell cranked. The engine ground for a few seconds, then caught, scattering the group.

"Gun it," the hitchhiker instructed.

Bell did, and everyone else covered their ears.

"Heavy foot."

Bell poured it on. Everyone but Simba ground the heels of their hands into their ears.

"That's it," the hitchhiker said. "She just passed some water."

Bell kept it up a little longer, then let it idle. The others peeled their hands off their ears and started to smile. Bell was beaming. "Purrs like a sweet little kitten," he said.

"Lots of old gas tanks accumulate water," the hitchhiker explained.

"Old," Ursula echoed, shaking violently. "Everything's old, grey, burnt-out. The whole world's nothing but an old, degenerate—"

"Stop your bitching," Piper interrupted. "You'll bring us all down."

"And besides," Chutney added, "there's dignity in age."

"Speaking of which," the hitchhiker said, looking down the road.

"Which do you seek?" Chutney inquired, slapping a friendly hand on the hitchhiker's shoulder. "Dignity or age? Or are you hoping, perhaps, for dignity sans age?"

"Age. A house. It's right up the road."

"We'll give you a ride," Chutney said quickly, looking to the others for expressions of agreement Piper could barely decipher beneath the hallucinations. "It's the very least we can do to repay you."

"Certainly is," Ronna confirmed with a warm smile. "Name's Ronna. What's yours?"

"Roscoe," the hitchhiker said.

"Nice to meet you," Ronna said, shaking the

dirty hand Roscoe hesitated to give her with such enthusiasm that even Piper, who never thought of jealousy, found herself looking around for Simba.

She spotted him in the back of the bus, apparently hiding out. "Dying," she'd heard him start to say, referring to the last time he'd seen Mushroom. So who had done the killing? Piper found herself walking toward the back of the bus, eyes on Simba.

At the very back, beneath the tailpipe was a large puddle of what must have been the water the hitchhiker said had passed through the engine. Was it the hallucinations, or was it really such a thick, reddish brown? Piper stooped and touched the puddle with a finger she then held to her nose. In a temporary cessation of the hallucinations, Piper experienced a moment of absolute clarity. It was the smell the bus acquired the night Josephine disappeared. Sticky. Absently, she wiped her hand on her workshirt. It was stained already and also brown. Bloodstains.

Piper looked up at the bus, then at the backside of Simba. She could just make out the leather thong around his neck from which, she knew, hung the antique dagger. Hadn't Simba been alone with Josephine that night? Had Josephine also been dying? A shudder passed through Piper. She felt a warm hand that gave her back a reassuring rub and looked around to discover Ronna at her side.

"You okay, Piper?" Ronna's eyes were true blue, open as a clear sky.

"Use your mind, Ronna, not your heart," Piper said.

Ronna smiled weakly. "I know. It's what I must learn from you, and I have been trying. I can change. What is it?"

"Simba."

Ronna bowed her head. "He's been so good to me. You tell me, Piper. Isn't there some place for emotion here?"

Piper, looking at Simba, felt something she had hardly experienced—an anguished tug at her heart. "Yes," she conceded.

"Remember the day we started this trek?" Ronna's voice was as soft as a breeze. "The day after my father raped and beat me?"

The hallucinations were back along with the intensity. Piper closed her eyes against the strength of her own feelings. "Yes," she said.

"Simba knew exactly where not to touch, what was sore, even if it was a part of me hidden by clothing. It was amazing."

"Perhaps," Piper mused. She opened her eyes. "Perhaps not."

"Meaning?"

"Meaning I can think of a not-very-pretty reason why Simba knew exactly where you had been hurt," Piper said.

Ronna stared.

Piper closed her eyes again, for just a moment. It was like telling a little kid there's no Santa Claus. "I was outside the bus myself or in town with Bell most of that first day. I only heard about it all very indirectly. You have to do the thinking, Ronna. Let's see if you can change."

"Watch me," Ronna said. Gone was the soft voice. Swarms of hallucinations failed to conceal the deep furrow in her brow.

"Consider everything Simba said," Piper suggested.

"No," Ronna said. "Nothing Simba said—at least not while I was conscious—was the key that day. It was Mushroom."

"Mushroom?"

"When we found her in the box and Simba asked what she was doing there. She said she was floating through the last of the sunlight when she heard the gravel crunch as this bus pulled into the driveway. Simba's the one who came in the bus."

"So?" Piper was lost, wondering if poor Ronna was, too.

"So the radio said forensic experts estimated the gangly boy's murder took place just before sundown. When my father hit me, presumably knocking me out, it was daylight. When I woke up in Simba's arms it was night. In between those times I had one memory of the gangly boy trying to get me away from somebody else."

Piper's mental feet landed squarely on the ground. "What time of day?"

Ronna's clear eyes didn't waver. "Just before sundown."

"Meaning there is a good chance that either Simba was there to overhear a scene which could not, I am sure, have escaped his attention or . . ."

"I was raped and beaten by . . ." Unbelievably, a smile flickered across Ronna's face. "Mighty Mouse?"

Piper fought to suppress a giggle, telling herself that it wasn't funny, then saw Ronna doing the same, and they both cracked up.

Suddenly Ronna sobered.

"What is it?" Piper asked.

"The gangly boy." Ronna's laughter had turned to tears.

"The guy Josephine was with," Piper added softly. "The guy Poppy was with . . . what did he call himself?"

"Siddhartha," Ronna whispered.

"A hideous, obnoxious man," Piper said, feeling tears on her own cheeks. "But it doesn't matter. He should have been allowed to continue his life, such as it was."

Ronna nodded. "I just remembered something more. Something that came out much later." She struggled to continue.

Piper rubbed Ronna's back.

Ronna took a deep, shuddering breath and stopped crying. "It was the first night we had sex." Ronna trembled. "Or at least what I thought was the first night we had sex."

"And?" Piper had trembled with Ronna and wanted to get them both away from that last thought.

"I felt bad about the fact that he'd never seen my face without all the bruises and stuff, but when I said so he stiffened. Odd reaction. Odder still when he then proceeded to supply a perfect

description of what I looked like normally."
Ronna fell silent.

Piper let her hallucinations wash over the puddle of old blood and the stains on her workshirt.

"Remember the day he got the speeding ticket?" Ronna asked.

Piper nodded.

"He even mentioned it that day, that he'd hallucinated what I looked like, thinking it was an acid flashback, but it wasn't at all psychedelic."

Piper mused. "An errant, Mighty Mouse memory?"

"A memory that slipped through one of Mushroom's walls. A memory not consciously his."

"Mighty Mouse's?" Piper asked.

"Mighty Mouse never came back."

"Then whose?" Piper demanded.

"I don't know. Maybe..."

"Maybe whose?" Piper persisted.

"Maybe Luke's."

Being in a patrol car again was swell.

Being in the company of two card-carrying members of the Conservative Party whose hate for anything pinko made Parsons himself appear liberal was, as he'd heard some young hoodlum back in Berkeley say, "boss and a half."

The fact that these two young officers were long on violence and short on the ability to sort out for themselves when and where to act was, from Parsons point of view, pure heaven.

Two banana-colored hearses rolled past them. A girl wrapped in nothing but a tattered Amer-

Twisted

ican flag leaned out the window of one. Her hair was long, but not as long as the hair of the bearded driver.

"Fucking Festival," the officer at the wheel squawked. His name was Fred. His voice was high-pitched and annoying, and he could never sit still. Actually, Parsons hated him.

"Fred, you're the son I never had," Parsons said, almost—he was so proud of himself—tearful. "The son I wish I'd had."

Parsons caught Fred's watery blue eyes with his sincere look. He was reminded of the first time he hooked a fish. The second cop, Mike, with his deliberate brown eyes and quiet—not to mention genuine—sincerity, was less neurotic.

"I hate hippies," Mike said decisively. "Glad you brought us in on this, Parsons. A lot of strange things happen at rock concerts. The last thing Nyland Heights needs right now is a pack of hippie ax murderers."

"I been feeling out law enforcement officials all the way across this country," Parsons lied. "Didn't find the kind of men I knew I could count on to help me with this thing until I met up with the two of you."

"You can count on us, buddy," Fred said, watery blue eyes moister still. "Can't think of a single thing on God's green earth I'd rather do than bust a bus load of no-account hippies. Hell, I just hope they put up a fight so we can have a little fun with them first."

"Won't let you down," was Mike's quiet, decisive comment.

"You're good men," Parsons said before drifting off into his own thoughts of Nyland Heights. A two-cop town. Neither officer over 25. Didn't find the kind of idiots I knew I could count on to do the dirty work and be green enough to be maneuvered out of the way when the time comes to take the credit, until I met up with the two of you.

The bus rolled by.

"Thar' she blows," Parsons said.

"Wheeee Haaa!" Fred stomped on the gas, squealed out onto the road and hit the siren. The way he was dancing around on the seat Parsons figured he was either in a lot worse shape psychologically than Parsons had dared to hope or he needed to go to the bathroom real bad.

Mike snapped the shotgun out of its holder on the dashboard without a moment's hesitation. Parsons studied the tight fingers he wrapped around the gun and the deep furrow between his brown eyes. Nothing like a trigger-happy partner to reduce the risks while neatly disqualifying himself from later collecting the rewards.

This was going to be fun.

Ahead of them the bus was weaving all over the road, more like they'd freaked the freaks out rather than they were trying to escape. Finally it lumbered off onto the shoulder like a beached whale.

Fred was the first out of the patrol car, revolver drawn. Mike appeared at his side with the shotgun. Parsons followed.

Simba was the first out of the bus, the stag

protecting the herd. A wide-eyed Chutney followed.

For a moment, while studying Chutney, Parsons almost felt something for another person, but he snapped out of it. "You're all under arrest," he announced quickly. "The arresting officer is Edgar E. Parsons."

"What for?" demanded the mousy owner of the bus.

Fred backhanded him, then looked back at Parsons with a grin and a wink. "None of your business," he said.

The electric green in Simba's eyes sparkled, and a fist twitched, but he held his ground like some dangerous animal that knew its time would come.

"Police officers aren't supposed to do things like that," said the Vancouver runaway whose boyfriend had been butchered. Her expression of disbelief suggested that the sickos were the police.

"Oh yeah?" Fred squawked before swatting her rear. "I hear hippie girls give it away. How many guys have scored off you, sweet cheeks? Under twenty and you're probably all floppy inside."

Still at Fred's side Mike started to laugh, then caught himself. His laugh had a creaky sound, like something he kept in the attic and rarely used. He leveled his shotgun at the group, swinging it from side to side, lingering when he caught the most fearful reactions. "Hands on your heads," he barked. "Now."

Ronna stepped out of the bus. Parsons flinched;

he hadn't quite worked through this one. She spotted him immediately.

"What are you doing, Dad?" Ronna asked. Her calm made him furious.

Mike and Fred wheeled on him. Parsons saw Ronna stare at the two younger officers in slack-jawed wonder, but not with the fear she should be feeling. Closing her eyes, she looked like she was meditating on some commie Eastern religion. When she looked up at Mike again her expression turned to joy.

"Rupp," Ronna called out to Mike, smiling and holding out her hand as if she expected it to be kissed.

Simba wheeled, a lover's jealousy in his eye.

Parsons laughed—inside, of course. Spaced-out hippie chick mistakes young officer who obviously has never seen her before for past lover, then claims older officer in background is father. Getting through the initial arrest without the revelation of their relationship was not going to be a problem.

It was then that Parsons noticed that the bus had been replaced by a horse-drawn wagon. He shook his head. The wagon disappeared, and the bus reappeared in its place.

What the fuck?

"Look, lady..." a thoroughly confused Mike was saying to Ronna. "I'm an officer of the law. My name is—"

"Rupp Hanlon," Ronna interrupted. "And I am Rachel Carnes. Soon to be your wife." She did some kind of a curtsy that looked like something out of the last century.

The cocaine addict leaned against the bus, shivered, then closed her eyes.

"You said you'd have the wagons hitched before sunup," Ronna was saying to Mike. "That my sister, Lucia, and I should meet you here."

Mike looked utterly bewildered. At last he spoke. "I hate hippies," he said again with quiet deliberation.

Parsons snickered, beating his heel into the dirt a few times for emphasis. Funny, he'd thought he was standing on pavement.

"Rupp," Ronna pleaded, giving Parsons a quick look that was anything but calm. "Please," she pleaded with Mike. "Close your eyes. Let your mind go. Look inside."

Chutney stared at Ronna. Parsons watched approvingly as a frown spread over Chutney's face.

The cocaine addict slumped against the bus, as if the bitch thought so little of being arrested that she was about to go to sleep. Parsons caught Fred's eye and jerked his head in her direction. The officer's eyes lit up. Fred winked back at Parsons, then danced over to Ursula with a grin and yanked her away from the bus.

Parsons wondered if he might have to reevaluate his hatred for Fred.

Ursula's eyes snapped open and sparkled. She smiled. "Jesse?" she asked, voice throbbing with emotion.

Parsons's head started to throb.

Fred frowned.

"You don't remember your own sweetheart, Lucia?" Ursula purred. "Or my sister Rachel?" she added, touching Ronna with affection.

Rachel...Lucia...Parsons felt dizzy.

"Jesse Hanlon!" Ursula protested. "Has all you promised in the sand come to naught? You were to join us outside Nyland Heights with the rest of the horses. We were to be in Hempstead by noon."

Horses...Nyland Heights...The Hanlon boys in the sand dunes...The hand Parsons put to his aching head shook violently, but he caught sight of Mike looking at him and tried to wink at him.

Mike frowned at Parsons, then arched an eyebrow at Fred, who also frowned at Parsons.

Ronna, whose face had been hidden while Ursula gave her a hug, turned back to the two young officers. "Look inside yourselves, both of you," Ronna begged with another fearful glance toward Parsons. "Do you think it is just by chance that we have all met again?"

Parsons figured neither of these boys would be any good at any looking-inside-yourself shit.

"Oh, Rachel, will it work?" Ursula asked Ronna.

Rachel? Parsons stumbled in the dirt of the road. He could have sworn he heard a horse whinnying close by.

"The crossroads!" Ronna yelled. "Don't you remember, Rupp? Lucia and I were to meet you at the crossroads."

A vision of the dusty intersection of two dirt roads hit Parsons like a thunderclap. He found himself sitting in the dirt of one of them. His eyes met Chutney's. "Eb," he said simply.

Chutney stared back at him for a long time. Finally he said, "Father?"

And it happened. The wagon replaced the bus again. Everyone's clothing changed. Desperately Parsons looked away from Chutney only to be caught by the hypnotic blue of Simba's eyes. Simba was wearing a spanking-new ancient sailor's suit and carrying a harpoon.

"Luke!" Parsons said. They were all there, all his children. Sweet Portia. Son Luke who had run away to sea. The two who had turned into witches, Lucia and Rachel. And ever-faithful, hard-working Eb. Joshua Carnes smiled up at his eldest son.

"Mike, this dude ain't never no how gonna' get the county seat to award us those raises he promised."

Jesse Hanlon! Yes, there were others there. Jesse's equally poor tenant farmer brother, Rupp. Zak, the hired hand. Alex, the slave. Joshua Carnes got to his feet.

"You're right, Fred," Rupp said in answer to his brother.

"Just look at him, Mike," Jesse said, staring at Joshua Carnes. "Look at his face. It doesn't even look like the same face anymore."

Joshua Carnes started toward them, knowing once again that he must do the thing that was right.

"You're right, Fred," Rupp said again.

"Cracked, he did," Jesse babbled nervously.

"Strain of the investigation," Rupp added.

"We got to get this sorry bastard outta' here," Jesse said, "before he discredits the fine name of the law."

Joshua Carnes hated the Hanlons, but beyond them was someone he hated more than anyone—his daughter Rachel.

"What'll we do with him?" Rupp asked Jesse.

"Protective custody. Lock the sucker up till we can get rid of him. Return him to his own jurisdiction while we take care of these no-account hippies ourselves."

Joshua Carnes found he had no ax, but he had something else.

"It'll ruin his career," Rupp pointed out. The Hanlons turned to each other for a moment, a moment when they no longer watched Joshua Carnes.

Joshua Carnes slipped the something else behind his right leg. He took another step toward Rachel, but suddenly his runaway son Luke was herding all but the Hanlons back toward the wagon.

"Bastard's career deserves to be ruined," Jesse finally answered.

The Hanlons turned back toward Joshua Carnes.

"The hippies?" Rupp asked.

"Of no account," Jesse answered. "They're crazy, but at least they don't represent the law."

"Let 'em go?" Rupp asked.

"For now," Jesse replied, dancing nervously toward Joshua Carnes.

Joshua Carnes heard a loud, unnatural sound he'd never heard before. He closed his eyes against it. When he opened them again, no one was left but the Hanlons.

Jesse winked at Mike and started toward Joshua Carnes.

"Harmless," Rupp declared.

"I know," Jesse said. "I always treat a fellow police officer with respect. God knows nobody else does."

Rachel. Where was Rachel? Joshua Carnes looked up the road and saw a strange thing. The dirt had been replaced by something hard and black with orange lines down the middle. A huge purple carriage with smoke coming out the back but no horses was moving away from them at a totally unnatural speed. Rachel's witchcraft?

The Hanlons were coming at them, but it appeared from their matching uniforms that they had joined some kind of militia.

It was getting confusing again.

Joshua Carnes shook his head. Dreams, weird dreams . . . Parsons pulled himself together.

The two young officers were shaking their heads at him, condescendingly.

Parsons whipped out the something else Joshua Carnes had hidden behind his right leg. It was Parsons's gun.

Chapter 12

In her hands is a basket filled with treasure—
beach grass, shells and driftwood, all lovingly
collected. But by her side is the greatest treasure
of all, the man who loves her.

He has gentle brown eyes with a wholesome
sheen and brown hair that blows freely in the
breeze off the flax pond. His strong shoulders are
framed by a wooden bridge, connecting the sand
pit to the back of her father's property but seeming now to symbolize her imminent escape from
that same property.

Suddenly shy, she looks down at her own
hands. Horrible—as rough, pink and burnt as
Mommy's. But that will be over soon. She looks
up. The sun is beginning to set.

"I'll join you outside of Nyland Heights with

the rest of the horses," his brother Jesse says, clinging excitedly to her sister Lucia. "We'll be in Hempstead by noon."

"We'll be on the ferry by seven o'clock and on the New Jersey side by midnight," Rupp says, his breath warming her cheek.

"Uncle Matthew is a preacher," Jesse says. "He'll perform the double wedding."

Through the gently moving golden grass she sees Jesse's cheeks flush as Lucia snuggles closer. "Tomorrow..." she whispers, turning back to herself and Rupp. Something inside her she thought was long dead suddenly takes wing and soars. She trembles.

"It hasn't come too soon," Lucia calls over to her. "Daddy and the overwork would have killed us, too."

If only Mommy hadn't died. Then they could have brought Mommy, too.

Jesse and Lucia kiss in parting.

"See you at sunup," Jesse says.

Rupp brings her attention back to him by wrapping his arms about her. He says nothing, but his brown eyes glow. His kiss is soft. As they draw apart she feels his muscles spasm, drawing her back.

"They won't suspect?" Rupp asks.

"No," she says and smiles. She and Lucia go.

The trees are pointed like Christmas trees, twisting strangely. A twig snaps. There is a shape that doesn't belong, a shape that moves and is more twisted than the trees themselves.

"Bell?" Ronna opened her eyes on the present; Chutney was at the wheel.

Ronna turned around in her seat. Bell stood at the back of the bus, muscles straining to hold apart two amplifiers so he could see out the rear window. Piper, jaw set, maintained an awkward stance at his side. Piper's knuckles, straining to hold the equipment over Bell's head steady against the motion of the bus, were white.

"Bell!" Chutney called again.

"What? Nothing, man, I swear on my grand-mother's—"

"Are you sure?" Chutney interrupted. "I can't see shit in these mirrors. They are positively en-crusted with hallucinations."

"If I snap my eyes, man," Bell started. "If I snap my eyes shut just right, then open 'em up and try real hard I can see for a coupla moments without the hallucinations getting in the way. No cops on our tail. Really!"

"Ronna?" Midas asked, seated behind her.

"Yes?"

"Ronna, I was wondering if . . . well, I mean . . ."

Ronna was wondering why Simba didn't in-terrupt to urge Midas to get to the point.

"I mean, if you don't mind my asking, was that older police officer really your father?"

Ronna shuddered. "Yes."

Chutney interrupted the hush that followed. "Simba?" he asked. "Right side?"

Ronna faced forward again, then looked to her right. Simba occupied the window seat beside her, but he wasn't looking out the window. Bizarre as it was, considering their size differential, he appeared to be hiding behind her. From what? Ronna considered the angle at which he had positioned himself. Then she looked in the opposite direction to find Roscoe, the hitchhiking auto mechanic, occupying the seat across the aisle and up one from theirs.

"Simba," Chutney called again.

"Nutha'," Simba muttered unintelligibly.

"What?" Chutney asked.

Roscoe turned around in his seat.

"Nothing," Simba yelled, sitting up so that he was visible to all.

Chutney made a left into an overgrown, circular driveway. "Is this what you wanted?" He cocked a burly brow at Roscoe, the hitchhiking auto mechanic.

Roscoe was staring at Simba, perplexed.

"This house?" Chutney persisted, but he still didn't get an answer.

"Hey, man, don't you remember me?" Roscoe asked Simba. "Pennsylvania? Night I was competing with some female hitchhiker further down the road for a ride?"

Simba turned ashen. Why? Mushroom? Hitchhiking?

"Here I was barking out directions and you're the one who told me how to find this house to begin with," Roscoe said.

House?

It was Simba's turn to look perplexed. "I told you about this house?"

"Affirmative," Roscoe said. "Don't you remember? I told you I was looking for adventure and asked you where you were headed. Your voice got strange and you told me about this house."

What house?

Ronna staggered out of her seat. She thought the bus was stopped but couldn't be sure due to the incessant rhythm of the hallucinations. She leaned over Poppy's seat on the opposite side of the bus, giving the child a reassuring smile she was far from feeling, and looked out the other side of the bus.

There it was.

"The house. That's it!" Ronna screamed, backing towards Simba. Something hit her head, and the bus spun around her, sickening. She felt herself swoon and then came darkness. She figured she'd fainted into Simba's arms again, forever the hackneyed gothic heroine.

That was even more sickening.

She was in a dream, on the beach at Santa Monica with her pail and shovel. Her mother was in the yellow cotton bathing suit with the elasticized gathering up the back. The beach was crowded. Ronna, giggling, ran along the edge of the water. She ran and ran, then she turned back to see Mommy, to see if Mommy was giggling, too.

Mommy wasn't there.

The beach was empty. Ronna, crying, ran along the edge of the water. She ran and ran, then she turned back to see if it was getting closer.

It was.

Ronna could never really see it and had no idea

what it was, but it had been chasing her in her dreams since early childhood. The terror she felt at the thought of it catching her was unimaginable. It was that terrifying thought that always propelled her out of her dream. Once awake it was always the same. For the rest of the night she would lie alone in her room sweating, her heart threatening to pound its way out of her chest.

In this dream she was running as fast as she possibly could, and it was getting even closer again. Suddenly a new feeling emerged; her running was sickening. The feeling that her running was sickening was only the teeniest hair's breath stronger than the terror she felt at the thought of it catching her, but that was enough.

She stopped running. Slowly, ever so slowly, she turned to face it, whatever it was. Dreaming or awake, it was the hardest thing she ever did.

Shaking, wild with fear, she strained to see what it was. All she could see was a formless grey cloud that, after a lifetime of running, finally caught up with her. There was a hideous moment as it engulfed her, then, like a night mist burnt away by the light of day, it simply disappeared.

It was nothing. It had never been anything more than nothing. It was only fear.

She stood alone, in an absolute void of nothingness, and laughed.

"Ronna!"

She opened her eyes again, this time to see Simba hovering over her, tucking her Mickey Mouse rug around her.

She tossed the old rug aside and got to her feet.

"Careful," Simba cautioned. "You bumped your head against my chin and passed out. Are you sure you're okay?"

"I think I just grew up," Ronna announced.

"You what?"

"Never mind," Ronna said, turning to go.

"Where are you going?" Simba asked.

"I want to see the house," Ronna said matter-of-factly.

"Don't you want to wait for the others?" Simba asked.

"No," responded a tranquil Ronna. "I need to be alone for awhile. I need to think. After I see the house, I'm going for a walk."

"Alone?" Simba asked.

"Alone," Ronna answered.

"In the middle of a thunderstorm?"

"I won't melt, since I'm not a witch," Ronna answered.

At that Simba jerked sideways, as if he were a puppet controlled by some other force.

"With your father in the neighborhood?" Simba asked.

Ronna shuddered a little at that but replied evenly enough. "He's less likely to find me if I'm off on my own, but there's something I have to tell you before I go."

"What?"

"I figured it out the day after Mushroom kept us up all night exploring past lives. I should have told you right away. Simba, I know you haven't experienced the past lives, but you must believe me. Josephine isn't the killer. It's my father."

"Your father? No, Ronna, it's—" Simba suddenly stopped making noise although his mouth continued moving as if he wanted to continue speaking.

Ronna jumped in, taking full advantage of the opportunity. "No, Simba, it's not Josephine. You saw how crazy my father is. Think about it. And, until I get back, at least warn the others by letting them know that's what I think.

The fear was in Simba's eyes. Ronna jumped out of the bus without him.

"Ronna?"

Vulnerability was in his voice and she turned back. Like a mist burnt away by daylight, the hallucinations cleared. There had never been anything much to them anyway. Ronna was able to look deeply into Simba's eyes and saw anguish churning in them. He opened his mouth to speak, then stopped.

"I do love you," Ronna said, but the moment the words left her mouth she wondered if they were true. Oddly, the old adage about how you can never go home again followed on the heels of this thought. Next, sorrow brushed by with the chilling realization that she no longer wanted comfort, Simba's or anyone else's.

Simba opened his mouth to speak, then stopped again.

"You've been so good to me," Ronna said. "That realization will never leave me." Those words she knew were true. "But I can't stand the traveling, this lifestyle. Guess I get off on having a mailing address and paying taxes." She was trying to keep it light, but the anguish in Simba's eyes had increased tenfold.

"Ronna," he choked out, "there is something I have to tell you."

She put a finger to his lips, her feeling for him then so strong it warmed her, too. "No, Simba, don't." Wanting to spare him a speech she figured he'd later regret, she gave him a gentle kiss, turned and left him.

She faced the house, obviously deserted, then marched toward it.

Three chimneys. The odd double porch in the front. Shutters slamming against the house in the wind. But most of all the trees—the twisted trees. Ronna walked to the left of the house into an old, fallen-down arbor. As she came around the corner of the house she faced a marsh, then the flax pond.

Thunder cracked, but Ronna didn't jump. She stood her ground and let the sound, and the lightning she knew would follow, wash over her like the big waves at Santa Monica beach.

"Unoccupied. What a perfect setting. We could do *Wuthering Heights* here." Behind Ronna, Chutney's rich voice echoed the thunder, then lingered in her mind. Chutney, once her elder brother Eb. She closed her eyes.

A shape emerges that doesn't belong, a shape that moves and is more twisted than the trees themselves. Sister Lucia is at her side, looking to her to figure out what to do. Ronna—nay,

Rachel—must think clearly. She must decide what to do.

That shape again. The mist. Her family in the clearing, barely visible through the painfully distorted trees. All present and accounted for except Mommy—and Eb, her brother with the twisted shape.

"Rachel, do we have to go back tonight? Couldn't we just sleep under the trees?" Lucia asks. "No more Poppa preaching at us, no more crazy hunchbacked Eb having his fits and seeing his witches."

"They would wonder," Rachel hears herself saying softly, "and search. No, we must go back. Remember, only one more night." And Rachel looks away from the group in the clearing and forgets about the shape in the trees, to look back at the flax pond and remember Rupp with the warm brown eyes. There is a great sense of elation, of a freedom soon to come.

Simba, Mighty Mouse and Luke watched as Ronna left. The walls, separating the three, had crumbled. Simba ached for her. Mighty Mouse wanted to protect her. Luke wanted to kill her.

Simba ground his fists into his temples, as if his brain was a puss-filled pimple he could pop to rid himself of the other two. He sobbed silently and without tears.

If he didn't do any drugs, if he didn't try to escape, could he maintain control? If he could, for how long? He looked down at his body—

strong muscles, huge frame—and started to shake.

"Hey, dude, what's your thing?"

Bell's voice came from behind him—or rather them.

"I don't know for sure," Roscoe answered. "I think that's what I'm looking for. I do know I love to fix things."

"Like what?"

"Motors, TV's, sound equipment, anything. I like to find out what makes 'em tick."

"A regular Edison," Bell said brightly.

Simba, and the other two within him, suffered. If only he had the strength to turn away from these people he cared for, to throw himself into the angry waters of the sound and swim away from the shore until he could swim no more.

Instead he watched Roscoe sizing up Bell's red headband and elegant goatee. "I'm really out of it," Roscoe said. "All of you make me feel like a kid with dirty sneakers and a comic book who finds himself in the middle of the senior prom."

For the briefest moment Simba forgot his troubles and smiled at Roscoe's honesty.

Now Bell was checking out Roscoe's brown leather bomber jacket and straight jeans. "Where you been, boy?"

Roscoe reached into his dark blue back pack and extracted a folder with a plastic covered discharge in it. "Three years in the Corps, two in Nam."

"A Marine?" Bell said, his face an unintentional testament to how little he thought of the military.

"I paid my dues," Roscoe said quietly.

During the uncomfortable silence that followed Simba found himself hoping Luke would, at least, have no reason to harm Roscoe.

"What's the Gizmo Delicious?" Roscoe asked, the soul of good-natured curiosity as he pointed to the writing on the side of the bus.

"Anything you want," Piper said, appearing out of nowhere to snuggle up to Bell.

She glared at Simba.

"A lovely experience," Poppy said.

"It's our band," Bell explained. "The best, the most."

"The worst," Ursula said as she joined them.

"The Gizmo Delicious," Bell interrupted, "is the meaning of life."

"You know the meaning of life?" Roscoe asked.

"Not yet," Bell said, "but we're getting there."

Roscoe reminded Simba of a fraternity hopeful, wondering whether this was the frat house for him. "Through drugs?" Roscoe asked, studying them carefully.

"What other way is there?" Midas asked, arriving with a clumsy attempt at a swagger. "Have you ever done drugs?"

"No," Roscoe answered, "I'm not into drugs. Except maybe an aspirin once in a while."

"Then you can start your life from that moment on," Poppy said, starry-eyed.

"It gives you compassion," Piper said. "The

301

colors are brighter. Sounds are clearer, stronger and more urgent."

"Your thoughts are purer," Poppy said. "Next time we get some, you'll have to try it, too."

Simba, Mighty Mouse and Luke reached into Simba's back pocket. One capsule left. Must not have counted right. Shouldn't they offer it to Roscoe? They didn't.

"This is the way to live. Off the land," Chutney said. "The new group, the commune way of living, is a base camp on the edge of time, a tiny platform in a vast universe of possibilities."

"The starting point for mounting expeditions into the unknown," Piper chimed in.

"The starting point for just plain mounting," Bell added, pinching Piper's rear.

Luke stared at Alex, his father's slave. Alex was wearing funny clothes again, but Luke still knew who he was. Alex. Not that funny African name nobody could say right that was supposed to mean a damn nigger could be a prince. Luke had known his father's slave that time on the fields of salt when the nigger had had the effrontery not only to do the thing that was wrong, but to do it with a white woman.

For just a moment, Luke was confused. Something about doing the thing that was wrong with a black bitch in a field and looking up to see his sister Rachel in the distance looking on—but he pushed it aside.

The race had to be protected. The buck had to be put down. Luke had started, using his dagger, but this buck was strong. Years of breeding them that way for work in the fields. Luke would have to depend on a white man's superior intelligence to finish the job. He'd wait till the nigger was alone and get him from behind.

Simba opened his mouth to scream, like he'd opened his mouth to tell Ronna about Luke and warn her away, but again no sound came out.

Luke stopped him.

Simba stretched his mouth as far open as it would go, hoping just one of the other people would notice him, but no one did. Suddenly, he was so acutely aware of the antique dagger around his neck that it seemed to burn. His hand twitched, then jerked toward the dagger, but Simba controlled it. Inside himself he heard his own bitter laugh. You can silence me, you sick fucking bastard, he told Luke, but force me to act against my will? Unfucking likely. I've bucked authority and fought submission all my life. Nobody can make me do anything.

Mighty Mouse was outraged. Simba wasn't sure whether it was because of Luke's intentions or his own language.

Thunder clapped, and Ursula jumped. Simba reached out to comfort her.

"Don't touch me, you friggin' murderer," Ursula hissed.

"Hang in there, Ursula," Chutney said gently. "Simba's not here to hurt you. He's here to help."

Ursula was shaking, clawing at her stringy dark hair. "Nobody ever believes me," she screeched, then collapsed in a heap of tears and twitches.

Sue Hollister Barr

Roscoe bent at her side. "What's wrong?"

"Cocaine," a few said in unison.

"Listen, I need a ride into Manhattan." Ursula's voice was tightly controlled and supremely reasonable. She even managed to smile at Roscoe. "The rest of them are too stoned to drive, but you're straight. I really admire you for that, and I need your help."

Luke watched Roscoe's involuntary shudder of revulsion as he listened to Lucia's honeyed words. Roscoe was Roscoe; he knew him as no other, had never seen him before this funny time. His sister Lucia was a witch. The intensity of her need throbbed beneath the forced softness of her voice, clashing. It made Luke shudder, too.

Luke remembered the first time he'd woken up in this funny time. The first thing he saw was Lucia, although he didn't know it was her then. She was walking toward him through a doorway. The room was full of smoke and people dressed in funny clothes. Luke fell back against a wall, hurting the back of his head.

"Hey, Simba, what's happenin'? Smokin' too much weed?"

Luke didn't know who Simba was or what the man was talking about, so he ignored him. He looked around and sniffed the air. Half the people were smoking the most perfectly rolled cigarettes Luke had ever seen. The other half were smoking cigarettes that looked ordinary enough but smelled of something Luke had never smelled.

Lucia was getting closer. He stared at her.

"Oh, out to get laid? You picked the right bitch,

304

man. Ole Ursula'll put out for anybody. Here, just slip her some of this."

The man handed Luke a small, clear packet of white powder. Lucia spotted it immediately and closed the distance between them.

She was wearing trousers.

She laughed and took his hand.

"Ursula, meet Simba," the man said.

"Hi," Lucia said, pulling his hand toward the trousers. "Need any help with that coke?"

Luke knew it was wrong to touch a woman there, but he had never seen a woman in trousers. He could see her . . . He could see everything.

Simba reeled, amazed that—in addition to everything else—he wasn't experiencing Luke's hard on. Mighty Mouse tsked.

"You okay, man?" Chutney asked, pulling the two of them back to the present.

"Yeah," Simba lied. He couldn't take it anymore. He wanted out, anyway he could. His hand strayed to his back pocket.

Luke was thinking about the second time he'd woken up in this funny time. He'd recognized the black bitch right away and thought the people with the funny clothes were in his own time. The furniture was right, although it was awfully worn out.

"My harpoon," Luke called out, suddenly at peace, thinking of his days as a sailor.

He had liked the sea. It was peaceful and quiet, not evil.

Luke crossed over some badly worn oriental rugs to get to the harpoon, then frowned. It wasn't his after all. He'd never seen one so rusty.

"Forget it, man," said a voice at his side. "Too much of a hassle to carry, and what the fuck are you going to tell the heat if of they just happen to cruise by and see you carrying it? Stick to the small stuff. Here."

It was a huge, muscular buck, handing him a bag made of paper. Telling him, a white man, what to do. Lucia was there, laughing at him. In that moment he almost recognized her, but he was distracted by the black bitch from the field who he'd been looking at when he woke up this time.

The freed woman wasn't in trousers; she was in what had to be undergarments. The yellow part at the top was made of some strange material that stretched over her breasts like a second skin. Luke stared, then shifted his gaze to the part of her dark buttocks that wasn't covered by the orange bottom.

"Hey, man, whatcha' lookin' at?" the buck asked, shoving him. "You got your own." He turned to Lucia. "Ursula, baby, come on over here and give this boy a quick hand job so we can get on with this here robbery."

Lucia put a hand on the front of his trousers. It was then Luke recognized her.

"Witch!" he yelled, backing up.

Hurt flashed in his sister's eyes, like a spark seen for a moment before igniting the blaze of anger that followed. "Witch? When you met me last weekend you didn't think I was a witch."

"I did wrong," Luke said, in agony as he remembered her pulling his hand to those trousers she had on. "But that is because I did not know you for who you are."

The black bitch elbowed in. "Simba, you full a' shit. Leave it to some no-account man to ball a girl and then decide he's too damn good for her."

Lucia seemed to be struggling with herself. Finally she approached him cautiously. "Like, maybe it was the coke. I know I took a lot." Her hand shook as she reached out to touch him. "I'm sorry. I . . . I like you, Simba."

Luke backhanded her into a chest of drawers. "Be gone, Lucia! Never doing your share of the chores. Lazy, shiftless, good-for-nothing. You leave all the housework for Portia, your youngest sister, while you and Rachel try to be ladies."

"Fuck you," Lucia yelled.

The buck laughed.

The freed woman glared at the buck.

The buck laughed more and reached out to fondle the part of her buttocks Luke had been looking at. That bothered Luke.

"Now you gonna decide you're too damn good for me, Josephine?" the buck asked the freed woman.

The freed woman jerked away. She looked ready to kill them both. "Ursula, girl, let's get away from these sorry-ass bastards," she said, taking Lucia's arm. "Mushroom'll wander back in here leaving her lookout post again any minute and these two smart-asses didn't even spot the jewelry up front."

For the moment, Luke and the uppity buck were left alone.

It was then Luke spotted the ax.

It was then Simba returned to the present and found himself swallowing the remaining capsule of LSD.

Luke didn't stop him.

Luke went back to reliving his victories, the times he had done the thing that is right with the help of the ax—the buck, the gangly boy, Siddhartha, Josephine and Mushroom.

Simba started to scream.

Luke stopped him.

Simba turned, ran and found himself at the front door of the deserted house.

We must do as we did before.

Simba jerked and shuddered. For all the science fiction he'd read that explored the supposedly cozy quality of hearing another person's voice inside your brain, the reality felt like the ultimate act of rape.

It was the first time Luke had spoken directly to him.

"What's this 'we' shit, motherfucker," Simba answered under his breath. He held up his hand. "Go ahead, move it." The hand twitched, nothing more. "I told you I've fought submission all my life."

You have submitted already, said Luke inside his head.

"Jive turkey!"

To your own weakness, said Luke. You took the drug. All I have to do is wait.

308

"Oh, shit!" Simba cried, remembering, then trying the door to the house in an irrational attempt to get away.

Luke laughed. What you have fought all your life, Simba, is reality. Forever escaping all things, even yourself. Forever wanting something more. Well, you found it.

Simba could have cried, had Luke allowed him to make that much sound. Instead Simba leaned back and forced the door with a smashing blow of his shoulder. It creaked open three feet, while his shoulder screamed with pain.

"Dynamite!" Bell/Alex appeared next to him with a flashlight. "Let's get inside before it starts to rain."

Run, Simba opened his mouth to say. Take the others.

Luke stopped him. Although they brushed shoulders, Bell didn't see Simba's mouth moving frantically in the dark.

"The world's one big freak-out," yelled Ursula/-Lucia behind them. "We're all going to die."

"Ursula's a drag," Bell confided.

Simba struggled to speak again and failed.

"Gizmo Delicious?" Ursula questioned. "Gizmo Delirious! Purple is the color for pimps and pushers and Needle Park."

"Here, man." Bell pressed the flashlight into Simba's twitching hand. "I better go help Chutney hold onto her."

Simba banged his head against the door repeatedly.

The door gave, opening all the way.

Home, said Luke. Go on, boy. Go ahead in.

"You can't make me," Simba said.

Yet.

"Ever," Simba said. Hope clawed its way to the surface of his mind. "The other times were different. Then there were the walls. Now I'm stronger."

We'll see who's the strongest.

Chutney/Eb and Bell/Alex pushed past on their way into the house with Ursula/Lucia held between them.

Chutney handed Simba one of the Coleman gas lanterns he had. "Where to, Simba?"

Simba's head twitched toward a large room, the interior of which was not visible from his vantage point. "In there with the big stone fireplace," came out of his mouth.

"What stone fireplace?" Chutney asked as he entered the room, then stopped to stare at something within. His eyes met Simba's. "How did you know?"

The others piled past Simba into the house.

"It sure is a big mother," said Bell, once Alex the slave.

"Looks like a lot of fireplaces," said Midas, once Zak the hired hand.

"Methinks that is what we need," said Chutney, once Luke's brother Eb. "Heat, heat, heat, heat."

Thunder rumbled. Ursula/Lucia jumped, then shivered. "Like, I can feel it going right through me, man," she whined. "Please, I can't take this shit. I'm out of strength. I'm out of everything."

"Breathe deeply," Chutney said, his actor's voice projecting.

"Come on, baby," Bell purred. "You and me is gonna' walk."

"Keeping score?" Piper, once the town whore, asked Roscoe.

"Kind of," Roscoe answered.

Simba, shaking, followed the others into the large room. In the flickering half-light no one appeared to notice his condition.

In the flickering half-light he thought he was starting to see geometric shapes.

"Methinks that this is the way to live," Chutney/Eb said, making himself at home as he placed his small, leather-bound book of verse on the dusty mantle of the big stone fireplace. "Off the land. By your wits. What we need is wood, wood, wood, wood."

"This place gives me the fuckin' shivers," Ursula yelled. "We're getting outta' here. Go to the Festival. Maybe someone there'll have some—"

"That will be enough," Chutney said, coming to Bell's aid as Ursula tried to bolt. "You don't make the decisions in this family; Simba does."

"Simba's a killer," Ursula wailed.

I must do the thing that is right, shouted Luke inside Simba's head. You, Lucia, may be the first.

Simba felt his mouth open involuntarily. He assumed he was about to yawn until he felt the wind whistle through his vocal chords. "Wood," Luke said aloud. "What we need is wood."

"Agreed," Chutney said. "Let's get a fire going."

"I hope we can get it started," Midas whined. "My plants are cold."

"And I thought musicians just lay around picking and strumming all day," Roscoe said with a smile.

"The Gizmo Delicious is a pain in the ass," Ursula hollered.

"A little hollow, that," Chutney commented. "A little played out. I think she's getting tired."

"Sodomy," Bell said regally. "Now that is a pain in the ass."

"Not if you do it right," Piper told him with a grin.

Mighty Mouse tsked—aloud.

Chutney heard, turned, winked and gave Simba a good-natured pat on the back.

"I'm cold and hungry," Midas complained.

"Who ain't?" Bell said. "But it's better than being a hypocritical slave to the establishment."

"At least my bed was warm," Midas went on. "Mother always—"

"First it's warm beds," Chutney interrupted. "Then it's a swell house and a car that leaves the Joneses in the dust. Or for those who manage to delude themselves into thinking being possessed by one supposed possession is any hipper than being possessed by another—a bookstore. Either way you're hooked on a bad trip that is not you."

"A rolling stone gathers no moss?" Roscoe asked.

"Precisely," Chutney said.

"You sure get around," Roscoe said.

Poppy smiled brightly. "We move so fast I can't

remember the last state we were in."

"Try a state of shock," Ursula quipped.

Chutney and Bell exchanged a look.

"Methinks she's getting better," Chutney said to Bell, who nodded.

"Gonna' make it?" Chutney asked Ursula softly.

"I don't know," Ursula said. "Maybe...I guess."

"Good," Chutney said. "The next problem is wood."

"Out back," Luke said, sending a shudder up Simba's back that was as involuntary as his speech. "There's a pile of wood all cut and ready."

"You're kidding," Bell said.

"No," Luke said. " 'Tis near the big tree."

Piper gave him a sharp look.

" 'Tis?" Chutney repeated, good-naturedly.

A few of them laughed.

"That reminds me," Poppy said brightly. "What were you before, Roscoe?"

"Before?"

"In your other lives," Poppy explained.

"Lives?" Roscoe sounded really interested.

Simba stood perfectly still, scared to death, feeling himself breathe. In. Out. In. Out. Could he control it? Slow it down? Speed it up? He tried, succeeded, and breathed a sigh of relief.

"I was lots of things," Poppy/Portia was saying. "I was an Egyptian queen and a Roman aristocrat and a..."

Simba tuned her out. Every ounce of his concentration was focused on his right hand, which just happened to be resting against his right thigh. Slowly, he lifted his little finger off his thigh, moved it sideways, and put it back down on his thigh at a considerable distance from his other fingers. This done, he breathed another sigh of relief.

"Talk about your good times," Roscoe was saying. "I've missed a lot."

"That's what drugs can do for you," Poppy said. "Open up the past. The question is—does the past influence the present?"

Simba's little finger sprang back off his thigh, jerked sideways and was slammed back down next to his other fingers. Luke laughed inside, then said aloud, "The question is—which is stronger? The now or the then?"

"That is the question, isn't it, Simba?" Piper said, staring intently.

"I'm not too sure," Roscoe mused. "I've never tried any drugs."

"I don't go in for that 'past lives' crap myself," Chutney said in his very best New York accent. "Too spooky. Brings me down."

"I just like to keep life simple," Bell put in. "Work hard. Play hard. Love hard." He grinned at Piper.

"I certainly wouldn't want you to love soft." Piper answered him but her eyes never left Simba.

"However," Chutney continued, "opening up one's mind through the use of hallucinogens is a time-honored tradition. The Indians used mushrooms to get in touch with the great spirits, to expand their awareness, to mellow out."

"No wonder they lost the continent," Roscoe said.

Thunder rumbled again, closer, and everyone jumped.

"Funky storm," Bell said. "We'd better get some sleep."

"Chores first," Luke snapped. "Better get some wood."

"That's right," Chutney said. "We're so stoned on this acid we keep getting distracted talking."

"You heard the man," Roscoe said, very much the Marine. "I'll help you outside, then I'm going to check out the beach. Let's move."

Roscoe, Chutney, Bell and Midas piled out the door, leaving the women with Simba, Mighty Mouse and Luke.

Piper picked up a flashlight, a big, heavy one. "Simba?" she asked.

"Yeah?" Luke was proud of himself for remembering that word, one he'd heard several times in this funny time. He knew the town whore suspected. Never again would he use the word " 'tis."

"My flashlight," Lucia snapped at the whore. "Take another."

The whore put the flashlight down but left her hand near it. Lucia let herself fall back against a wall, then slid down it to sit in a corner.

"Like, wow, Ursula, are you okay?" Portia asked.

"What's the use of living," Lucia answered, "if you're going to die like that?"

"Like, wow, Ursula, I don't understand," Portia said, "but I'll do your cards for you if you'd like."

His witch sister Lucia looked mean. His sweet sister Portia backed away, coming close to him.

Luke wanted to put his arm around his sweet sister Portia and tell her what a good girl she was for doing all her chores and Lucia and Rachel's besides, but the town whore was still staring at him. He didn't want to give himself away yet.

"Far out, Simba," Portia said, tugging on his arm in her enthusiasm. "This looks like such a marvelous old house. So elegant. So formal."

Simba's right hand found the back of Portia's neck, then massaged her shoulder in a gesture of brotherly affection. All three occupants of Simba's body participated and approved.

Even the town whore loosened up. She studied him, then headed for the door with another, smaller flashlight.

"Like, where are you going, Piper?" Portia asked.

"To the bus to get a few things," the whore said.

"Like, groovy. I'll see you later then," Portia said.

The whore paused on the threshold to give Portia a last smile. "Yeah," she said, then left.

Simba's arm fell away from Portia's shoulder.

"Shall you be making supper soon?" Luke asked her.

Portia made a pretty, if strangely styled, curtsy and looked up with a smile. "I most certainly shall, kind sir," she said.

Lucia snickered.

Portia struck a pose. "I fear I lack the proper attire, though."

Lucia snickered louder.

Portia turned toward her. "To go with this house," she explained.

"No fuckin' knowin' what she'll do next," Lucia hissed before warming, despite herself, in the face of Portia's innocent smile. "It is therefore advisable, kind sir, that you absent yourself from this room, be it ever so temporarily. Otherwise the dumb bitch is liable to strip naked in front of you."

Luke left.

The last thing he wanted to do was a thing that was wrong. Outside darkness helped cloak the hallucinations Simba was determined not to see.

"Yet," Luke said.

"Ever," Simba said.

The problem was that Simba didn't know who was telling his legs to walk toward the bus. He experimented, trying a sudden giant step without enough forethought to warn anyone who might be listening in. The wind kicked up just then, pushing him back. Or was it the wind? Simba successfully stopped dead in his tracks, breathed a sigh of relief, then heard Luke laugh inside. Was Luke playing with him? Letting him stop? Thunder cracked. Simba jumped. Luke laughed again. The lightning shot across the sky, highlighting—

along with a myriad of twisted trees—torrents of hallucinations. Simba was shaking. Something else had been visible to his left in those brief seconds of illumination, something he desperately hoped no one else had noticed.

"This land is your land. This land is my land." Simba sang, squeezing his eyes shut in his efforts to block all thoughts and all memories of things just seen.

Simba's right hand sprang to the dagger around his throat. "But this hand is my hand," Luke said, his words raping Simba's vocal chords yet again.

"Funny," Simba conceded, then laughed a sickly laugh. What else was there to do?

"To answer the question you kept trying to hide—yes," Luke said. "I saw the town whore over to the left, staring up at the stars. Alone."

Simba's laughter turned to tears. He first had heard Piper yelling during sex in an apartment over his head just as his own thoughts got to be too heavy for him. She had shoved the curtains aside to lean out the window and rest her tits upon the sill.

A deathlike cold passed over Simba as he became aware of what he imagined to be an ever so subtle shift in direction. Was it the wind? Was it his imagination? Was it the roughness of the terrain? The thunder roared; the lightning flickered on and off like the bulb swinging overhead in some seedy hotel room where addicts shot up and died.

In its light he saw Piper, still contemplating

the sky with a cuddly look like she was about to break into giggles. Now she was dead ahead.

Simba's left hand yanked the leather thong over his neck, freeing the dagger in his right. He felt his strides lengthen.

Simba tried to jerk his foot to the side, changing directions again.

Luke only tripped slightly and kept going straight.

Simba tried to straighten his right hand, in order to drop the dagger.

Luke clutched the fingers tighter.

Sickeningly Simba realized it was hard enough to physically control anyone in the heat of passion, let alone one that's inside you. Were it possible, it was going to take some time to get the knack, more time than it was going to take Luke to close the distance between them and Piper.

There was only one thing left.

"Why?" Simba asked.

She knows, Luke answered silently. And besides, she killed Mother.

A sharp and painful feeling passed through them both, and Simba knew that whatever else Luke was he had been a son who loved his mother.

"How?" Simba demanded.

Rage passed through them both.

She rejected Father, Luke continued. He came home and . . .

"And what?" Simba prodded desperately.

"Never mind," Luke snapped aloud, reaching Piper just as the thunder rolled.

319

Piper, turning at the sound of Luke's voice in the flickering lightning, never looked softer or more vulnerable. Luke started to raise the dagger. Simba fought, converting the motion to a staccato battle of muscular twitchings. In the lightning's last flicker Simba saw that Piper, wide-eyed, had pressed the hand with the antique quartz ring to her chest. Suddenly, the dagger dropped out of his hand.

Mother's ring.

It was Luke's thought, slow and painful. Again the thunder rumbled and the lightning flickered. Piper had vanished. From somewhere inside Luke's pain came Simba's laugh.

"Laugh now at my weakness," Luke said aloud, "but do not forget the log in thine own eye."

Log in thine own eye? Simba struggled to remember Bible School. A speck in your neighbor's eye . . . Something about forgetting your own imperfections. Lightning flashed again amidst a blizzard of hallucinations.

"Simba?"

It was a voice outside himself. Midas stood right next to him. Simba remembered how Midas's voice had jumped octaves when Simba told him they were going to paint his bus purple.

"Simba, you were right about the wood out by the big tree, but now they all want me to carry my share, and I'm cold and hungry and Mother always says I have a bad back. And besides, I just dropped a piece right here on my toe and—"

"And I owe you one, Midas. I didn't forget," Simba said, feeling real warmth. Forgetting about Luke, he leaned over to pick up the piece of wood, just as the lightning flashed again.

Luke snatched the dagger off the ground instead and swung it upwards, deep into Midas's belly.

"Simba?" The lightning's last flicker revealed a wide-eyed Midas who peered up into Simba's eyes like a child struck by a loving parent for the very first time. Just as the light failed, Midas looked down in time to see a part of his intestine flop out through the hole in his gut.

"Mother!" Midas screamed in the dark.

There was a moment of silence, then Simba heard him fall heavily. Simba started to lean over to try and help Midas, then remembered what Luke had just done under similar circumstances.

Could Midas have died so soon? Or did he—it would be in character—just faint? Simba didn't know much about knife wounds, but he figured he needed help fast and ran for the house.

A fire raged in the big stone fireplace of the large room. A woman stood facing the fire, her back to him. She had on an old, floor-length dress.

Witch! Luke screamed within at the sight of her.

Who is she? Simba pondered, confused by the clothing, the light and the hallucinations.

We must do as we did before, Luke instructed.

It was then that Simba found himself looking down slowly to discover his hand still held the dagger. A thick droplet of blood jiggled at the end, then fell to the floor, beautiful amidst an intricate lacework of ruby hallucinations. Turning the blade sideways, he discovered a clump of something greyish white stuck there. Did it still pulse with some leftover life, or was that an enhancement provided by the LSD?

Lucia, Luke answered him. 'Tis her fancy dress, the one she struts about in while sweet Portia does her chores.

Luke took a step toward the woman who still stood facing the fire.

Simba concentrated on the tightening of each fiber of muscle in his leg, letting it happen, remembering how Luke seemed to wait and catch him off guard. Just as the leg relaxed, Simba yanked it back to where it was before.

Lucia's your sister, man. I know that much. And, in this lifetime as Ursula, she's so fucked up on drugs she's not worth hassling over one way or the other. Mellow out, man. This is sick.

We didn't finish our chores, Luke answered, our work.

What work?

Cleansing the world of witches, Luke answered.

Simba was overcome by the futility of arguing with such a person. He shrugged, then sagged, letting his muscles relax.

"Killing the witches," Luke said aloud as he threw the knife.

The woman turned. "Simba! Like, wow, I found an old trunk full of clothes and—"

"Portia!" Luke yelled in anguish.

The old dagger caught Poppy in the throat, ripping it open.

"Aim," Luke lamented.

Poppy dipped her hand into her own throat, then marveled at the blood dripping off her fingers. "Far out," she managed to say, though the gurgly, breathless voice was hardly recognizable. "Like, the colors are so intense. I just love—" She wavered, staggered, then stabilized by clutching the mantle. A huge globule of red sprang from the hole in her throat, splattering the floor several feet away, but she didn't look particularly concerned or upset. Finally she crumpled to the floor, a broken toy.

"Oh, no, mouses in trouble." Mighty Mouse slipped into a moment when the other two were shocked into silence. In unison all three rushed to kneel in the puddle of blood at Poppy's side. Her eyes closed in a painfully slow motion. Her mouth slackened into a macabre half-smile, reminiscent one last time of the freckled innocence of Howdy Doody.

"Dead?" asked all three occupants of Simba's body mournfully.

The only answer was the fire crackling.

Was she breathing, or was it the rhythm of the hallucinations? Gently, all three lay Simba's hand on her chest.

Nothing. Then suddenly what seemed to be a burp inside her chest. Another huge globule of blood sloshed out the side of her mouth. Then she was still.

"Murderer!"

The three of them turned their communal body, clawing at the tears streaming down their communal cheeks.

"Ursula, I tried—" Simba started.

"Witch!" Luke interrupted.

All Mighty Mouse could do was tsk silently.

Luke spotted the knife, still caught in the side of Poppy's throat.

Simba stiffened every muscle in his body.

Ursula relaxed. "Don't bother fighting it. I'm next."

Simba looked at Ursula.

"Like, nobody ever believes me, man. It's the curse of my life."

"Lucia knows," Luke contributed, "because she's a witch."

"Yeah, yeah," Ursula said, coming further into the room. "I know. And I never do my chores."

Let him talk, Simba thought, concentrating on the rigid control of every other part of his body.

"You tricked us," Luke spat at her.

What's this "us" shit, motherfucker?

Ursula slapped a hand to her chest in mock horror. "Did I, now?"

"You tricked us into killing sweet Portia!" Luke accused.

Ursula looked disgusted, but then softened as she looked at Poppy. She looked at Poppy for a long time while nothing was heard but the crackle of the fire. "All right," she finally said, apparently to herself. "I'll try." She looked into Simba's eyes. "Hold him tight."

Simba did.

"Can you speak?" she asked.

"Yes, witch, I can—"

"Not you, ass wipe. Simba."

Simba struggled to maintain awareness of the rest of his body, while moving his mouth. "Yes, Ursula." The words were a clumsy struggle. "But just barely."

Ursula came closer, kneeling before them.

"Run," Simba forced out despite Luke's efforts to stop him. "Take the others."

"Believe me," she said softly. "There is only one answer."

"What?" came out of Simba's mouth immediately. He realized Luke had asked it, too.

There was a blur of motion. Poppy's head flopped sideways, thudding against the floor. Simba looked down to see the knife was now in Ursula's hands. He felt his own hands lunge for it and just barely suppressed them.

"Good," Ursula said, watching intently. She looked away for a moment, and Simba almost lost control when he was distracted by the extraordinary sight of tears in her eyes. "I always liked you, Simba."

She turned back to face them, clutching the knife in her lap. "Simba, close your eyes. Keep them shut, no matter what."

Simba looked at Ursula's hands, kneading the handle of the dagger. He thought he knew what "no matter what" was. Judging from the extra tension he was now feeling in all his muscles, he figured Luke knew, too.

"Thank you, Ursula," Simba said. He closed

his eyes tightly. It took all his concentration to keep them that way.

"Ursula," Luke said.

Let him talk, Simba thought.

"Ursula," Luke said again, sounding much more natural, much more like Simba. "Ursula, I didn't tell you before, but before you kill us I have a surprise for you. It's in my back pocket. While we were in Manhattan I got you a packet of co—"

Simba shifted all his attention to his mouth before Luke managed to say coke, but it was too late. His eyes flew open in time to see the cold determination in Ursula's face as she dropped the knife to lunge for his back pocket. Powerless, caught completely off guard, he watched in seeming slow motion as Luke scooped up the knife, firmly sliced her open just below the ribs, then plunged his hand all the way up into Ursula's warm, wet body and snatched out her heart.

All four of them watched Ursula's heart beat a few times in Simba's hand. Its gentle flutter reminded Simba of the wounded bird he'd cradled in his hands once when he was a kid.

At last Ursula fell slowly backwards, on top of Poppy's half-smile.

"No!" It was Simba screaming. He snatched up the knife and forced it into Ursula's lifeless hand. "Make it stop, Ursula. Please!"

"She no longer has the heart for it," Luke said.

Simba didn't even think of laughing this time. He sobbed.

"Holy Fucking Shit!" It was Chutney's rich

voice. He stood in the doorway, Midas in his arms. Bell was behind him, still holding some firewood and an ax.

"Oh, man," Bell said, "she's been in here, too."

She?

Luke rankled at that. Simba stared, mesmerized by Midas though he could feel Luke tugging at the muscles that controlled their eyes, wanting to look toward Bell for some reason.

The dagger had slashed the plain white T-shirt Midas wore, revealing the companion slash in his pot belly. His intestines no longer protruded from the hole. Instead, horribly, he had at last lost weight. The pasty skin of his abdomen flopped inward, rumpling oddly around the edges of a huge cavern. Organs were missing.

In death Midas's face had managed to maintain its final expression of outrage, marred only slightly by the tongue lolling out of the side of his mouth. Simba could almost imagine what Midas would have had to say about all this and how long it would have taken him to do so.

"Oh, shit, man!" Bell was saying. "Look at Poppy!"

Simba didn't. He shifted his attention to Midas's plain white T-shirt. Very unhip for 1966. No wonder the dumb little shit couldn't get laid. It was his own fault. If he'd just refrained from talking about his mother all the time, and—watched out for people picking daggers up off the ground.

Oh God, Midas, I'm so sorry, Simba screamed inside. He started to sob outside. From somewhere far, far away a small voice within him said something derogatory about men crying. His friend Chutney/brother Eb lay Midas down and put a hand on Simba's shoulder. It felt good to everyone, even Mighty Mouse.

"Any idea where she is?" Chutney asked.

She? Oh shit, they still think it's Josephine!

"Run! It's not Josephine," Simba got out before Luke clamped his teeth together so tight they hurt. Simba fought to reopen his mouth so hard it brought tears to his eyes. Chutney frowned, watching him intently and squeezing his shoulder by way of reassurance.

Two words! Two lousy words! The words, "It's me!" If only he could get his mouth open. But wait, to articulate the sounds in "It's me," all he had to do was—

"It's me!" Simba yelled through his teeth.

Chutney jumped back.

Bell's eyes widened, reminding Simba for one absurdly irrelevant second of some jolly black-faced cartoon character he'd seen on Saturday morning TV long ago. When Bell dropped the firewood with a clatter to better wield the ax, though, the image shattered.

Simba's insides churned with Luke's rage over Simba's supposed betrayal.

Chutney circled, wariness replaced only once by a heartbreaking look of sympathy he quickly vanquished.

"What do we do with him?" Bell asked.

"What's right is right," Chutney said sternly but with no resonance whatsoever in his voice.

"We erred in not turning this over to the proper authorities long before now." His gaze lingered briefly on each of the three corpses. "However crazy and prejudiced against hippies the local authorities may be—and from what we've seen so far I'd say we can count on a pretty high degree of both—I say we get the three of us in that school bus and pay them an immediate visit."

"Agreed," Bell said, tightening his fingers around the handle of the ax. "But first, Chutney, get the knife."

A tight-lipped Chutney scanned the room, spotting the knife resting in Ursula's grey hand. Simba listened to the fire crackle as Chutney's gaze crept another few inches across the dark wood floor to the twitching hand of Simba's that he and Luke fought to control. Bell, holding the ax high, and Chutney advanced as one with a stately, rather dignified step reminiscent of some ballroom dance of long ago. Simba, Luke and Mighty Mouse looked up at them from their vantage point of kneeling on the floor. Simba's hand twitched harder, flopping about the floor like a fish out of water.

You got the better of me before, Simba thought. It won't happen again.

Luke didn't answer. Simba felt what seemed to be a tick in the muscles around his eyes and found himself looking into Chutney's eyes.

"Eb," Luke called. "Don't you remember who you are?"

Not again, Simba thought, but he didn't dare

try to control his mouth with his hand only inches from the knife.

"Fuck that shit," was Chutney's answer.

Simba wanted to applaud.

"Ready?" Bell asked.

They were very close.

"Yes," Chutney said. His actor's voice actually cracked.

Simba could see the fear in his friend's eye. He wanted to say: It's okay. It's me, Simba, in control, running the show as usual. Another part of him wanted to say: It's not okay. I could lose control of that hand any second, idiots. Fuck taking me to the police; use the friggin' ax.

His hand made an exceptionally strong lunge for the knife, one Simba just barely managed to control.

Simba didn't say anything at all.

"Chutney, my man," Bell said, "here's what's happenin'. We're both going to get on the same side of him. That way if I have to use this ax, I don't have to worry so much about missing and getting you."

They positioned themselves. Bell spread his legs slightly and bent his knees, a fighter's stance. Simba looked up into Bell's eyes. Would he use the ax? Simba saw a no-nonsense neutrality infinitely more chilling than the most violent rage. Yes, he would use the ax. What would it feel like?

Luke was most obliging in supplying the answer through memory. Simba watched the face of Josephine's one-night stand from the antique store perform marvels no contortionist could come close to as it twisted through every imaginable expression of agony. Finally the man looked down to see the mangled mash of bone and gore that used to be his chest. His expression of surprise was so bizarre it moved Luke to a sort of mercy he expressed by using his dagger to deliver the last, fatal blow. As a final touch Luke lingered on the things he'd had to scrape off with his fingernails before stashing the dagger in his jacket pocket for safekeeping.

Simba was suddenly very conscious of the exact components of his body.

"We've waited long enough," Bell said, eyes glued on Simba. "Chutney, get the knife."

Chutney went for it. So did Luke.

Simba caught the swing of the ax in his peripheral vision. Sick with horror, he knew immediately that it wasn't Luke who hooked his arm behind Bell's knee, toppling him over the bodies of the two girls and into the fire. It was Simba.

Bell groaned and was silent.

Simba sprang to his feet. Chutney faced him. One hand was behind his back, the other held the dagger. He was staring straight at Simba but, for a moment, seemed to be looking through him.

"Grandfather," Chutney said simply.

Then his focus snapped back to Simba.

"Wait a minute, man," Simba said.

"No wait-a-minutes, no disclaimers," Chutney said.

"I want to help," Simba forced through teeth he thought would shatter under the pressure

Luke was exerting to keep them together. "To fight me, you must understand how the two people inside me fight each other."

Simba was struggling so hard to control his lips and tongue that he didn't realize until it was too late that Luke had scooped something off the floor. Luke then grabbed control of his eyes, not letting Simba see what it was, but Simba could still feel. His hand was gripping something wooden and essentially cylindrical. Luke let him look back at Chutney.

Something sizzled in the fire.

Chutney was looking at whatever was in Simba's hand. When he met Simba's eyes again, it was without even the slightest hint of his once-infinite supply of golden warmth. Even the fear had been replaced by an all-consuming determination. Simba recognized the will to live.

"Please," Simba begged him, "don't let Luke touch you with this ax."

"What ax?" Chutney asked.

Simba felt his eye muscles relax, so he grabbed control and looked at what he held. It was a piece of firewood. Confused, he looked back up at Chutney in time to see him pull the hand out from behind his back. Chutney held the ax.

Chutney hung the dagger around his neck so he could use both hands on the ax.

Luke took the first swing. Simba waited until he reached the weakest part of the arc, then jerked his muscles to throw the aim.

Luke missed.

Something began to smell.

Chutney swung. Both Luke and Simba held up the piece of firewood as a shield. The ax hit, breaking the firewood neatly in two, then continuing, somewhat off course, to graze the side of Simba's shoulder.

As pain shot through Simba's shoulder, it occurred to him dully that it was the same shoulder he'd used to force the front door open earlier. His hand sprang up to touch his wound, then jerked at the last minute—along with his other hand—toward Chutney. Taking advantage of the fact that it still hadn't completed its swing, Luke snatched the ax out of Chutney's hand.

"You son of a bitch," Simba yelled at Luke.

Fear was again visible in Chutney's eye.

"Listen to me," Simba begged Chutney. "Luke can throw knives very accurately, but you've got the knife. The door is behind you, my friend. Back slowly a few steps, then run."

"Thanks," Chutney said in a very small voice. He did as he was told. Just before he got to the door, Luke went to throw the ax. Simba waited for the weakest point of the arc again and jerked his muscles just as he'd done before.

The ax hit Chutney squarely in the back with a sickening thud, burying itself deeply. Chutney fell straight forward and was still.

"You son of a bitch," Simba cried at Luke.

"Aim," Luke said before he busted up laughing. Simba realized his mistake—jerking his muscles at the same exact point in the arc twice. Luke had compensated. At least Simba had been spared the expression on Chutney's face.

Something stank.

Simba turned slowly toward the fire. Bell's head must have hit something hard in the fireplace, knocking him out. Simba couldn't be sure whether he was dead or only unconscious, but one thing was sure.

Bell was really cooking.

He had on his Gizmo Delicious shirt; for a second Simba's heart sank at the thought of the band that would be no more. Then he saw the side of Bell's face that had settled into the fire. It appeared to have melted as if made of wax. The eyelids were gone. Flames caressed an eyeball that reminded Simba of a marshmallow, perfectly done. All and all, though, Bell didn't look any too delicious.

An ignoble end to a noble man, Simba thought. It was his last rational thought.

Luke laughed. Simba joined him.

Piper finally found the other ax. After a lengthly search of the bus, it turned out to be close at hand, carefully wedged up into the understructure of the last seat on the left. It was, perhaps, the only dry place left in the bus.

The rain had come, and everything else felt unbelievably soggy. The odd smell in the bus was stronger than ever.

Piper was partly under the seat still with her rear in the air, when the fast-failing light of her flashlight picked out something else wedged up under the seat. Piper reached up, plucked it out and unwrapped it. In her hand she held a sharpening stone.

Should she sharpen the fuckin' thing?

Simba was a lot stronger than she was. Should she even bring the ax, for that matter, taking the chance that he'd take it away from her? Maybe she should just hide it somewhere so at least he couldn't use it. Maybe thinking of protecting Poppy and Ursula by getting the ax had been a crazy idea. Much as it went against her grain, Piper had to admit that the concept of sexual equality evaporated in the face of matters involving physical strength. She should have gone to get the other men.

Piper was wriggling out from under the seat, when a glint of something under the seat across the aisle caught her eye.

A hallucination?

Since she was already on the floor, she crawled over to it.

Something had jammed it into the space between the seat leg and the wall. When her flashlight failed, she jiggled it back to feeble life, holding it over the thing.

Bone fragment.

Pieces of very old, very dried up tissue still clung to it. Disgusting. Yet she didn't remember anyone eating anything in the bus with bones that big.

The smell was much worse.

Piper yanked the bone free, held it and examined it under the flashlight. Was she hallucinating the tiny curled sliver of dry brown skin that stuck to it still? She dropped it, standing. Next she found herself heading toward the front of the bus with the ax.

It took her awhile to find the stain on the floor. She then examined the ceiling.

Nothing.

She propped the flickering flashlight on the closest seat and swung the ax.

Bull's-eye. Right on the stain. The floor buckled.

Piper swung again and again until there was a hole in the old floor.

The smell had never been worse.

Panting, she got down on her hands and knees again with the flashlight to peer through the hole.

Inches from Piper's eyeball, a dull, shriveled eyeball strained forward from a wind-dried, bug-splattered slab of Josephine's face to peer back at her.

Piper jerked away.

That slab had seen a lot of road miles. Every drop of moisture had either been claimed by the wind or had fallen below into the rusting gas lines.

No matter.

Piper snatched up the flashlight, jiggled it back to life, and headed for the food supplies up by the door. If that piece of Josephine was all dried out, she certainly wasn't going to investigate further and find the rain-soaked piece that was causing the smell. She wasn't going to let anything or anybody bring her down any more. Carrots.

Lentils. Aha! Wine. She curled up in the driver's seat, feet propped up in the steering wheel, and opened the wine.

It occurred to her that Ronna had changed but that she, Piper, had not. Well, no, that wasn't fair. She had changed by opening up to her feelings. That change had led her to opening up to other people, even—She broke off her thought to stare out the window, but no stars were visible in the rain. Still, Piper was honest enough to admit, in another perhaps more important area she hadn't changed at all—no bullshit. She just wasn't going to put up with it. Instead she took a good long swig of the wine—and another and another.

At first she felt great. The one last thing bringing her down, that smell, was solved when she kicked at the control that opened the bus' front door. Some rain came in, but Piper didn't care. She drank some more.

Between the booze and the acid, things started to spin. Piper decided she'd be more comfortable on the floor. As she struggled to achieve this without falling on her face, she thought she heard a footstep but couldn't be sure over the rain.

No matter.

She was just getting comfortable when a bright light flooded her and someone shoved something in front of her face. It took her awhile to achieve anything resembling focus, but she finally established that it was an ancient, crumbly clipping from a local newspaper.

"In the continuing investigation surrounding the death in Nyland Heights of Mrs. Joshua

Carnes, it has come to the attention of yours truly that there exist certain marked inconsistencies in the testimony of son Luke Carnes," it said in the flowery style of 19th century journalism.

"Fuck this," Piper said, speech heavily slurred. She lay her head back down and closed her eyes.

"Read," said a voice.

"Got anything lighter?" Piper asked grumpily. "Maybe a comic?"

"No."

Piper sighed. The hallucinations were spinning faster. She could hardly see anything, let alone fine print, so she got very close.

"This correspondent for one would like to know why father Joshua Carnes chose to decline offers of assistance from prominent experts in the field of mental malaise when it is all too clear that son Luke is desperately in need of such assistance."

Piper addressed the person behind her. "Simba? Luke? Whoever? I don't give a shit." Piper put her head down again and watched the hallucinations spin faster and faster.

"You should, swine of Satan."

"Sticks and stones can hurt my bones," Piper sassed, "but words will never harm me."

"I have more than words."

A chill moment of sobriety passed through Piper, during which she spotted the ax where she'd left it on the floor, but then it passed. The hallucinations were whipping about now, a geometry text gone mad in a centrifuge. Piper closed her eyes.

"Work."

"Yeah, it's a bitch," she agreed.

"All that work. It is getting harder every year. All we got left is work and evil. No joy, only selfishness."

"A real drag," Piper commiserated, then yawned.

A hand scooped up the newspaper clipping. "Mrs. Joshua Carnes...Work killed her. Lucia and Rachel, never doing their chores, they helped."

Piper dozed off for a moment, then jolted herself back into consciousness.

"Sweet Portia looks more like her mother everyday. Does all her chores and Lucia's and Rachel's besides. Hands are starting to turn ugly, just like her mother's."

"Bummer," Piper said.

"You killed her mother."

"I thought it was Lucia and Rachel," Piper mused, stretching.

"You are not listening, swine of Satan. I only said they helped."

"Well, sor-ry!" Piper snapped, but she found her eyes opening. The intensity in the other person's voice had triggered something groggy in Piper but not quite dead.

"Work," Piper said quickly. "You said work killed her."

"No, you don't understand."

"But I'd like to understand," Piper said softly, hating herself. "If you could just help me to."

Piper heard laughter. "They never figured it out."

She was turning slowly, trying to look upward without drawing too much attention to herself. The floor undulated beneath her like a water bed. Never in her life had she been even half as high. On the heels of that thought came a sickening despair.

"She killed herself. Oh, she needed very careful instruction and a lot of coercion—she was far too stupid to figure out anything on her own—but she killed herself. The two of us watched. She didn't quite get it right, and she kept wanting to back out, of course. It took awhile."

Piper heard a click. The bright light was gone. As they plunged into darkness vertigo brushed by. Again, for a moment, Piper was perfectly sober. Silently she felt around for her flashlight, found it and flipped it on.

Nothing.

She jiggled it.

Still nothing.

Gently, she put it down. Her fingers crawled across the floor towards the ax, or at least toward where she thought the ax would be. Just as her fingers closed on its handle something hard stomped on them.

"Shit!" Piper rolled away, holding her fingers.

"My eyes adjust a lot quicker now. All that night driving."

Piper was on her feet, making a beeline for the open door. The rain had let up. The air was fresh, and the moist earth smelled sweet. Her eyes began to adjust. Through that door was the world outside, rich and full of promise. Clouds scudded across an open sky. She could see a single, bright star. Piper reached for the door frame, ready to vault the steps and come down running.

The impact propelled her through the door and into the mud, face down. At first she didn't know what had happened and blamed it on an over-zealous jump. It wasn't until she tried to get up, and the first shooting pain coursed through her back and arms, that she realized something was terribly, horribly wrong.

Something was stuck in her back. It didn't take Piper long to figure out what. She managed to get to her knees. Remarkably, it didn't hurt much; it was just that her body wasn't working right. Then there was a tug at the ax. That hurt. Another tug. The ax came free. That was when the agony began.

Piper rolled across the wet ground anyway, desperate to escape the next blow. When her back hit the ground, something hard and wet, prob-ably a large twig, slid deep into her body. She realized the old cliché about seeing stars was no exaggeration.

Think! Piper screamed inside herself. Never had she been in a situation she couldn't think her way out of.

High over her head she caught a glint of the ax descending. Piper knew she was injured severely but probably not fatally—yet. Raw will to live bubbled inside her, an ache that crescendoed into an anguished inner scream as she felt herself los-ing consciousness. The acid. The booze. The in-jury. Just as she realized fully that being alive really was everything, she lost all power to do anything about it.

Were her eyes closed, or was her vision gone? Was she still on her back in the mud? She couldn't feel her body. She could be sitting now, or standing, for all she knew. By the time the blade reached her face, cutting at an angle through the bridge of her nose and crushing her right cheekbone, she almost savored the dull, dreamlike quality of feeling something.

Then there was a third blow. Idly she marveled at the shudder of her skull, just before shattering. She could feel the contents of her head, shoved in different directions by shards of bone as if a jar of strawberry preserves had been dropped on the kitchen floor. And then she could feel no more.

Was it a dream? Parsons didn't understand what was happening. He'd been to the house. Of course it just had to be full of antiques. He hated antiques.

He had found the clipping.

But he still didn't understand what was going on with him.

Finally he dropped the ax in the mud. On his way back to the house he stepped in what was left of the frizzy-haired hippie's face and ground his foot around a bit. That made him feel a little better.

He rubbed his paunch.

It was wet.

Damn, but killing people was messy.

Chapter 13

"They won't suspect?" Rupp asks.

"No," she says and smiles. She and Lucia go.

A twig snaps. There is a shape that doesn't belong, a shape that moves and is more twisted than the trees themselves. Sister Lucia is at her side. Rachel must decide what to do. Her family is up ahead, everyone except Eb with the twisted shape. This time Rachel doesn't look away from the group in the clearing. This time Rachel doesn't forget about the shape in the trees. Slowly, ever so slowly, she turns to face it. This time Rachel doesn't feel; she thinks. The twisted shape in the trees is Eb. He has been spying and will tell Father and Luke about the elopement. Rachel thinks harder. Eb is crazy and will twist it all besides, make it seem like witchcraft.

Father and Luke are also crazy.

The night that Mommy died Father and Mommy were alone in the big bed in their room. There was a lot of rustling around. Rachel put her ear to the door. Mostly she couldn't make out the words, but she caught a few. Mommy was trying to make Father feel all right about something he couldn't do. Then there was more rustling. Then there was more Mommy begging Father to feel all right about the thing he couldn't do. More rustling. Then Rachel heard Mommy get out of bed and come over near the door. Rachel could hear her heavy breathing and almost all of her words then. Mommy told Father that this happened to all men from time to time and that it was nothing to worry about. Rachel looked through the crack in the door. Father got out of bed and hit Mommy. Hard.

Rachel then heard something Rachel had never heard before. Mommy started to scream at Father about everything, even the lady in the carriage with the shiny purple dress. Finally Mommy used a Bible quote to convince Father that he shouldn't hit his own wife. She ended by saying she wanted to leave Father and that she was afraid to be alone in the same room as Father.

Father shoved the door open in Rachel's face, not even seeing her. Rachel scampered down the hall. Father came back with Luke and a knife and slammed the door behind them. Rachel put her ear to the door again. Father told Mommy that the only way a truly God-fearing wife could leave

344

her husband was through death. Then he and
Luke moved away from the door. Again, Rachel
couldn't make out all the words, but she caught
a few.

Overwhelmed by her feelings, Rachel had decided she heard wrong since none of what followed made any sense. Now she looks at it coldly.
It makes sense if she accepts that her mother's
death wasn't the accident her father had at first
claimed or the suicide the papers later exposed.
No, her father, in the presence of their son, forced
his wife to execute herself.

Father and Luke are very crazy.

"Rachel, do we have to go back tonight?" Lucia
asks, looking to her to figure out what to do.

"No, we mustn't go back tonight," Rachel
hears herself saying. "We must run back to Rupp
and Jesse, before they launch the boat, and escape tonight."

Ronna snapped herself out of her fantasy re-
vision of Rachel's memory. She returned to the
room with the firelight flickering across the
creamy old walls. The faded, crumbly plaster
looked as if it would be soft to the touch, like
flannel. The fire crackled. Ronna looked down,
aghast at the carnage.

She yanked what was left of Bell out of the
flames and dragged Ursula off Poppy. It was Poppy's smile, undaunted by death itself, that had
stopped her cold.

Did poor Poppy just love death?

Tears blurred Ronna's vision, but she straightened Poppy's twisted legs, kissed her brow and got to her feet.

There was a step in the hall.

It took Ronna exactly five seconds to grab the dagger that hung around Chutney's neck and position herself behind the door.

"Where is everybody?"

It was Roscoe. Ronna smiled, relieved. Besides, now she had help. One of them could look for Piper while the other went for the police.

Poor out-of-it Roscoe. Something in his innocence touched her heart, like Poppy. He was big and strong and could probably save her life, but—she looked at the remnants of a very muscular Bell—could also lose his own. Besides, he had nothing to do with this, no counterpart in the 19th century. Ronna made a decision. Before he entered the room with the four corpses, she dropped the dagger and darted out to meet him.

He was soaked from the rain, and she used her shirt sleeve to dab him dry. "Where have you been?" she managed to scold lightly.

"Stupid, huh," he conceded. "Took a walk along the water. Got caught in the storm."

"Hell of a time to take in the sights," Ronna managed, thinking furiously. What should she tell him? No self-respecting ex-Marine would leave a woman behind if he knew the truth.

"Had to think," Roscoe said. "Get off on my own. Sometimes I feel so out of it that being with people is lonelier than being alone."

"Considering peace and awareness through drugs?" Ronna asked dryly.

"Think I'll stick to aspirin."

"Good idea," Ronna exclaimed. "Listen, Roscoe—"

Roscoe interrupted. "Why do people get into weird stuff like drugs and reincarnation?"

"Oh, because they don't think plain, old, ordinary life is enough. Look, Roscoe, we've got an emergency here, and I need your help."

Roscoe snapped to attention like an obedient scout.

"It's, uh, Ursula. She flipped out. She's been running around with a knife threatening to kill people."

Roscoe stepped closer. From what Ronna could read of his face, he was ready to slay dragons in her behalf.

"We've, uh, got her under control now, but someone's got to get the police. And you'll have to go to the next town because it can't be the local police. You saw their attitude. They're not only liable to arrest us on suspicion of looking like beatniks, but they're liable to kill us. Anyway we're all too stoned to drive."

"Sure you'll be all right if I leave you here?" he asked.

"Sure."

"Promise?" His voice had deepened and softened.

"I promise," Ronna answered.

Roscoe drew back, sighed and looked at her, but what he said was, "Where are the keys?"

Shit! "One moment. I'll get them. You better

stay here. I think Ursula's asleep now. Better that only one of us goes in."

Hopefully he'd write her nervous chatter off to the supposed emergency with Ursula. Ronna dashed back into the room with the crackling fire.

Who drove last? Bell. Double shit! Bell was still smoking. She went for the front pockets of his skin-tight jeans, immediately burning herself on the metal rivets. Struggling to get her hand in the pocket, she punched through his crispy skin. The smell of roast pork assailed her. Warm juices ran down her arm to drip off her elbow. It was sickening. The burnt clothing smelled bad; Bell himself smelled of Sunday dinner long ago.

No keys.

Back pockets.

Nothing.

Triple shit.

Nonplussed, Ronna listened to the fire crackle, then imagined she heard another step in the hall.

Without thinking, she started to reach into the fire with her hand. The juices dripped into the flames and sizzled. Ronna grabbed a short piece of firewood that was close at hand and started poking around in the embers. A glitter near the hearth caught her eye.

The keys.

They must have fallen out when she dragged Bell out. Though they hadn't been in the flames, they were hot enough. She jiggled them about in her hands as she scurried across the room, dodging corpses. Running out the door, she ran right into Roscoe, who was on his way in.

He held her for only a moment too long, then backed away, sniffing. "Dinner?"

"Old family favorite," Ronna said. "You can have some when you get back."

"Great. Any idea where the police station is?"

"None whatsoever," Ronna answered.

"Fair enough. I'll find it." He took the keys.

"Watch out. They're hot. Dropped them on the hearth."

He nodded smartly and turned to go.

To Ronna, it felt like Simba's description of his mother's leaving on the first day of kindergarten. "Roscoe?" she called.

He turned back. "Sure you want me to go?"

"Yes," Ronna said, "but one last thing."

"What?"

"Hurry."

He nodded and was gone.

Ronna slipped back behind the door and retrieved the dagger, hanging it around her neck.

Where was the ax?

Perhaps more to the point, where was Simba? And Piper.

Better to find than be found, said a new voice in her head, a voice Ronna recognized as an inner attempt to be her own parent or caretaker.

She crept into the hall and heard the bus taking off. Remembering she'd heard Roscoe's footsteps, Ronna hugged the wall, figuring the floorboards would be better anchored and less creaky there. A shutter slammed against the house in the wind, but she didn't jump; she didn't make a sound. By the front door she paused and listened.

She heard nothing but the faint crackle of the fire in the living room and a light whistling of the wind.

Ronna backtracked into the living room, tiptoeing through the corpses—Chutney spreadeagled and face down, Midas, who looked like he'd had a Caesarean, Ursula, whose depressed look suggested she might have committed harikari, barbecued Bell, and Poppy the Eternal Optimist. Inappropriately, the flickering firelight lent them all a warm and cozy glow. Ronna slipped through the archway at the other end of the room.

Cool moonlight washed across the next room, catching the dusty sheet covering a dining room table. Ronna froze in the shadows, listening. The wind said "hush" coming through the broken windows, but the leaves ignored it, rustling rebelliously in the corners of the room. Ronna rushed through the moonlight, exiting the room.

Next was a place of darkness so thick it seemed solid. Ronna stood perfectly still and waited. A gentle peace entered her soul. Puzzled, she finally realized that exploring a deserted house at night reminded her of the adventures of a rabbit in some gentle children's book she'd read long ago. As her eyes adjusted, a stairway appeared in front of her like a developing Polaroid picture.

Ronna ascended a few steps, sticking to the wall and testing each step for creakiness before putting her weight into it. Suddenly out of nowhere something touched her face. She clawed at it, a small sound escaping her, and she put her weight on an untested step. Naturally, it creaked.

Quadruple shit.

Ronna's heart pounded so hard she feared it could be heard. She waited again. For the first time she touched the dagger around her neck. After testing the handle, she gingerly ran her fingers over the blade. With her heart pounding hard, she knew exactly where it was located in her chest. Her fingers measured off the length of the still-sticky blade. Her memory played back the exact locations of the openings she'd seen in each corpse. An icy chill passed through her when she realized what she was doing. She was planning.

Finally her heart was still. She tested the next step, then the next.

Something touched her face again. She froze, silent. Nothing creaked. It was still on her face. Slowly she put her hand to it, snatched it away, then rolled it about between her fingers.

Cobwebs.

Relieved, Ronna smiled in the dark, brushed cobwebs aside as she went, and headed for the moonbeams at the top of the stairs.

The moon had carpeted the second floor hallway in white, the color of faded porcelain. Ronna hid in darkness on the last step, listening carefully. Utter silence rang in her ears.

Was the house really empty? Should she have checked outside instead? She'd assumed no one was out there because she herself had been out there, first in the back, then in the front, and then in the back again just before she came in to discover the bodies.

Ronna pulled the leather thong over her head, freeing the dagger. Gripping it in her hand, it occurred to her that another person could snatch it away. She undid the knot in the leather thong and wrapped it securely around her wrist, tying it again with the help of her teeth.

Nobody was going to take that dagger away.

Ronna stepped into the moonlight. She walked the length of the hall to the upper level of the double porch at the front of the house and looked out. All was still except the twisted trees, whispering secrets in the wind. The bus, of course, was gone. "Hurry," she mouthed in silent prayer, then bit back despair and retraced her steps back down the hall. From the back of the house, she peered out over the marsh and flax pond. Then she stared down at the clearing at the back of the house. The sole tree in the clearing was the biggest, most gnarled of all. Again all was still.

Except in Ronna's mind.

"They would wonder," Ronna/Rachel hears herself saying as she returns to her family, the obedient, dependent child. "Remember, only one more night." And Ronna/Rachel forgets about the shape in the trees to look back at the flax pond and remember Mike/Rupp with the warm brown eyes. There is a great sense of elation and a freedom soon to come.

This is what really happened, Ronna paused to tell herself. All was still.

Rachel and her sister Ursula/Lucia enter the clearing. No one notices. The hired hand Midas/Zak and the slave Bell/Alex are bending their backs with the two-man saw, showering sawdust into the wind. Father and their two brothers, Chutney/Eb and Simba/Luke, are feverishly chopping wood. Axes bite into logs, and chips fly.

Father is splitting his logs with a steel wedge and a sledge hammer. He swings his sledge with a vengeance. "Are they lazy because they are witches?" he asks. "Or, being witches, are they lazy? Or is it the Hanlon boys, leading them astray?"

Tiring, Luke swings, but the log doesn't split. "Rachel and Lucia? Witches?" he asks.

"It is what Eb says," Father says., "Eb could split that log without half trying. You, Luke, are not used to real work. Sailors never are."

"No, Poppa, I guess that is true." Luke swings again, this time harder. Still the log doesn't split.

"What kind of work do you do on a whaling boat?" Father asks, working furiously.

"Rowing, harpooning, climbing, rigging, stripping blubber," Luke says proudly.

"Nothin' that's any use here," Father says flatly.

Luke finally splits the log and proudly stands back. Bell/Alex and Midas/Zak take a breather, too. When Father gives them all a stern look, they all get right back to work.

"Eb is a good worker," Father says. "Never quits. Better'n all the rest of you."

Poppy/Portia comes out of the house. "Dinner is about ready. Are Rachel and Lucia about? I could use some help."

"See what I mean?" Father says. "Never can depend on them."

"Yes," Luke agrees, swinging as hard as he can.

"I cannot abide their disrespect. Ever since your ma died," Father says.

"I hate them for it," Luke says.

"We must punish them once and forever," Father says.

"Yes," Luke says loudly. He stands closer to Father, trying to match his tempo.

"He has been brooding all day," Zak says. "They shall catch hell tonight."

"I ain't never seen him so mad," Alex answers.

Rachel and Lucia look at each other, elation gone. Here all is work and anger, anger against them. Without a word they start to back out of the clearing. Turning they run into Chutney/Eb. They have waited so long that he has caught up with them, cornering them.

"Poppa," Eb calls, "I caught them."

"Caught them doing what?" Father asks.

"They were with the Hanlon boys in the sand dunes," Eb answers.

"Yes, Father, we were," Rachel says humbly, hoping to abate his terrible rage with this admission.

"Sinning?" Father asks Eb.

"They was gigglin' and laughin'," Eb says.

"Yes," Rachel says, hanging her head.

Luke turns toward her, muscles like the strings of a harp playing under his naked torso. He looks her up and down. "And I came home to this?" he asks angrily.

"And breathin' hard," Eb continues, "like, you know, Poppa."

"Did they make witches' signs?" Father asks.

"Stakes and all," Eb answers. "They are gonna run away with the Hanlon boys. And they hate you, Poppa. And you, too, Luke. They said it right out. And they shrieked. And they laughed."

"Ebenezer," Rachel exclaims, "are you crazy? I beseech you, do not tell such lies."

"You have sinned against me, my house and the Lord for the last time," Father says.

"No, Poppa!" Lucia screams. "We have not done those things he said."

"Seize them," Father says. "I will kill them."

"I will do it," Eb says.

"No, I will," Luke says.

All was no longer still. Ronna snapped back to the present. She heard a voice.

Or did she just think she heard a voice?

All was again still except the pounding of her heart. She turned. Before her loomed another set of stairs.

Better not to be seen, said the voice inside her. Ronna stepped out of the moonlight into the shadow of the stairwell, oddly comforted when a cobweb brushed her face. As soon as her eyes adjusted she started slowly up the steps. At the top no moonlight greeted her, only a dankness as thick as a tomb. Ronna made her way toward the window at the end of the hall.

"Here. I am here," said a voice.

Ronna didn't know what came after quadruple shit.

"Poppa?" It was Simba's voice.

Whew. Not talking to her. Simba's voice came from behind a door somewhere, presumably talking to himself. Or, more precisely, among his various selves. Ronna stood perfectly still, but her heart went wild.

Which door?

"I did like you wanted, Poppa."

First door to the right.

"Did you do the thing that is right?"

No, it seemed further away now and muffled. Maybe the second door.

"With all but two, Poppa."

Definitely the first door.

"One. I did the thing that is right with the whore."

Piper! Tears stung the corners of Ronna's eyes. One? Only me. No point hanging around.

"Dragged her this way and that. She ignored me again, like the night I had to explain to your mother how to use a knife. We must not let the one that is left get away, Luke. I will kill her."

Ronna was on her way past the door. It opened. She knew immediately that the man blocking her escape was Luke. He said, "No, I will."

Ronna drew her right hand behind her back to hide the knife. "Simba?" she asked. Not the vaguest hint of recognition passed through his eyes. Something creaked in the room beyond.

"Witch!" Luke said, and before she knew it he'd grabbed her left hand and swung her into the room. Ronna landed in a heap in the corner, but her right hand was still behind her.

Luke, of course, had the ax.

No! yelled a million little voices inside Ronna—a chorus of memories, consciousness, and all that she had done and been. She panned the room in search of a way out, another weapon, anything. Luke advanced slowly. There was a closet door, partially closed. A Coleman lantern illuminated the room from atop a heavy oak chest of drawers. A seaman's trunk sat at the foot of the bed, beyond which was a window she had no chance of reaching. Metal hooks high on the wall next to her held sailor's clothing and equipment, including a harpoon. Luke brought the ax up over his right shoulder, positioning his left leg forward for balance. Only then did Ronna see the obvious. Inches from her left hand was the hooked rug on which he stood. He swung. She yanked. He fell. The ax skittered across the floor. He rolled for it. She dove for it, forgetting about concealing the knife attached to her wrist, and reached the ax at the same time. The knife got in her way. He did something she didn't understand by jerking downward when her hand was facing upward on the ax handle, and suddenly he had the ax to himself. They stood facing each other.

Sickeningly, Ronna realized a knife doesn't stand up well against an ax, and he was much stronger and heavier. His momentum alone... The window. Ronna took a step in front of the seaman's trunk at the foot of the bed. He swung. Ronna jerked back to the side and threw herself on the ax handle, continuing its forward motion. Luke fell across the bed face down. The ax slipped through his fingers. Ronna heard glass shatter. Luke grabbed her wrist, pinning her to the bed, but it was the left wrist. Ronna struggled to juggle the knife handle into her right hand, hesitated for only a second, and crossed her arms to plunge the knife into the back of someone she told herself was no longer Simba.

He was already turning toward her. The knife penetrated his shoulder, in a place Ronna just then realized had already been injured. It then deflected off bone just as he shuddered in pain. The combination threatened to dislocate her wrist. Suddenly she found him on top of her, his hands pinning down both her wrists.

"You shall die for that, witch," Luke said.

They both looked at the knife. Ronna was glad she'd tied it to her wrist. They both looked toward the window and Ronna's heart sank. Yes, the ax had broken through the window, but it had come to rest on the sill. Panting, they looked into each other's eyes, and Ronna went for the only weapon presently at hand.

"Look at me, Luke," Ronna said softly. "Who am I?"

"A witch," he said.

"What's my name?"

"Rachel," he said.

"What's my last name?"

"Carnes," he said.

"Same as yours?"

"Yes," he said with difficulty. "You are my sister."

"Yes," Ronna said with alacrity. "And the last

person you helped kill, hoping Poppa would then love you as much as Eb, was our mother."

"No!" His grip on her wrists tightened. Her right wrist screamed with pain. "The whore killed Mother."

"Piper, I mean the whore, never even met Mother," Ronna said evenly. "Whatever the whore or anybody else did to Poppa, did that justify his coming home to take it out on poor Mother in such a way?"

"She killed herself," Luke stated.

"No, Luke. Remember that night accurately. Poppa made her do it. And what have you been doing ever since? First you ran away from Poppa, by going to sea, then you came back to obey his every wish. Why? Still competing for his love, no matter what you have to do to get it? Or afraid if you displease him you might be the next one he forces to use a knife?"

Luke released her left wrist so that he could use his right hand to backhand her. Ronna watched his elbow move away from his side and across her body, but she didn't waste the moment defending herself against a slap. Instead, she shot her left hand around his armpit to reach his back. There she forced her fingers deep into his cut shoulder, clawing ruthlessly at anything her searching fingers could find inside. He jerked away from her, yelping with pain, just as she managed to hook her fingernails under something fibrous. It was slimy and fought to escape her grasp by tightening at her touch, but she held on and gave it a yank.

Luke released her right wrist. Ronna's left hand twisted and tugged, while her right fumbled for the dagger's handle. At last twisting his shoulder free of her grasp, he fell backwards against the window sill exposing his neck. In a flash she reviewed freshman anatomy and aimed the knife for his jugular. He twisted sideways; the knife slipped under his collarbone and got stuck. He clutched at it, cutting the fingers of his right hand. She tugged, trying to get the knife, and the hand of hers it was tied to, free.

The knife sprang loose, propelling Ronna backwards with her head aimed for the foot of the bed and the seaman's trunk. In the midst of falling backwards, she watched helplessly as Luke's trembling right hand grappled for the ax, knocking it further out the window. Just before it was too late, he caught it.

Ronna's head hit the trunk, dazing her slightly. She scrambled off the bed anyway, heading for the door. The closet door creaked open further to collide with her. Then the wind blew through the broken window. She turned. Luke was coming at her like a kicker after the opposing team scored a touchdown. His foot caught her square in the lower abdomen, doubling her over as it lifted her off her feet and propelled her into the opposite wall. She thudded against the wall, just missing the metal hooks, and slid down to the floor. Nauseous and dazed, she watched Luke positioning his hands on the ax handle, his right hand still shaking.

"Remember when we were little," she said,

"and you and Eb would look out for your sisters? Poppa's not here to hurt anyone anymore. The love of a man who could force his wife to disembowel herself is not worth striving for. You don't have to do this."

"Poppa is still here," Luke said. Blood oozed from his collarbone and coursed over his right hand in rivulets, but he seemed to have achieved a stable grip on the ax.

Ronna struggled not to vomit in reaction to the kick. She shouldn't have let Roscoe go . . . silly, silly heroics . . . maybe they could play tag . . . roll in the grass . . . something about four-leaf clovers. "Oh, Simba," she called, overcome at last by a sense of weakness and futility, "if you could only see what's happening. Come back. Be my strength." Ronna looked into Luke's eyes.

They weren't Luke's anymore. Ronna could tell. Then again, they weren't Simba's either. Still, Luke twitched all over as if his muscles were fighting each other. Someone had stayed the ax.

"Here I come to save the day," said the corny, somewhat silly voice of Mighty Mouse.

Ronna smiled in wonder, took a deep breath and looked about. One of the metal hooks over her head held a harpoon. In a single motion she stood, snatched the harpoon, and swung in up under Luke's ribcage.

It sounded like someone had halved a watermelon. Blood sputtered from the wound. The twitching took on a new quality, less voluntary, then Luke toppled over backwards and was still.

"Sorry, Mighty Mouse," Ronna said sadly.

His blood puddled, then ran down the cracks between the floorboards as far as the opposing walls. Still open, the hypnotic blue eyes pulled Ronna back to them. The face was still haunting.

Ronna wrapped her hands around the harpoon again. "I owe two of the three of you this much." She pulled the harpoon out. It wasn't easy. Fortunately she hadn't shoved it in as far as she thought she had. As it was she had to press her foot against his ribs for leverage and work it back and forth like a double fishhook. Her right wrist was killing her. Halfway through she untied the knife and let it drop to the floor. She was then able to tug harder. More of him got ripped up, but she figured it didn't matter anymore.

Mesmerized, she looked back into the eyes with tendrils of electric green. They seemed to look back at her, accusing. She remembered Simba, her head on his bare chest, rocked gently by his breathing, his arms tightly wrapped around her. Ronna couldn't hold it back anymore. She turned from him, squatted facing the wall, and puked her guts up.

Simba seemed to be sitting in a dark room all by himself. Through the door and all the way down an equally dark corridor, he could see the one point of light. Apparently someone had left the TV on. Simba couldn't make it out any too well at that distance, but it appeared to be one of those grade D horror movies shot from the monster's point of view. The monster appeared

Twisted

to be pursuing a girl who looked a lot like Ronna. Just now the monster was apparently lying down and the girl was squatting with her back to it, puking against a wall.

I've heard of not turning a chick on, but this is ridiculous, Simba thought. Ole monster must be pretty ugly.

Now the point of view shifted higher, then tilted downward to angle on an antique dagger with a leather thong attached to it that someone had dropped on the floor.

Ole monster must be sitting up, just about to sock it to the bitch, Simba thought. What a cliché.

A hand with rivulets of blood on it could be seen picking up the knife.

Simba picked his nose.

The camera angle shifted to the girl's back again, showing off her ass.

Simba checked it out. Yup, just like Ronna.

The dagger descended for a magnificently fatal lunge. The girl leaned over to puke again at the last moment, wrecking it. Still, not a bad beginning. The bitch got a nasty cut. She turned, and the camera went in close to catch her scream.

Yup, it was Ronna.

"No, Luke, no! You son of a bitch!" Helpless, banished to some inner void, Simba stood in the dark and screamed.

But just then someone must have turned off the TV and, with it, turned Simba off as well.

* * *

"But I'd much rather stay here with you."

"We can go back together, Mommy."

"That's true."

Hair soft as sunbeams fell across her face. Lips as velvety as a horse's nose kissed her nose. Piper tilted her head up to look into eyes as vast and pure as the sky. The air was fresh; her daughter's cheeks smelled of fresh cream and cuddliness. Together, they smiled, then giggled, then tickled each other.

"Mommy, can we be twins this time?"

"Might be harder to find women down there who've just conceived twins, but sure. Why not? We'll do it. Identical or fraternal?"

"Oh, identical, Mommy. Don't you think?"

"Sure. Boys or girls?"

"Oh, let's be girls again, Mommy. It's more fun."

"Yes, my treasure, I most hardily agree." Piper became pensive. She turned away from the bright, pure light at the upper end of the corridor. Instead she looked back down from whence she came. Behind her stretched a long corridor carpeted with clouds. At that end was darkness.

This time Piper was going to change. She wanted to face it and feel it all, even the darkness.

Piper looked back up at the one she had once named Star. The bright, pure light shone upon her still-rounded cheeks. She was smiling, translucent, long brown hair fluttering in a breeze that came from who knows where.

"Dearest," Piper began, her voice raspy-and low, "last time I passed through here—wherever here is—you must already have started another life. How sweet it was of you to wait for me this time."

Silken arms encircled Piper's head. "This time I didn't want to miss you," Star said. Piper could feel both of their hearts beating together. Again, she became pensive.

"Maybe you can help your mother," Piper said.

"Sure, Mommy, what can I do?"

"I want to understand it all. Maybe you know some things that I don't, having spent some time so close to the bright, pure light of the ultimate truth. Like, do you know if we'll remember all this in our next lives?"

"Not supposed to," Star said.

"If we're not supposed to, what just happened down there? Or do you know about—"

"I know, Mommy," Star interrupted. "That was different."

"Because?"

"Sometimes people don't let go of the life before, like ghosts."

"Why?"

"Maybe it's 'cuz they haven't learned the ultimate lesson, Mommy."

"Which is?"

"Accept. Let go."

"Hmmm. Pretty heavy. I may need another couple of lifetimes on that one myself."

Star took Piper's hand, tugging her back down the long corridor toward the darkness below. "Well, then, come on, Mommy. Let's go."

Together, they started back down over the clouds.

Beyond the closet door the gelatinous splatter that was once Luke's head was clearly visible. It was amazing what could be done at close range with a shotgun.

The soldier held the shotgun. Ronna stared at the results, then up at him.

"Yes, I can kill people," the soldier said. "And without much of a reaction. I've killed a lot."

Ronna stood. "Anyone can kill, given the right conditions. I thought I just did, and he was my lover. You saved my life, Roscoe. Thank you."

"Well, I couldn't leave it to the scrawny old codger I left dozing on the steering wheel of his patrol car out front."

"Scrawny old codger?"

The soldier nodded yes. "What the sleepy town next to this one calls a sheriff. I'd be amazed if he weighs more than eighty pounds, is less than ninety years old and drinks less than a fifth of gin a day. I snatched the shotgun off the dash and came in to check myself. What the hell happened here?"

"Long story," Ronna said. "Adventure's over here. If you're thinking of hitching back west, I'll tell you along the way."

"Talk about your good times," he mused. "Where are you going?"

"Berkeley, California. I've an English paper due in a few weeks—and a mother I haven't called for ages. And a diet I'd better start." She turned to go.

He grabbed her from behind. "And a knife wound that needs attention." He whipped the appropriate supplies out of his pack and doctored her back with an efficiency suggesting much experience. "Done, soldier. Let's move out!"

They left.

Joshua Carnes kicked the closet door the rest of the way open. Again it creaked.

Damn. More night driving.